Praise for Naomi Williams

'I inhaled *The Woman in Ward 9*. Such a clever, chilling and unputdownable thriller ... with a killer twist that made me want to read it all over again'

CLAIRE DOUGLAS

'Wrapped itself tighter and tighter around me until I could hardly breathe'

S. E. LYNES

'Dark, twisted and razor-sharp. You'll be racing towards a nail-biting ending and then you'll want to read it all over again'

LAUREN NORTH

'Keeps you guessing right until the last word. Don't expect to sleep if you take this one to bed'

G. D. WRIGHT

'Dark, gripping, and utterly unputdownable ... Prepare to be hooked!'

EMILY FREUD

'Dripping with tension and a creeping sense of unease ... an utterly gripping, mess-with-your-mind thriller'

A. A. CHAUDHURI

Naomi Williams grew up in Yorkshire and now lives in London with her family. She studied English at university and started her career teaching English and Drama, before becoming a full-time writer. *The Eyewitness* is her second psychological suspense novel.

ALSO BY NAOMI WILLIAMS

The Woman in Ward 9

THE EYEWITNESS

Naomi Williams

HEADLINE

First published in Great Britain in 2026 by
Headline Publishing Group Limited

1

Cataloguing in Publication Data is available from the British Library

Paperback ISBN 978 1 0354 3189 2

Typeset in Sabon by CC Book Production

Printed and bound in Great Britain by Clays Ltd, Elcograf S.p.A.

MIX
Paper | Supporting responsible forestry
FSC® C104740

Headline's policy is to use papers that are natural, renewable and recyclable products and made from wood grown in well-managed forests and other controlled sources. The logging and manufacturing processes are expected to conform to the environmental regulations of the country of origin.

The authorized representative in the EEA is Hachette Ireland,
8 Castlecourt Centre, Dublin 15, D15 XTP3, Ireland
(email: info@hbgi.ie)

HEADLINE PUBLISHING GROUP
An Hachette UK Company
Carmelite House
50 Victoria Embankment
London EC4Y 0DZ

www.headline.co.uk
www.hachette.co.uk

For Katherine Bridge
With love and thanks for decades of friendship
and support, and for being the best research buddy
I could wish for

Prologue
The Watcher

I'm not a stalker. Okay, I am, if you want to split hairs, but I'm not like those losers who hunt down celebrities, shadow randoms in the street, or hound people on the internet. My stalking is a means to an end, that's all. I once did something I thought I'd been able to leave behind, but now there's a risk I'll be found out. And I don't want that. I've worked too hard for it all to be taken away from me now. That's why I'm watching, observing, silently tracking. I'm alert, eyes wide open, waiting for the right time to terminate the threat. It's more fun than I thought it would be.

So you see, I'm not just a stalker. I'm much more dangerous than that.

Chapter One

My fingers tingled with cold on the short walk from my private practice on Bath Street to Grind, the café bar on the corner near Old Street tube station. Max was sitting at a table near the glass frontage, a brown-and-cream-checked scarf wound round his neck. Even the sight of him lifted my energy levels with a familiar, unwelcome dopamine release. I'd hoped I was past that by now. He was looking down at his phone, the light from the screen illuminating his angular cheekbones and narrow nose. As if sensing my presence, he glanced up. Through my billowing breath I could see the warmth in his smile.

When I pushed open the door, the balmy air blowing from the air-conditioning unit overhead was like a warm flannel across my frozen face. 'Happy New Year,' I said, approaching the table, arms outstretched. 'God, it's cold.'

'Happy New Year, Beth.' Max stood and gave me a quick hug, kissing me on both cheeks. It momentarily struck me that we embraced outside work as a matter of course. When we met inside Moorfields Eye Hospital, where we both did

NHS shifts aside from our private practice, we wouldn't dream of even an air kiss. Social behaviour was a strange thing. Who decides what's acceptable, and when? Max tugged his scarf tighter, despite the stifling heat compared to the frigid air outside. 'It's going to be like this until the end of the week. I spoke to my sister, and at least it's raining in Wellington. I hate freezing my bollocks off when they're all on the beach. That doesn't show me in the best light, does it?'

'I know you better than that.' I wagged a finger at him. 'If your family in New Zealand were basking in sunshine, you'd be happy for them. You couldn't help yourself.'

He grinned coyly. 'God, is that my brand – Mr Nice Guy?'

'There are worse things to be.' I knew that for a fact.

'I'll take your word for it.' He glanced through the window at the hoary sky. 'Might even snow in London this week.'

I shivered at the thought. 'Are they still doing mulled wine in here?' I sat on the leather stool and scrutinised the drinks menu. 'Urgh. It doesn't look like it.'

'That's because it's January,' said Max. 'No mulled wine after Twelfth Night. It would be bad luck.'

'Hm, I don't want any more of that, thank you very much,' I said, keeping my eyes on the menu. I didn't want to see his reaction. We both knew what had happened to me was more bad judgement than bad luck.

I ordered a hot chocolate with Bailey's, the best alternative I could find. I hoped it would thaw my fingers, which were now turning red and itching, and provide the shot of alcohol I needed following the first clinic after the holidays. 'What's this mysterious thing you wanted to discuss so urgently?' I said, when the waiter took our menus and sauntered back behind the counter.

'A new patient. A tricky one, so I wanted to discuss the case with you face to face. I was hoping you'd be willing to take the private referral, but . . .' He paused, his brow furrowing.

'Why not you?' Max and I were both ophthalmologists with added training in neurology, both experienced in dealing with the complex interaction between the eyes, brain and nerves. He'd been practising a couple of years longer than I had, first in his native New Zealand, then here at Moorfields. Anything I could do, he could do, and private patients meant good money.

He licked his lips. He always did that when he was nervous. My shoulder muscles tensed. Max glanced out of the window then back at me, clearing his throat. 'The patient is a woman called Rachel Cartwright. She's been referred by a private GP who usually sends all his eye patients my way, but Rachel will only see a female consultant.'

Max stopped speaking as the waiter approached with our drinks. He put them in front of us, and I cupped the tall glass, my palms warming as the rich smell of chocolate and whiskey rose with the steam.

'Do you know why?' I asked when we were alone again.

'Apparently she's had traumatic experiences with men before.'

'Oh.' I let my gaze drop to the froth on top of my drink, watching the tiny bubbles dissolve into the brown liquid. I wondered whether Max classed what happened to me eighteen months ago as traumatic. Maybe that was why he wanted to speak to me in person, rather than discussing this over the phone or email. I took a breath, then looked Max in the eye. 'Go on,' I said. 'Tell me more.'

Chapter Two

Max's grey eyes fixed on me. His pupils were large. Inside was bright compared to the dark winter evening beyond the glass, so his iris dilator muscles were contracting. I wondered if he was analysing my eyes in the same way. Probably. It came with the job. I lowered my gaze in case he read the truth about how I really felt in mine.

'The patient, Rachel, is a lawyer – in criminal law, I think,' he said.

'I reckon that would be quite enough to make you cautious around the male of the species.' I looked up and arched one brow. I knew plenty of men who would immediately give me a *not all men* speech after a comment like that – a few fusty senior consultants I'd worked with since qualifying ten years ago came to mind – but not Max. He was a good man, an ally. 'I'm not sure I could do that job, especially if I had to defend someone I suspected might be guilty.'

'She might say the same about slicing an eyeball open with a scalpel,' said Max, grinning. 'Horses for courses.' The phrase sounded oddly British in his Kiwi accent.

'Fair point.' I sipped my drink and smiled, remembering the senior school biology class where I first handled a cow's eyeball. Most of my classmates were repulsed, some backing away, squealing, but I was intrigued by the gelatinous ball that contained a world of fascinating elements working together to create the magic of sight. That's when I first considered a career in ophthalmology. When Moira died so suddenly later that year, I thought about going into neurology, but when I understood quite how often I wouldn't be able to save people I returned to my original plan. Finding my aunt's lifeless body destroyed me. She'd always been the picture of health, the most vibrant person I knew. But under the skin of her animated face and the bone of her skull an invisible clot was preparing to block the blood flow to her brain. I wanted to be a doctor, but I didn't have the constitution to face death on a daily basis. I suspected I chose to work with eyes because, with modern technology, I could see inside. To feel safe, I needed to be able to believe my own eyes. What was hidden scared me.

My drink was sickly-sweet and the sugar and alcohol combination was already warming my insides. 'What's Rachel presenting with?'

'Blepharospasm. Quite acute. Her eyelids are clamping closed for long periods.'

I nodded. 'Okay. Not too atypical. Primary or secondary?'

'Primary, I think. She doesn't have any other conditions that might be causing it, not that we know of, anyway.' He took a gulp of beer. I didn't know how he could face a cold drink. I was chilled through to my bones and the warm air from the unit above the door now seemed wholly inadequate to heat the vast room.

'Okay. It could be a trauma response, then? It wouldn't be unusual for earlier trauma to come out later as a conversion disorder somewhere in the body. I've seen it before.'

'Yep,' said Max. 'I'm inclined to agree, but apparently she's adamant it's an eye condition and insisted on being referred to a female ophthalmologist.'

'A woman who knows her own mind,' I said. 'I like it.' I lifted my glass and swallowed the last of the thick liquid at the bottom. A cloying residue clung to my back teeth. 'It won't do any harm to give her a thorough examination. I could always refer her on to a psych if all the tests are clear. I'd be sensitive. I wouldn't mention anything psychological until I'd ruled out physical causes.' I knew from bitter experience what it was like to be told things were in my head when I knew damned well they weren't.

Max shifted on his stool. 'There is one more thing.'

I looked up. His mouth was a thin line.

A group of what appeared to be students entered the bar, a young man with a scruffy beard holding the door open for his friends, letting an icy blast into the room. I had to resist the urge to ask them to close the door as the bearded one held it wide for a straggler to join them. I wrapped my arms round myself. 'What's that?'

'The timings of the blepharospasms. Most of the cases I've seen are regular, but this one's pretty specific.'

'In what way?'

'Her eyelids clamp completely shut for forty-eight hours, then open for forty-eight hours.'

I leaned my elbows on the table, pulling back when the coldness of the marble seeped through my shirtsleeves. 'That's odd.'

'I know.' He finished the last of his pint. 'I did a bit of digging and found an article about a man who had a similar thing. Don't judge me . . . It was in the *Sun*.'

I tucked my chin into my neck. 'Hm, the *Lancet* or the *Sun*, which of those two would any self-respecting medical professional consult?'

He smiled sheepishly. 'Yeah, well, this man's eyes clamped shut for days at a time, but it didn't say whether they opened for exactly the same length of time. All I'm saying is, it might not be completely out of the realms of possibility that this is a medical rather than psychological issue.'

'What was that man's treatment, according to this esteemed medical journal?'

He nudged my foot with his boot. 'When did you get so cynical?'

I sat up straight and yanked my shoulders back. 'Sorry. I am taking this seriously. How was he treated?'

He bared his teeth in a grimace. 'He had most of the muscles removed from his eyelids.'

'Ouch. Grim. I won't be mentioning that at the first appointment.'

'So, you will see her?' His eyes widened in hope.

'You've piqued my interest. What sane eye doctor wouldn't want to investigate such a mysterious case?'

He nodded. 'Yep. Shame she'll only see a female medic. It's the kind of thing I'd like to get my own teeth into.' He put his hands on the table and let out a resigned breath.

Max had more experience than I did and I suddenly felt less sure of myself. 'If it's okay with you, I'd like it if we could confer on this. I'd appreciate your input.'

'You're more than qualified to do it on your own.'

'Thanks, but, as you say, the presentation is unusual, so if I knew I had you to thrash things out with, I'd feel more comfortable.' I picked up a teaspoon and tapped it on the back of his hand. 'I mean, I'm not paying you consultation fees, or anything. Let's get that straight right from the start.'

'Charming. I was expecting a massive introduction fee at least. That's my early retirement plans down the drain.'

'Ha! No chance, buddy.' I leaned in. 'You'll help, though?'

He shook his head and gazed up through his lashes. 'If you need it, of course I will.'

I knew he would without asking, because that's the kind of man he was. 'Right, excellent. Send over the details and I'll get her booked in this week.'

Chapter Three
The Watcher

You are a few minutes late this morning, which is deeply frustrating because the cold feels like acid on my skin. When you haven't shown by eight thirty, I consider going into Grind to buy a takeaway coffee to stop my fingers getting frostbite, but then I see you hurry up the steps from Old Street station and all thoughts of cold disappear. The chase is on. I love the spike of adrenaline I get when you first come into sight. It's better than a shot of espresso.

You walk fast, white air billowing from your mouth. That grey beret suits you. I can't say the same for the puffa jacket. It doesn't exactly scream medical professional, but it is minus two, so I suppose needs must.

I follow you as you pass the tired but beautiful terracotta Leysian Mission building. Tired but beautiful could describe you this morning. Your blonde highlights are still bright from when you had them done before Christmas, but the make-up I can imagine you applying in that dingy flat you had to move to last year hasn't quite hidden the purple smudges under your eyes.

I've watched the skin in your tear troughs start to sag over the last few months. It's a shame, but I'm not surprised. Losing your husband, all your friends and then your home would take its toll on anyone, and you're more sensitive than most, aren't you, Beth?

As I follow you along City Road towards Moorfields, the edge of the building on the corner appears like the blade of a knife. The sight makes me shiver in anticipation, because however bad things have been for you up until now they are about to get a whole lot worse.

Chapter Four

I muddled through the week, cursing myself for leaving advertising for the new receptionist/assistant role until the New Year. When my ex-husband, Joel, and I shared the private practice, he'd been in charge of staffing. I pretended to myself that's why Freya went with him when he moved to his new premises, but, really, I knew it wasn't just about loyalty. It was about my betrayal of him.

There was no point looking back. I had two interviews pencilled in between appointments on Monday, so I had to get on with it until then. I checked my schedule and saw that Rachel Cartwright was my first patient. Blepharospasm, that was right. We'd booked the appointment for that morning because it was what she described as an 'open eye day'.

I glanced around my consulting room to make sure everything was in order. My grey beret had fallen off the hook on the back of the door, so I picked it up and hung it over my puffa jacket on my way out to collect Rachel from the small reception area at the top of the stairs.

The three small armchairs that constituted our waiting

area – my waiting area – were empty. I didn't allow my eyes to travel to the closed door behind which Joel's old consulting room sat, but the memories came despite my best efforts to keep them at bay. We were so excited when we hired this floor of the building in Bath Street. It was just round the corner from Moorfields Eye Hospital, where we both did our part-time NHS work, and consisted of three floors of rooms rented by clinicians and a basement full of state-of-the-art technology, which we could book out when the treatment called for it.

The image of Joel's hollowed-out face when he packed the last of his things and waited for the lift down to the ground floor for the final time appeared in my mind's eye. On top of the dismantling of the life we'd dreamed of and built together, it was crippling me financially to leave Joel's room empty, especially on top of Mum's care-home fees, but I hadn't had the time or the energy to find someone else to work alongside. If I thought about it hard enough, I was probably self-sabotaging. I didn't deserve to succeed, and I acted accordingly.

I turned at the sound of footsteps on the stairs. A woman with black-brown hair that fell to her shoulders in ringletty curls reached the top step, put her hands on her hips and huffed. 'Sorry I'm late. There was no one on reception. I wasn't sure where to find you.' She wore wide black palazzo pants and a blood-red rollneck that skimmed the waistband of her trousers. A bold lipstick matched her top. I felt corporate and dull in comparison, in my navy tailored suit.

'Oh, I'm so sorry,' I said. 'I'm interviewing receptionists

next week. We used to have a rota, but I've been relying on the other practices to fill the void and I expect they're pretty annoyed with me by now.'

'That's all right,' she said. 'As long as I haven't missed my appointment.' She pronounced the consonants clearly. Her accent had the kind of polish that hinted at a good education.

'No, don't worry. Rachel Cartwright?' I heard my attempt to match her accent with my own and hated myself for not being confident enough in my ability and status to just be myself.

'Yes.' She smiled. A speck of red lipstick was stuck to her incisor. If we'd met in a ladies' bathroom I'd have quietly let her know, and she would have thanked me and wiped it off. I could see her in my imagination, leaning in towards a mirror, rubbing at her tooth with her finger. 'Mrs Sanderson?'

Every time I heard my married name, guilt speared me. I had no right to that name any more. 'Yes. Good to meet you. Please, call me Beth.' Most of my colleagues encouraged patients to address them as either Doctor or by their title, but I preferred to use first names with mine. I had no interest in the power being a consultant automatically gave me. I'd only ever been interested in doing the best I could for my patients, helping them, curing them where I could, and for that I needed them to be relaxed. That was hard to achieve in a clinical environment, so it was my job to make it happen.

There was something very intimate about being an

ophthalmologist. They say the eyes are the windows to the soul and, while I thought that was a fanciful concept, there's no denying the body part I specialised in was unlike any other. Even though I knew the workings of every element, the way they came together to allow us to experience the beauty of the world still had a hint of mysticism. Added to that, from the moment I started treating someone, I was close to their face, felt their breath on my cheeks and mouth. Being so near to another individual inevitably felt personal. Not only that, but my patients trusted me with the most fragile part of their physical being. There's a reason our first instinct when we're frightened is to close our eyes.

I stepped forward and held out my hand. As Rachel shook it, I made a quick assessment of her face. Her hair coiled to the side from a cowlick above a line-free brow and fell to her shoulders in curls and the odd soft ringlet. I knew from the scant information Max had emailed over that she was in her mid-thirties, just a couple of years younger than me, and I suspected she might already be using Botox. That was interesting, since that would be my first suggestion as a treatment for blepharospasm. I didn't judge her for trying to stop the clock. Most people I knew had regular appointments for filler and Botox, men and women alike. On the floor below, the practice's main source of income was aesthetic surgery and fillers around the eye area. Rachel was an attractive woman with a heart-shaped face, evenly spaced features and clear skin. I imagined her field of work was fiercely competitive, hard enough for a woman to break into, never mind succeed in. Pretty privilege was a thing, and I didn't blame her for wanting to hold on to one of the few privileges women had in business.

'Come this way.' I led her into my room. She scanned my workspace and I followed her gaze, feeling proud of the calm, welcoming environment I'd created. The eye exam chair and equipment on the left-hand side could look stark and a little daunting, but I thought the large kentia palm in the pot by the window and the blue chairs I'd got in the sale at the Conran Shop made the other side of the room more homely. It was a clinical environment dressed up as something else, but what things looked like affected how people responded to them. I wanted them to feel safe here, so I made it look safe. It was certainly a sharp contrast to the tiny box of a consulting room I was allocated for my NHS work, with its scuffed paintwork and smell of disinfectant. 'Take a seat.'

She perched at the edge of the chair I gestured to, and I sat in the other, rather than at the swivel chair at my desk. I wanted her to know she had my full attention. A pad and pen lay on the circular glass table in front of us, but I would only pick that up if I felt there was a detail I might forget. I planned to write my notes up after the appointment. She knitted her hands together in her lap, the skin on the back of them ridging where the tips of her fingers pushed down. A ring on her middle finger with at least five good-sized diamonds glinted. There was no wedding band. 'Thank you for seeing me,' she said.

'My pleasure.' I smiled, hoping to put her at ease. Ripples

of anxiety seemed to pulse through the air between us. 'From what little I know of your case, it sounds like you've been having a difficult time.'

'You could say that.' She gave a short laugh. Her skin turned red where she dug the tips of her fingers into her knuckles. 'It's been hell, to be honest. Whatever this is, it's ruining my life. I can't carry on like this.' Her voice broke and she gazed down at her lap.

I had the impulse to lean forward and touch her hand. Her nails were pressing into her flesh so hard I was afraid she would puncture the skin. 'I'm sorry you're experiencing that,' I said. 'I'll do my best to help you get to the bottom of why you can't open your eyes sometimes.'

She looked up, tears brimming on her lower lids. 'Thank you,' she said again, the words wobbling. Her distress was tangible, and I was acutely aware her gratitude was premature. The way she stared at me, with such vulnerability and hope, made me fearful that I couldn't meet her expectations. And I found I wanted to help her, very much indeed.

'The results of your most recent eye test were in the notes sent over from your GP, and you don't need glasses for reading or distance, is that right?'

She nodded.

'Okay. Why don't you tell me when the spasms started,' I said. 'And we'll take it from there.'

Chapter Five

The more we talked, the more composed Rachel became, and soon I could see the articulate, confident woman she was when this strange condition wasn't afflicting her. She was likeable too, punctuating her conversation with self-effacing smiles and regular eye contact.

'So you have no idea why the spasms started?' I said, after she explained how she woke up one morning completely unable to open her eyes.

'None.' She released her grip on her hands and let them fall on the black fabric of her trousers. 'It's the weirdest thing. I mean, I've never heard of anyone experiencing anything like this before.'

'Blepharospasm isn't that uncommon,' I said. 'If that helps?'

'Yeah, I've read about the eye-twitching, and I know the spasms can make some people's lids close for long periods, but it's the timings. I mean, two days is so specific. It's freakish. If someone else told me about this, I wouldn't believe them.'

'The body works in mysterious ways,' I said, watching her eyes, trying to detect anything uncommon in the working of the muscles or the movement of her irises, but nothing stood out. 'Look at menstrual cycles. You could ask why women bleed every twenty-eight days. Why do we sleep for around eight hours? All animals have set but different gestation periods. The body has a built-in clock, and just because we know about the reproductive cycle and the circadian rhythm, it doesn't mean they're any less mysterious when you think about them objectively.'

'Hm.' She didn't look convinced, and I didn't blame her. Her chin puckered. 'It's frightening. Losing control over your body, your sight, and not knowing why; it's really scary. And you don't really think about how much you rely on your sight until you lose it. I mean, it takes three seconds to make a first impression of someone, apparently. We don't need a person to even open their mouths before we've decided who they are, based on their looks alone.'

I nodded. 'That's a very good point.' I felt bad I'd never considered that before.

'What was your first impression of me?' she said.

'I'm not sure it's the same when you first meet a new patient,' I said, embarrassed by the seemingly personal question. 'I was assessing you from a clinical perspective rather than an interpersonal one.' What had actually gone through my mind was that I wished I was as attractive and put together as she was. I'd immediately admired her style, the way she spoke, her easy manner. She appeared at home in her own skin in a way I couldn't help but envy.

'Okay, yes, but outside of here, you would only take three seconds to work out if I was your kind of person, just by the way I smiled, or dressed, or the aura I gave off or whatever. You'd probably have decided if I was a potential friend or a potential serial killer and respond accordingly. But when my eyes are closed I can't reasonably assess if the Deliveroo driver is the kind of man who loves his wife and reads his kids bedtime stories, or if he jacks up in a squat after every shift. I know it's not as simple as that, and I know we shouldn't judge someone by how they present, especially since there are going to be bad actors in all walks of life, but I'm just trying to explain why it leaves you vulnerable in ways you wouldn't think. It's a lot harder to spot a serial killer with your eyes closed.'

'I understand.'

She smiled. The speck of lipstick was gone, and I was glad. I didn't like to think of anyone else noticing it. 'I somehow knew you would.' She lifted her hands. 'Which proves my point. I trusted you on sight.'

'I'm very glad to hear it.' A warm feeling settled over me.

'I need to be treated by someone I can really trust. The first day when my eyelids wouldn't open, the panic was . . . Then they opened again two days later and I thought that was it, a weird one-off. Then it happened again, and the pattern was so exact. Knowing that I'm going to sleep some days, but when I wake up I won't be able to see, it's terrifying, to be frank.'

I could imagine. I wasn't a big fan of the dark myself and I thought that made me a more sympathetic doctor when it came to treating people with sight loss. 'Can you think of anything you were doing differently when the spasms first began?'

'Not really. I'm a senior associate at my law firm and I'd been working hard, spending a lot of time on the computer and on case notes. I have to read a lot of material. I probably do more than I need to, but I feel compelled to do the best I can, because the outcome of a trial affects so many people's lives. Could that be the problem?'

I understood exactly what she meant. We were similar in our committed approach to our jobs, and I liked her all the more for it. 'We'll know more when I've examined you.'

She exhaled a long breath. 'There's no way around the reading. I'm up for partner, and I can't tell you how much I want it. It's between me and this complete dick.' She clamped her hand over her mouth. 'Sorry, that was probably inappropriate.'

'Depends,' I said. 'On whether he's a complete dick.' I followed her lead even though it wasn't how I usually spoke with patients. Humour was good for relaxation.

A throaty laugh took me by surprise. 'Oh, he is,' she said. 'The worst kind of public school boy; misogynist know-it-all. Bloated with privilege, educated beyond his intelligence, if you know what I mean?'

I nodded. I knew exactly what she meant. I met plenty of doctors who were from generations of medics, all sent to the same public schools and individually tutored to pass the exams, but who didn't have an ounce of smarts between them. Joel and I had always prided ourselves on coming from working-class backgrounds, through the state-school system and studying bloody hard while doing shitty part-time jobs to get our medical degrees. We thought it made us better doctors because we had a greater understanding of the real world. 'I know exactly what you mean.'

'I thought you would.' The side of her mouth lifted in a conspiratorial smile, like a bright red tick. 'So it's between me and that idiot, and I hope you don't think I'm being arrogant, but I think I deserve it. I've had to work harder than him, because, you know, the old boys' network and, well, the patriarchy. And I'm good at my job.'

'And you've been off work for how long now?'

Her smile dropped. 'Since mid-December. It's not like I can go in part time, on the days when I know my eyes will be open, because the law doesn't work like that. Once a trial starts, it's full on.' She wound a dark curl round her finger. The movement made her look childlike, unguarded. 'As far as work knows, I took my holiday entitlement over Christmas and now I'm on a two-month sabbatical before my next big leap. I phrased it like that so they thought I was taking some time to charge up before I get partner. You've got to convince them you expect to succeed, so I'm faking it till I make it.' She made fists. 'I've got to have sorted this out by the end of February, or that's it. I won't get another chance like this. And if this carries on I won't be able to practise. My career will be over.'

'I understand.' I did. My imposter syndrome told me I should never have been made a consultant in the first place. If my drive to help people hadn't been so strong, I would probably never have allowed myself to reach for the lofty heights I was at now. Most days, especially when I came up against the older generation of medics who acted like they were born for the role, I had to remind myself I was a fully qualified consultant, just like them. I still expected to be exposed as a charlatan. I sometimes wondered if my actions eighteen months ago were my way of stopping the endless wait for it all to go wrong: I simply did something so stupid that my life imploded.

She leaned forward. 'I've got to get my life back.' She let go of her hair and the curl sprang back into shape. 'Before all this started, everything seemed to be coming together. I'd just moved into this beautiful place – my ideal home – work was going well, then, boom, I can't open my bloody eyes.'

'You moved shortly before the blepharospasms started?' That was interesting. 'Have you ever had allergic reactions?'

'Nope.' She shook her head. 'The GP suggested I tried taking antihistamine when it happened because I'd recently moved to somewhere new, but it didn't make any difference.'

'And you haven't had any swelling, breathing problems, rashes?'

'None.' Rachel lay her head on the back of the chair and closed her eyes. 'It's like something out of a nightmare. Everything I'd worked for was within reach, and now I can't grasp it. And, on top of that, I've been feeling like . . .'

'Like what?'

She glanced over her shoulder at the window. The light made her irises a vivid translucent blue. 'Nothing. It's just . . . it affects everything: my state of mind, how I react to things that usually wouldn't bother me. It's scary, not being in control of your own body.'

It was interesting that she mentioned her state of mind. I wondered how much that had to do with what was happening to her or whether, as she seemed to think, it was the other way round. 'Okay. Let's start with some basic eye tests. I know you've had one since this started, but I'd like to do my own, just to confirm everything is as it should be.' I stood. 'Come over and sit in this chair.' I moved to the optometry chair and tapped the leather arm. I picked up the remote control to close the blackout blind. 'I'm going to make it dark in here, then we can get started.

Half an hour later, all the findings in Rachel's previous eye test were confirmed. 'You have more photosensitivity, which is sensitivity to light, than average, and there's some minor slackness in your eyelid muscles, but that's not surprising since you're spending fifty per cent of your time in the dark.'

She stared at the computer screen intently as I took her through the images of the topography of both of her eyes. 'You can see here' – I pointed at the line made up of various degrees of grey crossing the screen, moving my index finger from left to right – 'the layers of your optic nerve are smooth and straight.' I tapped to the next image. 'And the macular scan is healthy, so the retinal imaging hasn't thrown up anything unusual.' I moved to the next image and enlarged the picture. 'There's a freckle on the peripheral retina of your left eye, but when I look at the layers of retinal tissue' – I changed the perspective on the screen – 'the freckle disappears at the superficial level, which tells me it's flat, so that's absolutely nothing to worry about, although I would advise regular check-ups to make sure nothing changes.'

She nodded. 'So . . .'

I reached for the remote control and the blind mechanism buzzed as it lifted. Daylight flooded the room, making us both blink. 'So I'm afraid I don't have any answers for you yet.'

'Yet?' She viewed me with wide-eyed hope, making me desperate to find answers for her. That was why I went into medicine, to help people and give them hope. Everything in my life had crumpled into hopelessness after Moira, the aunt who all but brought me up, suffered a fatal stroke at only thirty-two. The only way I could see out of the despair was to try to stop anyone else experiencing the hell that followed after I discovered her lifeless body.

Ophthalmology might not sound like a life-saving discipline, but it could be. It was also the one where I could best cope with my own emotions. I was not good at losing people. And an eye exam could help identify all kinds of health conditions. Certain changes in the eye, like damage to the blood vessels in the retina, could predict if a person was more likely to have a stroke in future. Saving someone's sight was incredible. Saving their life was even better. I watched Rachel and understood there was more than one way to save a life. I'd been existing, rather than living, for the past year. If I could stop Rachel from that fate, I would. 'I'd like to examine you while you're experiencing a blepharospasm, if that's okay.'

'Of course, but I'm not sure how that would work, practically, I mean.' A shallow crease formed between her perfectly shaped brows. 'The GP did home visits, so that helped. I'm not sure how I'd get here when my eyes are closed. I could get a cab, I suppose, but my new house is in St Katharine Docks, right by the water. I'm not in a hurry to try to find my way out on to the street when my eyes are closed. I've only just managed to navigate the inside.'

'Perhaps a family member or a friend could come along with you?'

She glanced down at her hands. 'I don't have any family left, and most of my friends work in law, so I don't feel like I can tell them what's going on. If people find out I can't do my job properly, then I risk losing everything I've worked for. It's a pretty dog-eat-dog business. You can't afford to show any weakness.' She looked up. 'That sounds awful, doesn't it? Like I don't trust anyone, or I value my career more than friends? I haven't always got the work–life balance thing right, I'm afraid. I've let friendships outside work slide.'

I nodded. I wished I could say I'd let my friendships slide because of work. In truth, my friends had come along as a package with Joel when we met at university. An upbringing like mine didn't tend to foster lasting friendships; I was too focused on managing Mum's drinking and erratic behaviour and pretending everything was okay at home so no one called children's services. Understandably, the people

I inherited with Joel had chosen to walk away when they learned what I'd done. I didn't blame them. Most of them were medics with strong ethics, just like I had once been, and Joel was the injured party, so it was only right they sided with him and cut me off. I missed them to the point of aching, though. Without them and my husband, loneliness was swallowing me.

'I could come to you?' The words were out of my mouth before I'd really considered it. Had I learned nothing from the last time I'd agreed to see a patient at home?

Rachel's eyes brightened. 'Really? That would be amazing.'

I wasn't being reckless. She needed further examination and this was the best way. I retrieved my iPad from my desk and opened the calendar. 'When do you anticipate another episode?' It seemed strange to be able to plan for exactly when her eyes would clamp shut. But bodies were strange. My moods were often defined by the moon. Was this any more peculiar than that?

I typed in the appointment date for the following Thursday along with Rachel's address. She was suffering, and whatever was causing it was real, whether it was medical or psychological. I was a doctor. It was my duty to relieve suffering. When we shook hands at the end of her appointment, her thanks were so heartfelt that, however unorthodox a home visit was, in this case, at least, I believed it was the right thing to do.

Chapter Six

On Saturday morning my guilt mixed with dread, as it always did on the drive to my monthly visit to Mum's care home in Chelmsford. In my mind, I replayed the phone call I received from Mum's neighbour three years ago, telling me she'd been found in a heap outside her front door. She'd had a stroke, just like Moira.

'She's too mean to die,' Joel had said in a moment of gallows humour when Mum was hooked up to machines in ICU. He held me close, understanding how complicated my feelings were. I'd spent so much of my young life trying to make her happy, and make her love me. When she was on the brink of death, I had no idea what to hope for. It wasn't until later that I accepted what I truly wanted was the beeping of her heart monitor to stop and for her to slip away. What kind of daughter wants that? It didn't seem fair, though, that both her and her younger sister had been struck down by the same devastating condition a few decades apart, but Moira had died and Mum was still here, living, breathing, judging.

'I bet she'll stay alive to spite you,' Joel had predicted.

I'd thought the comment a little cruel at the time. Now I could see he was right. She'd trapped me into being responsible for her health and happiness again, just like she had when I was a child. At least this time it wasn't a conscious choice. I wouldn't want to live like she did now, entirely dependent on other people. I pitied her. That didn't stop me wishing the stroke had killed her and hating myself for it.

Looking back, I could pinpoint Mum's stroke as the moment when everything started to go wrong. Joel and I had never argued about money before, but his resentment at me insisting Mum moved into the best care home available, whatever the cost, put distance between us.

'We can't afford it,' he said, exasperated at the mounting bills for private nurses, and endless prescriptions, after the money from the sale of her tiny flat was spent. 'Not on top of the mortgage and the rent on Bath Street. And it's not as if she ever did anything for you. You've got where you have despite her, not because of her.'

While I'd said similar things myself over the years, it still sounded cold coming out of his mouth. I'd earned the right to criticise. He hadn't. She was helpless again. She needed me, and the old co-dependent feelings returned, making me stand my ground. I took on extra shifts at Moorfields and more patients at Bath Street to pay the extortionate bills, and soon Joel and I were passing strangers, and I became starved of both a mother's love and a husband's.

I tried to stop replaying what followed in my mind as I parked in front of the imposing stone mansion house.

Instead, I focused on the scaffolding that had been erected on one side and the man painting a window frame brilliant white. That would be reflected in next month's bills, I thought, as I climbed out of the car and braced myself to go inside.

Mum was sitting in the pale blue high-backed chair in her room, grey hair in lank ribbons to her shoulders. She turned her head to me and her eyes trailed from my face to my trainers and back again. I couldn't help glancing down to assess what she saw. I imagined her thinking I'd lost weight and looked scrawny. She'd want to know why I was wearing trainers like a fourteen-year-old lout instead of proper shoes. She rarely spoke now. My theory was that she couldn't bear the wavering in her voice since the stroke had left her without full control of any part of her body. She probably wouldn't lower herself to voice her disdain anyway. She'd let her withering expression and my low self-esteem do it for her.

'Hi, Mum.' She turned her head away. I opened the plastic bag gripped in my fist. 'I've brought the things Marie asked me to get.' I took out the expensive hand cream and lip balm Marie, the care home manager, had listed in an email. Mum used to say luxury products were a waste of money, but she'd embraced her consumer side in the last year. I was using supermarket-brand shampoo and conditioner at home, in an attempt to cut costs, but I didn't feel like I could turn up without the items Mum specifically asked for, not when I only visited once a month.

It had occurred to me that maybe Marie was the one

with expensive tastes, but the Rituals diffuser Mum asked for last time was still sitting on top of the chest of drawers opposite the bed, the sweet cherry blossom aroma fighting with the underlying smell of unwashed body. I concluded she'd developed a hankering for Jo Malone just to spite me. I was a sap for indulging it. She'd always told me I was weak.

She held out a shaking hand. The gesture wrongfooted me. Did she want me to hold it? A moment of pathetic hope lifted my chest. She had been capable of affection when I was a child. On rare occasions, she'd cup my face in her hands and stare deep into my eyes, telling me that I was all she had in the world. I would thirst for those moments, savouring them when they came, tucking them away in a special pocket in my heart to bring out to replay when her kindness drowned in a bottle. I hadn't been offered so much as a soft word in years, though, and I should have known better than to hope by now. Irritation flashed in her eyes and she waved a pointed finger at the hand cream I was still holding.

Heat burned my cheeks as I squeezed a blob on to her palm and watched her clumsily spread the thick cream over the back of her hands, where green veins protruded. The thin skin rippled like a breeze over water.

'How's Joel?' She looked me directly in the eye, and I could tell by the set of her jaw and the straining tendons in her neck that it cost her to keep her head still. That's the effort she was willing to go to to inflict maximum pain. The slur in her voice reminded me of my childhood, only this time it was because of muscle weakness, not alcohol.

'I haven't seen him in a while.'

She made a guttural sound and curled her lip. 'You never did know when you were well off.'

I wanted to ask when she thought I was well off; when she sent me to school in charity-shop shoes while she spent her money at the off licence, or when she stopped me from bringing schoolfriends home altogether because we made too much noise and mess? Things were even worse after Moira died. Mum had relied on her for free childcare, and when Moira was gone I was left to make my own way in the world as Mum used her younger sister's death as an excuse to drink herself into oblivion. My childhood died alongside my aunt. I spent my teenage years desperately trying to be enough to keep my mother alive. Friends and a social life went out of the window when she became my full-time job.

Studying was my escape, something I could control and get some validation from, but I almost didn't go to university. If it hadn't been for my sixth-form biology teacher taking me under her wing, encouraging me and helping with the applications, I would probably never have gone to medical school. Mum seemed to recover while I was away. Joel never understood why I couldn't walk away from her, but it was never that easy. When you've spent so much of your life trying to make someone care about you, it becomes a deeply ingrained habit, an addiction, almost, always chasing the soaring highs of a gentle touch or a kind word. I never did manage to kick it, even when her contempt for me became the foundation of our relationship. At least now I'd lived up to her expectations.

She closed her eyes. Her pupils moved under her papery

lids. I thought of Rachel and imagined Mum's eyelids clamping shut, and a frisson of panic rushed through me. It must be truly terrifying not to be able to open your eyes at will. I sat in the silent room, contemplating that, until a woman wearing a blue tabard knocked on the half-open door.

'Tea, Magdelana?' she said.

Mum opened her eyes, and the side of her face most weakened by the stroke drooped, making the smile she offered into a grimace. 'Lovely. Thanks, Pearl.'

'And one for you, my darling?' Pearl smiled at me.

'She hasn't got time,' Mum slurred. 'She's always too busy to stay for long.'

'Shame.' Pearl's smile dropped, her disapproval clear.

'I can stay for a cup of tea,' I said, my voice artificially bright.

'No, don't stay on my account. I don't want to keep you from your busy life.' Mum managed to sound hurt and weary. She'd always been good at making people believe what she wanted them to.

I had the urge to argue, to tell Pearl what I sacrificed to keep Mum in that place, but it passed as quickly as it came. Instead, I nodded. 'Okay.' I folded the empty carrier bag into a small square, avoiding Pearl's judgemental gaze. 'I'll see you next month, then.'

I heard Pearl's quiet tut as she turned to go, then the heavy tread of her footsteps in the corridor outside. Mum closed her eyes again. They remained shut as I left the room.

Chapter Seven

After visiting Mum, I felt even more empty and alone. As a distraction from my frayed thoughts, I spent the rest of the weekend trying to make my flat more like a home. I drove through the Blackwall Tunnel to the Ikea on Greenwich Peninsula, touring the cavernous superstore trying not to notice couples discussing what to buy for the homes they shared. When Joel and I bought our beautiful flat in Tredegar Square seven years ago, we'd been giddy with its potential. It was small, but it was in one of the East End's most prestigious locations. I remember how mind-boggled we were that a pair of state-school kids had been able to buy a two-bed place with beautiful ceiling roses and original iron fireplaces with tiled surrounds. How optimistic we were, how happy.

We scoured the antiques warehouses in Bermondsey for pieces we loved until it was as near perfect as we could get it without hiring an interior designer. If we'd known our punishing work schedules as we both scrambled up the ladder to become consultants meant we'd hardly ever be at home at the same time, would we have made different choices about our home, our career trajectories? Would I have made a different choice about Mum? I feel like I would have changed anything to avoid the solitary life I was currently living, but I can't be sure. The need to take care of her was so ingrained, and I was still doing it, even now.

Moving out when Joel called time on our relationship and we sold the flat was one of the worst days of my life. I think it was one of his too. His expression of loss when he stood in the street and gazed up at our home for the last time will never leave me.

I said, 'I'm so sorry,' for about the thousandth time.

'I know,' he said. 'It's all such a waste.' Then he turned away and got in his car.

I couldn't move. I stood on the pavement as he started the engine and pulled away from the kerb, hardly able to comprehend the enormity of my loss. It was like grief. It still is.

Joel moved to a top-floor flat on the outskirts of London. I went for a higher floor too, renting a place in a gated development off the Roman Road. It was a new-build and I hated every inch of its white painted blandness. But it was the best I could afford and it was not too far from work, and now, instead of lying with my head in my husband's lap watching a film like we used to on a rare night off, my Sunday evening was spent alone, trying to put together a pair of cheap, walnut-veneer bedside tables. I gave up after one. I'd split a nail and stood on a screw, and I didn't even need the second table, since I was a sad divorcée living on her own.

In a fit of nostalgia, I picked up my phone and tapped in Gemma's number. Gemma and Joel shared a student house when I met him, and she was someone I used to see regularly since she was a GP living nearby in Bethnal Green. I opened the message thread and scrolled up. I couldn't help but smile at her messages: a list of white rectangles, one after another, each containing one sentence at most. My replies were in green, much longer, answering all her points in one message. She'd laughed at me about that, telling me I texted like a grandma. 'It's supposed to be like the beats of a conversation,' she'd said over an impromptu dinner out one weekday evening. 'Like a stream of consciousness.' She'd turned her phone screen to me and pointed at my well-punctuated words. 'Not something you might get from the doctor to tell you your chlamydia test came back clear.'

'If you're sending out texts like that to your patients,' I said, 'I think you should be investigated by the GMC.'

She'd laughed then and told me a story about a man who'd presented at her surgery with thrush, thinking he'd caught an STD, and clearly traumatised that his wife would find out he was cheating with his piano teacher. She spoke through glugs of wine and bites of naan bread, and it had all seemed so normal. Months later, our friendship was over. I scrolled to the last message she sent. *I'm sorry, Beth, but I need to be there for Joel. He's broken. I wish you well, but please don't contact me again.*

Similar messages came from all our not-entirely-mutual friends. They'd been his, first and foremost. Everyone wished me well, but no one was willing to spend time with someone as flawed as me. I didn't blame them. I blamed myself.

When I reached Bath Street on Monday morning, I realised I hadn't spoken to anyone other than Mum, Pearl and the cashier at Ikea all weekend, and he didn't even look me in the eye when he sullenly told me to have a good day. I had a sudden image of me tripping over the scattered components of the second bedside table, hitting my head and dying on the cheap synthetic carpet. I probably wouldn't be found until after the third stage of decomposition. My body would have time to self-digest, fluid-filled blisters would form on my skin and internal organs, then I'd bloat with gas, until I eventually liquefied. That's when the smell would be enough to alert the people in the other flats. Strangers would find me and gag. I gave my head a shake and told myself off for being self-pitying and maudlin. The image of my soft tissues melting stayed with me, though.

I'd arranged the interviews for the role of receptionist and assistant in the morning. The first candidate, a young woman who'd appeared promising on paper, looked bored throughout, was monosyllabic in her answers and chewed gum throughout our entire exchange. I found myself gritting my teeth at the sound of saliva churning in her mouth. I didn't bother pretending I would be in touch. Inwardly sighing, I cut the interview short. 'I don't think your skills are compatible with the role,' I said. 'But thank you for taking the time to come in, and all the best with your job search.'

She stuck out her lower lip and said, 'Oh, I thought that went all right.' As she left the building I heard her on the phone to someone describing me as a 'stuck-up cow' and was quite offended. I didn't want to be a stuck-up cow, I wanted to be a kind and friendly employer to someone who was equally professional, someone who I could have an adult conversation with. Surely that wasn't too much to ask?

I'd barely recovered from the disappointment and indignance when the sound of the intercom buzzing alerted me to the arrival of the next candidate. I went to the glass door and was pleasantly surprised to see a man with a round face, and circular-rimmed glasses perched on his nose, which served to accentuate the softness of his features. He looked to be around my age. A grown-up. He was wearing a dark blue suit with narrow trousers and a crisp white shirt. He was talking into a phone, but finished the call hurriedly and smiled at me through the glass. When I opened the door, he shoved the phone with its distinctive black-and-white case into his pocket and offered his hand to shake. His skin was cold, but his smile and demeanour radiated warmth. 'Aaron Fletcher?' I said, opening the door wide for him to enter the square reception area.

'Hi. Yes. I'm here for the interview.' A draught of spiky air followed him in, making the follicles on my arms bristle.

I pushed the door closed. 'Great. I'm Beth Sanderson. Please call me Beth. Thank you for coming in today.' I thought about the conversation I'd had with Rachel Cartwright about first impressions. She was right. I liked this man immediately, and I was getting absolutely no signs he was a serial killer.

'My pleasure. I'm pleased you're considering me for the role.' I followed his gaze around the sparse reception, with its blocky white desk and one large palm in a terracotta pot. 'Reception is down here, I take it?'

'Yes. You'd sometimes be down here, and with me on the third floor the rest of the time.' This was a good start. I could already feel my mood lifting. 'Follow me, and we'll get started.' I took the stairs because, however nice he seemed, I didn't feel comfortable being in the confined space of the lift on my own with a man I didn't know. I knew it was pointless because we'd soon be in my consulting room together. I made small talk as we climbed the three flights. 'Have you come far?'

'Not too far,' he said, his deep voice echoing in the stairwell. 'I stay with my girlfriend in Shoreditch during the week, then go home to Hertfordshire when I'm not working. It's a long story, but I help care for a family friend who's not well. That's why I'm looking for something part time.'

'That's kind of you.'

'Not really. She did a lot for me when I was growing up. We've been through some rough times together, so it's the least I can do.'

We reached the top of the stairs and I gestured for him to go through to my room, trying not to show that my breathing was a little laboured. He didn't seem to have been affected by the ascent. Fit: that was a plus point.

'Take a seat.' When we were both comfortable, I picked up my iPad from the coffee table and tapped on the app where I'd written my questions. 'You've already told me why you want to work part time.' I hesitated over whether to ask the next question in case it was insensitive, but decided to go ahead anyway. 'If your circumstances change for any reason, would you then be looking for something with more hours?'

He smiled, dimples appearing on his round cheeks. 'I understand why you'd ask, but I can reassure you, if my circumstances change, I'd be more likely to look for an additional part-time job, rather than something nine to five. I have no interest in doing one type of work all day, every day. I've done that for years, and I know it's not for me. Not any more. One of the things that appealed to me about this job was the variety. I like that it will be partly reception, because I like people, but I think assisting you would be interesting too. I've done mainly administrative work before, as you can see on my CV, but this looks like it will be' – he glanced up to the left and smiled – 'meatier. I loved biology at school, and the workings of the human body have always fascinated me. I mean, sight; it's incredible, isn't it?' He grinned. 'And helping people always feels good, doesn't it?' He nodded, as though affirming his own thoughts. 'I think this job would really suit my skills and my interests.'

I looked into his brown eyes, enlarged by the round lenses of his glasses, as he spoke, agreeing with everything he said. Within five minutes of meeting him, I knew I'd be asking Aaron Fletcher to become my right-hand man.

Chapter Eight
The Watcher

I see you approach St Katharine Docks from the entrance opposite Moretown. I prefer the West Basin entrance with those ridiculous grey elephants with white tusks on top of the gate piers. I'm surprised they haven't been smashed to pieces by the woke mob, now I come to think of it. The whole area harks back to colonial Britain, and those elephants are a gauche reminder of the numerous vainglorious thieves in our collective history.

I've come across modern-day thieves in my time. None of them are likely to have statues erected in their honour by the powers that be. That said, they build their own swaggering palaces in Essex and Kent as permanent monuments to their wealth and power, and their remote-controlled iron gates aren't so different to the ones erected here.

You move towards the railings, stopping and gazing out across the water. I'm not surprised you pause to take in the view. It's a beautiful sight. Small yachts and houseboats are moored around the periphery of the dock, and across the way the windows of the Dickens Inn shine orange against its black wood cladding.

I notice you're not carrying a takeaway coffee cup. That's unusual. From what I've seen, you have quite the caffeine dependency. Doctors always seem to develop unhealthy habits, and you, Beth, are no exception. You're always tired, aren't you? You want to watch that. You can't afford to be practically sleepwalking through the day, not with people like me around. And with your training you should know that no amount of coffee can substitute for a decent night's sleep. When did you last have one of those? I bet you can't even remember what it feels like to wake up refreshed and looking forward to the day ahead.

I can. I started today with a real pep in my step, thanks to you. My plan is entering the next stage, and I'm buzzing as I watch you pause next to the deep, dark water. The weather is milder than it was last week, and you're wearing a long camel-coloured coat. It suits you better than that awful puffa jacket. You take your phone out of your pocket and check the screen, then look around you at the warehouse conversions to the right and ugly modern flats behind you. I have to duck away to ensure you don't see me. My heart starts to thunder in my chest at the risk of being found out. If you see me, my plan will fail, and all my careful manoeuvring over the last few months will have been for nothing. It's quite thrilling, this high-stakes game of cat and mouse . . . although I'm not sure you'd agree if you knew that I'm watching every move you make, or if you had any idea about what's in store.

Chapter Nine

It was years since I'd been to St Katharine Docks. Eight years, to be exact. I'd forgotten how pretty it was. I had a memory of walking around outside the warehouse conversions with Joel, discussing whether we should get a one-bedroom place in Docklands and be more central, rather than a bigger place in the East End. I remember the property prices being astronomical, which wasn't a huge surprise since I could see Tower Bridge and the Shard from where I stood by the fence overlooking the basin. I wished I'd grabbed a coffee on the way there. It was too late now. I glanced down at my yawning reflection shimmering on the surface of the black water below. My features merged and distorted, like the reflection in a hall of mirrors at a funfair. It was me, but it wasn't me. That's how I felt all the time now, as if I could no longer pick the new version of me out of a crowd.

I pushed the thought away and checked Rachel's address again on my phone, surmising that her home must be in the middle of the quirky terrace directly on the water to my left. Like the others on the short row, the lower level had two patio windows with black railings across the lower third. Below the windows the brickwork was divided by a rusting ladder which disappeared into the dock. An iron circle was attached to the wall beyond the ladder and below that the brickwork darkened, algae clinging in a green cuff before merging with the murky water below. The sight of a wooden duck house attached to the wall a few houses along made me smile.

What made the row of houses particularly striking were the two-storey turrets that protruded above the second patio window. Clad in the same dark wood as the Inn across the way, they stood out like dark watchtowers, topped by weathervanes silhouetted against the slate-grey sky, a ship in full sail. The highest floor of the turrets had windows on all five sides. I imagined what someone could see if they were standing in the centre of that room. It must offer an almost panoramic view across the dock. I understood why Rachel chose to live there. They were extraordinary houses in a stunning location. They must cost a fortune. I remembered what she said about making partner. This place would need a hefty salary for someone living alone. I earned well, but I'd found keeping my flat and the practice going along with Mum's care home fees almost impossible, so money was often on my mind.

I walked along a stone path flanked by bushes swamped in variegated ivy, and round to the back of the houses, which were plain in comparison to the front, with stippled cream plasterwork and overhanging windowless dormers. Four red brick steps led up to Rachel's black door, a chrome doorbell to the right. I pressed the bell and waited.

A minute later, the door opened a crack and Rachel stood, shielded by it, hardly visible behind the wood. 'Hello?' Her voice was hesitant, very different to that of the confident woman I'd met last week. I was reminded of what she'd said about first impressions. If this were our first meeting, I would have formed a very different opinion of her. I supposed that demonstrated how flawed most humans' ability to judge character often is. The warm, articulate woman I met first was the same woman who was cowering behind the door now. People had more than one side, and what's visible in any one moment is only a tiny part of the story.

'It's me – Beth.' She opened the door wider. Her eyelids were fully closed, her face clean of make-up.

'Come in.'

'Thanks. I'm coming inside now. I'll close the door behind me.' I spoke to her as I would any visually impaired patient, making sure she knew what my movements were. 'I'll pop my coat on the banister.' I shrugged off my long coat, taking in the room as I did. The door opened directly on to a bright space, a white-painted staircase with a beige runner was ahead and to my right was a large room with the two patio doors letting in light from over the water. There were no overhead lights or lamps on, which made the back of the room darker. I was drawn to the view beyond the windows, but stayed where I was, waiting to take Rachel's lead.

'Have a seat,' she said, moving forward and running her fingers along the back of one of two cream sofas. 'Sorry if the room looks a bit odd. I've moved things around so I don't bump into everything. You should have seen me back when all this started. My shins were black and blue.' She sat down gingerly. 'I tripped over that coffee table.' She waved a hand in the direction of a dark wood table next to the wall. 'I hit my chin when I fell. Had a massive bruise for weeks.'

'Very wise to set things up so there's nothing in the way,' I said, sitting on the other sofa and scanning my surroundings. It occurred to me that I would probably act differently if Rachel could see me. I remember reading about the Hawthorne effect, the way we modify our behaviour when we know someone is watching us. It would be considered rude to gawp around the way I was now. If Rachel's eyes were open, I would focus on her and steal glances rather than openly assessing, letting my eyes rest on the small desk with an office chair in the space under the stairs, then the oval mirror over a long console table with a simple beige lamp on one end.

A row of clothbound books sat on the narrow table, wrought-iron weights at either end keeping them upright. The bookends appeared to be repurposed sections of railway line. I peered at the books' titles. You could tell a lot about a person by the books they chose to display. These seemed to be all classics, for decoration purposes rather than reading preference. I was disappointed not to learn anything new about Rachel from them.

'Excuse the state of me, by the way,' she said. I turned back to her as she tugged at the bottom of her navy hoodie, which she wore with matching joggers. There was no denying she appeared very different to when she came to see me last Friday in a sleek outfit and full make-up. She'd apologised twice already too. Her entire demeanour had altered with her loss of sight. She was diminished somehow, and I found that moved me. 'I have to keep clothes simple on closed-eye days. I plan everything I need the day before, lay out my clothes, prepare food in advance, all that kind of thing.' She raised her brows, and I watched to see if her lids lifted, but none of her eyeball became exposed. 'I should be glad that at least there's a pattern to all this. I can plan ahead. Small mercies, I suppose. But it seems like every time it happens, even though I know it's coming, I'm starting again, stumbling about in the dark.'

'That must be hard.' My patients who were born blind, or who lost their sight, whether gradually or suddenly, were mostly on a one-way trajectory. It took time, but they gradually came to terms with their sight loss and navigated the world according to their new circumstances. Rachel couldn't do that. 'If you'd like me to take a look around, I could see if there are any obvious hazards.'

'That's a good idea,' she said. 'Although . . . maybe not today. This is going to sound stupid, but the rest of the house is a bit of a state. The benefit of living on three floors is that, if you make one tidy, you've at least got a livable space. The kitchen's on the next floor up, then the bedrooms are above that. Even though I've been here since November, I haven't unpacked all the boxes yet. I keep planning to get around to it, but I only have half the time to get things done now, and even when I can open my eyes I don't have the energy to face unpacking a home I might end up losing if this carries on much longer. I still can't believe this is happening.'

The muscles in her jaw tensed and I got the impression she was trying not to cry. My heart went out to her. I could imagine the excitement she'd felt when she moved into her dream home. The memory of that feeling was still easy for me to access, and I wouldn't wish for anyone else to have all that hope and potential torn from them.

'Don't worry. I'm not here to judge your living arrangements. I'm happy to check things are safe.'

Colour bloomed on her cheeks. 'Thanks, but . . . I hope you don't think I'm being ungrateful . . . I'm just so used to being independent, and I'm finding all this, well, I feel like I'm losing my agency, if you know what I mean.'

I shouldn't have pushed her. 'Of course. I'll do my examination and leave you to it.'

She swallowed. Her chin puckered as if still working hard to stop tears coming. 'Sorry. I'm being awful, aren't I? I am grateful you're here. Honestly.'

I moved to sit next to her and put a hand on her shoulder. She flinched. I lifted my hand. 'Sorry,' I said, mortified. 'I should have told you I was moving closer. I shouldn't have touched you without your consent. I'm so sorry.'

'No, I'm sorry,' she said. 'I'm a walking nerve ending when I'm like this. I've never suffered from anxiety before, but when I can't open my eyes every sound makes me jump. It's like I've been plunged into the darkest part of the night and I'm locked there, feeling like a frightened kid for two days at a time. I swear, I'll have a heart attack if this goes on much longer.'

'I'll do everything I can to get to the bottom of this,' I said, resisting the urge to comfort her. It was easier to fight my natural empathy when I was in a clinical environment. Seeing someone in distress in their own home was tough for me, but I needed to remain professional. 'Sorry if this seems like a personal question, but have you ever used dermal fillers or Botox on your face?'

She grimaced. 'I haven't had any fillers. Not yet, anyway. I'm not discounting it when I get more saggy . . . but I did have Botox a few times. Do you think this is because of that?' Her bottom lip slackened. 'Have I done this to myself?'

'No, I doubt very much that's the cause. In fact, Botox is one of the go-to treatments for blepharospasm.' I spoke quickly, not wanting her to blame herself. I knew all too well how destructive that could be.

'Really?' The crease that had formed between her brows relaxed.

'Yes.' I examined her face. Although her skin was smooth, the muscles around her eyes and on her forehead moved fairly naturally. It didn't appear to be paralysed. 'When did you last have Botox?'

The crease reappeared between her brows. Another sign it must've worn off. 'It was last summer, I think. Maybe June.'

Botox only lasted three to four months, although if it

was used for protracted periods, the muscles could train themselves to contract less. 'And how many years have you been getting the injections?'

'Oh, not many,' she said. 'Maybe two. I only have them here.' She touched her forehead. 'Because I noticed frown lines and I didn't want to look cross all the time.'

'You didn't have any around here? I'm just going to touch your face lightly so you know where I mean.' I placed the pad of my finger on the faint lines at the corner of her eyes.

'No. Honestly.'

'I believe you,' I said. 'Don't worry. Do you notice the light penetrate your eyelids at all? Everyone's eyelids are different, but the skin there is the thinnest on our bodies. At least some light usually passes through. I wear an eye mask to sleep in the summer, because even the early-morning light wakes me up.' I didn't know why I'd disclosed that personal detail.

'That's one of the scariest things,' she said, turning her head to the windows. The light illuminated the purple and blue spider veins on her eyelids. 'I know the windows are in that direction, because I see the blackness turn more of a kind of dark red.'

'Okay. That's a very normal response.'

'That's not the scary part.' She rubbed the hem of her sweatshirt between her thumb and forefinger. 'Sometimes I see dark shadows moving in front of the windows.'

My scalp tightened. I glanced over at the curtainless windows.

As if reading my mind, she said, 'I've been meaning to

measure up for curtains for months, but I haven't got round to it.' She folded her arms around herself. 'I wish I had. There's so much glass in this place.'

I relaxed a little when I realised that outside that window was a drop straight into the dock. 'Well, it would take Spider-Man to be close enough to cause a shadow through that window. There's nowhere to stand. It goes straight down to the water.'

She nodded, her arms crossed, fingers clutching her forearms. 'I know. I'm being stupid. Unless someone moored a boat right outside, or had a telescope on the other side of the dock, they couldn't see in from there.'

'Exactly.'

'So what's causing the shadows?' she said, her voice little above a whisper. 'If it's not someone outside, then . . .'

She let the question hang in the air. I turned my gaze back to the cold water of the dock, glad she couldn't see the unease on my face.

Chapter Ten

I turned back from the window to face Rachel. Her fingers still gripped her arms and her lips were pale and pinched. She was obviously frightened.

'It must be hard not to let your imagination fill in for your sight,' I said, giving myself a mental shake. Rachel wasn't seeing shadows through the patio doors, and she certainly wasn't seeing them inside her house. Not human shadows, anyway. 'The reflection of the water could cast ripples across the walls, or you could simply be reacting to the change of light when the sun disappears behind a cloud.' I spoke gently, hoping my words were reassuring. She would hear if someone was inside, surely? Neuroimaging studies of people who couldn't see showed activity in the areas of the brain normally associated with sight when they were asked to locate sound. 'And hearing tries to compensate for loss of sight, so I'm sure you'd hear ... anything unusual.'

Rachel released her arms and rubbed her hands back and forth over her thighs. 'I don't know if I would. Everything sounds strange when I'm like this, and I'm still getting used to the noises of this house.'

I knew what she meant. I had excellent vision, but I still jumped at the slam of my neighbour's door closing, or someone shouting out down by Regent's Canal, which ran alongside the block I'd moved into. Our old flat had been in a converted Victorian house. The walls were solid stone and the square was a quiet haven in the bustle of the East End. The walls in my new place off a busy road seemed like little more than chipboard in comparison.

'And it can get quite busy out there at night, over where the bars and restaurants are,' she continued, waving her hand in the direction of the dock. 'One of the reasons I moved here was because of all the lovely places to eat and drink, but when I'm in the dark the sound of footsteps nearby makes the hairs on my arms stand on end. Do you know what I mean? Even laughter sounds sinister when you're defenceless like this.'

'I understand.' I thought back to what Max told me when he asked me to take Rachel on as a patient. He said she'd had traumatic experiences with men, or something similar. I wondered what those experiences were, and how much they played into what she was feeling now. It was on the tip of my tongue to ask, but I decided not to. She had come to me because she was certain her symptom was physical, not psychological. I wouldn't allude to anything until I had discounted a medical cause. 'If it's okay with you, I'd like to try to lift your eyelids. Is that all right?'

She shifted her position so she was facing me on the sofa. 'Go ahead.'

'Just a second. I'll get my ophthalmoscope out of my bag.' I went back to where my bag sat on the pale wood floor next to the other sofa and got out the pocket-sized device that would let me see to the back of her eyes, if I could successfully open them. The chrome handle was cold against my hand. I moved to the other side of the sofa, away from the windows. Since there were no curtains, I wouldn't be able to make the room dark enough to get the best view, but there was nothing I could do about that. 'If you could turn towards my voice,' I said. 'It's a little darker if you move your head this way, so I'll be able to see better.'

She turned and raised her head. 'Okay. Can you run me through what you're doing, please? I'm a bit jittery, I'm afraid.'

'Of course. It must be pretty scary letting someone inside your home, then allowing them to examine the most vulnerable part of you. I'll try to be clear and gentle.'

'Thank you.' Her voice was thick with emotion.

'I'm going to sit close to you now, then I'm going to carefully touch the area around your eyes first. Is that okay?' She nodded. I sat next to her. 'Sorry if my fingers are a bit cold.' I put the ophthalmoscope on the cushion, then curled my fingers into my palms to try to encourage heat into them. 'I'm going to check the muscles. I'm looking for progressive external ophthalmoplegia, or ptosis, where the eyelid muscles weaken and droop.' I was ninety-five per cent sure she didn't have ptosis because her lids didn't relax over her eyes, but it was worth manipulating them again now the spasm was in effect. I touched her dark brows with my index fingers, then lifted them. The skin on her eyelids became taut, and a tiny sliver of eyeball appeared between her lashes. Her irises moved from side to side, as though desperate to take advantage of this tiny window on to the world. 'Can you see me?'

She lifted her chin. 'No. Everything's blurry.'

'That's to be expected when your eyes have been closed for a while.' There was the slight weakness I'd identified before, but nothing to explain the symptom. I took my fingers away and the slit of white, black and blue disappeared. She exhaled a disappointed sigh. 'Now I'm going to open your right eye using my thumb and index finger, okay?'

'Okay.' Her voice wavered and I could feel her brace beside me.

'I'll be gentle. Try to relax.' I switched on the light of my ophthalmoscope and took it in my right hand, using my left to nudge her eyelid apart. There was a lot of resistance. The orbicularis oculi muscles were clamped tight in a contraction. Sweat dampened my top lip. 'Stop me if this hurts.' I tried to prise them apart.

'It's okay.' I let go when she winced, then tried again as delicately as I could. 'I've tried to do this myself, but it's not easy, is it?' she said. The muscles in her jaw tensed as she gritted her teeth.

Nervously, I pushed my thumb and index finger apart with more pressure. Part of her blue iris came into view, then the pupil and the white shell of the sclera. Her muscles twitched hard under my fingers as they tried to blink.

'I hope this isn't too uncomfortable,' I said. 'You'll naturally want to blink against the light, but I'm going to keep your eyelids open for a second so I can take a proper look.'

'It feels like there's too much air on my eyeball,' she said. 'Does that sound weird?'

'Not at all. It will feel dry because your lids aren't smoothing it over with aqueous humour, the liquid that coats your eye.' I lifted the light. 'This will be very bright. I'm sorry.'

Finding it increasingly difficult to keep the eyelid from slipping from under my fingers, I peered into the back, but, as I expected, the retina was healthy and I couldn't detect any other abnormalities. I let go and her lids snapped shut. Feeling like I was performing torture, I repeated the process with her other eye, and got the same results.

Her eyelids became slippery with tears and it was harder to hold the lid in place. Liquid seeped from the canthus at the corner of her eye. She rubbed it away with a trembling hand.

'I'm sorry this is so distressing for you,' I said.

'Thank you,' she said.

My heart broke for her. 'Do you have anyone who could stay with you while we're investigating what's causing this?'

'No,' she said. My mum always said I worked too hard and should make more time for friends or relationships. But did I listen?'

A small part of me envied her for having the kind of

mother who gave sage, well-meaning advice. 'Could your mum stay, or another family member?'

'She died five years ago. There's no one. I really can't risk anyone from work finding out about this. I spent so long building my career, and now it's all going down the toilet because of some completely arbitrary condition no one can help me with.'

'Don't give up yet,' I said, desperate to offer her some hope. 'I haven't.' That was true. I had drawn a blank so far, but I was not a quitter. 'I'm going to go away and do more research. I'll do everything I can to help you.'

'Thank you,' she said, moving her hand until she found mine. She gripped it tightly. 'I can't tell you how much I appreciate this. I'm not coping that well, if I'm honest. When I'm on my own, the anxiety is . . . well, it's affecting me more than I could have imagined.'

Tears fell on to her cheeks. I took a breath in, then said, 'If you give me your phone, I'll put my number in. You'll be able to ask Siri to find it then, if you need it, won't you?'

'Really?' The hope in her voice brought a lump to my throat.

'Of course.'

She took an iPhone from the pocket of her joggers and held it near her face. 'Siri, open contacts.' She turned the screen towards me. 'I had to change face recognition so it recognised me with my eyes closed.'

'You can do that?'

'Yeah, you have to turn off *require attention* in settings. I just have to hope no one else wants to get into my phone while my eyes are closed or I'm asleep, because it would open if it was pointed at my face.' She held it out for me to check. 'Has it done it?'

'It has.' I took the phone from her and put in my details. 'I'm under Beth Sanderson,' I said, handing it back to her. 'I'll call my phone now and store your number in my directory.'

'Thank you so much. I promise I won't call unless I really, really need help.'

It was only when I was walking back towards Waitrose, where I'd parked my car, that a thought made sweat collect on my top lip. The last time I had given my personal number to a patient had been the start of the end for Joel and me. I wiped the moisture away. I had no husband to lose this time. The friends had left with him and I'd already lost the home I loved. I only had Max and my job left, and I'd given my number to Rachel because I was trying to do that to the best of my ability. I was a doctor. I had a duty to help her. Since I had to try to keep Max at arm's length, my work was my only reason to get up in the morning.

No, giving my number to Rachel was the right thing to do. Anyone with a shred of humanity would have done the same.

Chapter Eleven

Aaron had been quick to learn the system, picking things up the first time I explained them, and he was warm and professional with the patients. Added to that, he was punctual, well dressed and even smelled of something tangy and citrussy, which lingered pleasantly in rooms after he left. I patted myself on the back for employing him, glad that not every decision I made was a dud.

'I like the new boy,' said Clara Angus, an elderly woman with wet macular degeneration that was progressively eroding the centre of her vision. It was the end of her appointment, and she was in good spirits since the condition hadn't worsened significantly since I last saw her. 'If I was thirty years younger.' Her soft cheeks plumped in a cheeky smile.

'Boy?' I said, raising an eyebrow. 'He's in his mid-thirties.'

'When you're eighty-four, everyone looks like a child.' She patted me on the arm with a liver-spotted hand. 'Thanks for that prescription. I'll send William out for it this afternoon.' She gave a theatrical sigh. 'If his old legs will carry him as far as the chemist.' Her watery eyes glittered with mischief. 'If I had a toy boy like your Aaron, he could run there and back in a pair of those little shorts the rugby players wear.'

'Behave yourself,' I said, laughing, then feeling wrong for doing so. If an elderly man said that about a younger woman, I wouldn't be amused. Still, Clara was from a different era. 'And he's not my Aaron. He's got a girlfriend and he's an employee, a valuable one, so don't you scare him off.' I stood. 'Now, remember to put those drops in every morning, first thing.'

'You're no fun,' she said. She unhooked her leopard-print walking stick from the chair arm and heaved herself to standing. 'I'll make my next appointment with young Aaron on my way out, shall I?'

'You do that. And no shenanigans when I'm out of sight, you hear me?' I followed her to the lift near the top of the stairs. I rarely used it myself because my life was sedentary enough, but it was invaluable for patients like Clara, and those with significantly impaired sight.

Ten minutes later, Aaron knocked on my door. He came in holding a mug, and the rich aroma of filtered coffee filled the room. 'Thought you might need this.'

'Oh, thank you.' I was unusually tired. Whenever I woke in the night, Rachel's case would creep into my thoughts, and I didn't seem to be able to shift it and go back to sleep. It wasn't just the puzzle of her blepharospasms keeping me awake, it was her fear. I couldn't shake the sense that she really believed she was seeing someone's shadow beyond her closed eyelids. I smiled up at Aaron, seeing my face reflected in the lenses of his round glasses. 'I imagine you need something stronger than coffee after being accosted by Clara Angus.'

He put the mug on my desk and laughed. 'Don't worry about that. Old ladies are my speciality. The woman I care for is over eighty. There's nothing I haven't experienced before.' The smile melted from his face.

I imagined what was going through his mind. From what I'd seen of him, and as evidenced by the warm drink steaming on my desk, he was a thoughtful man. 'It must be difficult, watching someone you care about going through a difficult time.'

His shoulders rose and fell. 'It is what it is. I do my best for her. Can't do anything more.' He breathed in sharply. 'Right, your next patient isn't until this afternoon, so is there anything specific you'd like me to be getting on with?'

'Yes, actually there is. Follow me.' I stood and led the way to Joel's consulting room. I had to stop thinking of it like that. It was my other consulting room. I pushed open the door, trying not to let thoughts of when we first took over this floor overwhelm me. We were like giddy teenagers. We'd had sex on the desk against the right-hand wall, giggling when the legs rocked and we thought we might break it, but carrying on anyway. Three years later, when we were both exhausted from trying to combine our NHS shifts with our burgeoning private practice, this was the only place we regularly set eyes on each other. We'd fallen into an unhealthy pattern of only discussing patients, the care-home bills, or whose turn it was to put the rubbish out. The sex stopped. We rarely even touched.

I brought myself back to the moment and the plan I'd formulated in the early hours of the morning. 'I'd like you to research something for me.' I turned on the computer on the desk. 'I've got a patient whose eyes close for forty-eight hours, then open for forty-eight hours.'

Aaron blinked. 'Really? I've never heard of that before. Is it always for that exact amount of time?'

'Yep.'

'Wow.' His brow creased. 'Is that common?'

'Not common, no. At least, not the timing part.'

'I know that bodies can malfunction in weird ways, but that sounds . . . I don't know, a bit implausible.'

'Let's keep an open mind.' I cut him off, mildly disappointed with his response. I also felt strangely defensive, and I couldn't work out if that was for Rachel or myself. Either way, it wasn't his place to judge. I watched the screen come to life. 'She's convinced it's medical, rather than a psychological response, so that's what we'll investigate until we've excluded everything. I'd like you to help me research unusual eye conditions, and neurological problems which could affect the muscles around the eyes. I'll send you a list of the ophthalmic terms you might want to use, but it's worth using lay terms as well because I'm interested in articles from magazines and papers too.' I paused. 'I've seen the one from the *Sun* about the patient who had most of his orbicularis oculi, the sphincter-like muscle arranged concentrically around the upper and lower eyelids, removed.'

'No way.' He pushed his glasses up his nose, frown lines etched across his brow. 'God, that's grim.'

'It is. I'm hoping my patient won't need anything like that.'

'I completely get that,' he said. 'I'm on it. You only want eye-related stuff, though?'

I thought about it. 'Primarily, but if you think something you find could be relevant, I'm all ears. This patient needs help as quickly as possible. It's affecting her work as well as her life, so time is of the essence.'

'Got it,' said Aaron. He intertwined his fingers, drawing them back until his knuckles made a sickening crack, then sat and held his hands over the keys. 'Is it weird that I think this is the best job ever?'

I grinned. 'I would say it's ideal. Right, let's get to work. First one to solve the mystery gets a gold star.'

Chapter Twelve

That weekend, I finally had a chance to go through Aaron's findings on unusual eye conditions and collate them with my own. I sent the documents I thought might be useful to my cheap little home printer so I could lay them out and see them all at once. I thought that might help me recognise any similarities or patterns.

In the small kitchen off my living room, I turned on the Nespresso machine I'd brought from our old flat. It was too big for the space, but I didn't care. Caffeine was the only thing that kept me going sometimes. The display came to life, then the message telling me the machine needed descaling popped up. I sank back against the scratched aluminium sink and closed my eyes. That was always a half-an-hour job, one I'd be more inclined to do if I'd had a fucking coffee.

I balled my fists at the sound of the printer stuttering in the other room. This could not be happening. I kicked myself for not using the office printer to churn out all the articles and research papers. Eventually, after a YouTube tutorial on how to locate and remove a sliver of paper that had come away when I ripped it in frustration, I had the reams of print-outs I needed. I washed the ink from my fingers, took the paper through to my bedroom and spread the findings out on top of my duvet cover.

Armed with highlighter and pen, I sat cross-legged on the bed and picked up the first sheet. It was an account from a doctor who came across an elderly woman with muscle weakness, myasthenia gravis, which prevented her from opening her eyes, in an emergency room in the US. The doctor thought the transmission between the muscles and the nerve endings had been disrupted, which meant the patient lost the use of the muscles that controlled the eyelids. I read on, falling down a fascinating rabbit hole of neurotransmitters, enzymes and autoimmune responses, highlighting every part I thought could be useful.

There was a lot of information about the positive effects of Botulinum toxin, but no suggestion that regular cosmetic use could cause the spasms. Quite the opposite. And Rachel was clear she hadn't had any treatment for months and had only used it for a couple of years. I read through the rest of the sheets, highlighting passages and making notes in the margins.

I read up on the effects of dry eyes and allergies, still sure that neither was causing Rachel's involuntary eyelid closure. Could it be corneal irritation? Even if that was causing the initial spasms, I couldn't see how anything I read about could make sense of the specific timings she was experiencing.

Neurological disorders like peripheral neuropathy and compression nerve syndrome were possible. Electromyography, a diagnostic test that evaluated the health and function of skeletal muscles and the nerves that control them, would be a good place for a neurologist to start when I'd ruled out an eye condition, which I was still unwilling to do quite yet.

I was surprised when I looked up to find the light of the afternoon fading through the window. I'd been so engrossed I'd forgotten to eat lunch. I grabbed a quick sandwich and took my notes through to the living room, scanning all the documents again. There were elements I could equate with what was happening to Rachel, but only tenuously. I needed another pair of eyes on this. I opened my phone and sent a message to Max. *You free for lunch tomorrow? Want to pick your brains. It's on me. X*

Dancing dots appeared, followed by Max's reply. *The Strand, 1pm?*

I sighed, wishing I hadn't said I'd pay. Lovely as it was to take advantage of Max's membership of the exclusive private club, a lunch would set me back more than I could afford. Since I was the one asking for the favour, I tapped out, *Great. See you there! X* and pressed send.

Chapter Thirteen

The following day, I took the District Line tube from Mile End to Temple and then rushed through the miserable gloom of a typical January Sunday up to the Strand. An uneasy feeling made me turn and look behind me as I neared Max's club; the sensation of being watched moved like insects over my skin. My heart rate increased as I scanned the faces of people passing by. A tall woman in a hijab smiled at me when I caught her eye; a man pushing a bike glanced swiftly away. I scoured the pedestrianised area outside King's College, but didn't see anyone I recognised. I gave my head a shake. Listening to Rachel talk about someone being in her house had brought back my own experiences. That was all. No one was following me. I was just being paranoid.

I pulled myself together and pushed through the revolving door to the building's brown-hued reception, bracing myself to face the beautiful people behind the desk. Whenever I met Max there, I felt instantly intimidated by the youthful receptionists with their polished skin and effortlessly cool clothes. For some reason, I needed to justify why I dared to enter the hallowed halls of the rich, successful and creative – which I knew was ridiculous. It was a throwback to my upbringing, I supposed. I could imagine my mother asking why on earth anyone would want to be a member of an exclusive club. The word *exclusive* would turn ugly in her bitter mouth. It would change from desirable to somewhere that excluded people like us. It would be a judgement, and a reminder that I didn't belong. Moira would have laughed at that. It never failed to astound me that two sisters could be so polar opposite in outlook. If she were still alive, she'd remind me I was just as good as anyone else. Better, since I had a medical degree, and a private practice to my name. She'd tell me to own it, and have a cocktail for her.

Approaching the first receptionist to look up, I lifted my chin and harnessed my inner Moira. 'Hi. I'm here to meet Max Larson.' The woman, who had the most pronounced cheekbones I'd ever seen, glanced down at her screen, then back at me.

An obsequious smile made her cheeks protrude even further. 'I'm afraid Mr Larson hasn't arrived yet. Please take a seat until he gets here.' She gestured to a row of fold-down, theatre-type seats to my left. Cowed, and cursing Max for his tardiness, I moved towards the area that told anyone passing through that the people on those chairs were not exclusive. They were lesser beings, excluded until the person who was important enough to be a member arrived. Thankfully, before I had chance to lower the seat, I heard Max's voice.

I turned, and all resentment disappeared at the sight of his apologetic expression. 'So sorry I'm late.' He kissed me on both cheeks, then glanced at the receptionists. 'Wouldn't Cerberus and Co. let you go up?'

'I didn't ask. I just did what I was told,' I said. 'I'm a good girl, I am,' I added in a cockney accent.

He grinned, then gave his name at the desk and ushered us both into the lift, pressing the button for the eighth floor. 'How's things?' he said as the lift ascended.

'Good, thanks.' I saw myself standing outside, sure I was being watched, then yesterday, surrounded by work papers instead of friends and family. I thought about telling Max that the most exciting thing about my Saturday had been descaling the coffee machine, but I didn't. I couldn't. 'You?'

'Yeah, not bad. I went on a date last night, actually.'

My stomach flipped. I sent urgent signals to my facial muscles to remain impassive. The lift door opened and he strode out. This was the first time he'd mentioned dating someone since he'd told me he was in love with me. Even before his declaration, my feelings for him had slowly crept up on me, until one day I realised that seeing Max was the only thing I still looked forward to in life. He knew me, and what I'd done, but he still cared about me.

It was six months after my split with Joel when Max told me how he felt, and it was all I could do not to tell him that I felt exactly the same way. But that wouldn't have been fair. I'd loved Joel enough to marry him, and look what I did to him. The years of Mum telling me that my father left us because of me had burrowed deep into my self-structure. Rationally, I knew that was unlikely to be true. No matter how brattish a toddler I was, it was hard to believe that I was bad enough for him to desert his family. The more logical explanation was that he couldn't tolerate her drinking and her bitterness. I'd never know for sure because we got news of his death before I reached double digits, so my mother's truth stood unchallenged. And logic doesn't apply to the subconscious and, somewhere deep inside, what she said became part of my belief system.

Whatever the truth about my father, one thing Mum said was right: I ruined everything good. My marriage was proof of that. I wouldn't let myself hurt this kind, thoughtful man too. I let him down as gently as I could, pretending my feelings for Joel were still too strong, extending the period of time between our regular catch-ups. Much as it hurt to draw away, I didn't trust myself not to lean forward and kiss him in a moment of weakness, and that would be selfish. The irony was he was the one person I wanted to share how I felt with, but I couldn't exactly complain to him about how lonely I was after rejecting him.

Telling me about his date felt like a step back into solid friendship territory, and I should be grateful for that. It's what he thought I wanted, what I did want. It was a move forward. If only my thumping heart could catch up with my brain. Instead, it felt like it had dropped into my stomach. It was all too fucking sad. 'Ooh, tell me more.'

He turned left and started up the stairs. 'Not much to tell. She was a kiwi too, and she was nice enough.'

'Nice enough?' We reached the top of the stairs, and I

glanced right towards the roof terrace, where the raised swimming pool glistened an unnatural cyan blue against the battleship-grey sky.

'Yes, nice. She was nice.'

'Hardly a glowing endorsement.' We carried on into the main room with its floor-to-ceiling windows and glorious view across the city. A man with a shaved head showed us to our table and I tried not to stare at the ornate tattoos circling his neck, or the flesh tunnel earrings that stretched his lobes to twice their natural size. The table was next to the window, and beyond the balcony a dark blue flag with hints of red and white drooped above the Australian Commission. 'Will you see her again?' I steeled myself.

Max took the menu from the bald man with a smile, then stared down at it. 'Maybe.' He put the menu down and sighed. 'Sorry, I don't know why I brought that up.'

'It's okay,' I said. I was trying to convince myself as much as him. It wasn't even remotely fair that I didn't want him to date other women, and I certainly didn't want to let him know I felt that way.

'No, it's weird. We've been dancing around each other like a pair of emotionally immature teenagers for a year now.' He glanced out of the window, clearly embarrassed. He turned back to me. 'Fuck it. I don't really know how to be around you any more. I wish I'd never told you how I felt.'

'It's okay,' I repeated. 'It's fine.' He looked away again, and I didn't blame him. My brain floundered around for the right words. I reached out and touched his hand, but immediately saw that was a mistake when his gaze rested on my fingers over his. I withdrew my hand and dropped it into my lap. 'If my head wasn't already a mess . . .' What was I doing? I shouldn't be giving him hope. 'I'm so grateful for your friendship.' He kept his eyes on his hand and nodded. Silence pulsed between us. 'Seriously. I owe you so much. What you said to Joel, I won't forget it.'

'You're a good doctor. It wouldn't have been right to let him destroy your career out of spite.'

I forced myself to smile. It hadn't been spite that led Joel to seriously consider reporting me to the GMC before Max talked him out of it. It had been his keen sense of right and wrong, a sense I'd shared until I blurred the lines. No, not blurred: crossed.

'Well, I'm grateful. I just want you to know that. Who knows where I'd be without you stepping in? Me and Mum would both be out on the street, probably.'

'How is your dear mother?' He glanced up. 'Have you seen her recently?'

'Yep, last weekend.' His shoulders dropped a centimetre and I could tell he was glad of the change of subject. 'She was very much . . . herself.'

'That good, eh?' He grinned. Before I stepped back from him, I'd shared much of what happened during my childhood. He'd listened and sympathised, and even offered to recommend a therapist. I probably should have taken him up on it. For some reason I'd always resisted getting help for the issues resulting from what happened back then, what was still going on between myself and my mother. I was sure a therapist would have plenty to say about why I avoided getting help.

Now, sitting across from this gentle man, I allowed myself to imagine him visiting her with me one day. He was the kind of man she admired, despite herself. Joel was too working-class-made-good for her to truly respect him, despite all he'd achieved. And he wasn't cowed by her. She hated that. I suspected she resented him for making me happy too. He partially rebuilt what she tore down, which meant she had less power over me for a while. Max was from a different background entirely, one she pretended to loathe, but he'd know how to manage her. He would be interested and attentive, and she would succumb to his charm because of her own vanity.

'I wasn't even allowed to stay for a cup of tea. I was told I was too busy.'

'Ah, the old make someone else the demon so you can be the martyr technique? Number three in the elderly parents' handbook, I believe. It's a tactic. Try to forget it, if you can.'

He had a knack of making me feel like I wasn't to blame for anything, and I loved him for it. I caught that thought and threw it away before it could reach my heart.

'I'll do my best.'

'Make sure you do.' He wagged a finger at me. 'What was it you wanted to run by me?'

A vision of tears seeping from Rachel's closed eyes appeared in my mind's eye. 'I wanted to talk to you about Rachel Cartwright, the woman with the forty-eight-hour blepharospasms.'

'Oh, yes.' He raised his eyes to mine. 'Any luck finding out what's going on there?'

I leaned down to take the folder containing my research notes out of my bag. I opened it and put the papers on the table, over the cutlery and perfectly folded napkin. 'I was going through this lot yesterday, and—'

'Yesterday?' His eyes narrowed. 'Saturday?'

'Yes, I wasn't busy, so—'

'Are you billing the time?' He cocked his head to the side.

Heat rushed to my cheeks. I stared down at the papers in front of me. It was a thick pile, the margins filled with notes, and yellow highlighter blocking out long passages. 'It's an interesting case. Research is part of the job.'

The waiter came over. 'Any drinks?'

'I'll have a margarita picante, please,' said Max.

I wasn't sure a cocktail was a good idea at lunchtime, but maybe tequila would dull the feeling of discomposure Max's questions brought out in me. 'I'll have the same, thank you.'

When the waiter was out of earshot, Max leaned his chin on his hands. He had the stubble he only allowed himself to grow at the weekend, the dark shadow flecked grey near his ears. We were old enough for grey hairs. The years were passing, and I would grow old alone. His clear eyes searched my face. 'When I asked if you'd treat this patient, I didn't expect you to spend your weekends working for free.'

'I know.' I resisted the urge to shove the papers back in my bag.

'I'm not having a go.' The kindness in his voice made

me feel worse. 'I worry about you, that's all. Last time you got so involved in a case—'

'That was different,' I said, my chest tightening.

'I know, but it started like this, with you getting . . .' He scanned the room as though looking for the right words. 'Over-invested, caring too much.'

Defensive anger flared in my gut. 'I am not over-invested.' The waiter put our drinks down in front of us and I took a gulp, the acid of the lime and the heat of the chilli hitting the back of my throat and making me cough.

'Go easy.' Max sipped his drink demurely, as if showing me the way.

I wanted to tell him he wasn't my mother, but my mother wouldn't tell me to go easy. She'd tell me I was an idiot for knocking back an expensive drink as if it were water and that I deserved everything I got. That was what she said after Joel left, that I'd been reckless and selfish. She told me I'd made my own bed so I should damn well lie in it. It was almost as if she relished my downfall, as if she'd been waiting for it. She had no idea how lonely I'd been, how Joel and I had stopped behaving like a couple long beforehand. I doubt she would have cared if she had. I viewed Max across the table, the anger melting away. He was the only one who'd stuck by me. He wanted the best for me. I lifted the glass back up, took a tiny sip, then raised it to him.

'I worry about you, that's all,' he said. 'I don't want you to get too emotionally involved with a patient again, not after last time.'

'I'm not going to fall into bed with Rachel Cartwright,' I said. 'I'm boringly heterosexual. You know that.'

'Yes,' said Max, in a tone that told me there was a *but* coming. He crossed his arms, and I braced myself for a lecture. 'You're a brilliant doctor, Beth, and that's partly because you have this compulsion to help people. Most of us are so jaded by the time we become consultants that a patient is a puzzle to solve, rather than a human being like us, with people they love and who love them back. If I'm being honest, I'm glad I'm desensitised to some degree. That serves me better. It's harder to cut into the eye of someone you've started to care about, isn't it?'

'I can slice into anyone's eyeball quite happily,' I said, shimmying my shoulders. 'Don't you worry about me.' I leaned in and lowered my voice. 'I'm not getting too involved.'

His gaze dropped to the papers on the table, then up at me, his brow lifting minutely. 'You can't save everyone, no matter how many weekends you work. Just don't start caring too much for this woman, Beth. No good can come of it.'

'I won't,' I said, as if the idea was preposterous. He didn't look convinced, and I didn't blame him. He knew me well enough, and we both knew I was lying.

Chapter Fourteen

The next day my mouth was dry, and my brain sluggish. Max and I had shared a bottle of wine, then another large glass after our cocktails yesterday, and I hadn't drunk enough water. Despite his gentle chastisement, he'd gone through my findings with me and, when the bill came, he'd insisted on paying, and it was all I could do not to throw my arms around him in gratitude. I didn't usually drink much, and when the soporific effects of the alcohol took hold I found myself looking at Max through a soft-focus lens, wondering if it would really be so bad if we got together. Thank goodness I hadn't acted on drunken impulse. Not only would I be bound to fuck it up romantically, but Max was pretty much the only friend I had left, and if I lost him then I really would be alone.

Aaron was already there when I arrived at work, looking well rested and cheerful. I envied his clear, bag-free eyes. My head throbbed and I had a craving for carbohydrates. 'This is probably deeply unprofessional,' I said, 'but you wouldn't pop out and get me a pain au raisin and a latte, would you? I'd have grabbed them myself on my way in, but I was running late, and I need to catch up on my first patient's notes.' I was always prepared for the patients in my clinics, so this was out of character and unprofessional. Even I could accept I'd been obsessing about Rachel so much I'd let my interest in other patients slide. If Max was right, and I did care too much, I needed to share that out more equally.

'No problem,' he said. 'Late night?'

'No, just a long lunch. It's embarrassing, really. I'm such a lightweight. I met up with my friend Max and I don't usually drink much, so I was sloshed on half a bottle.' I didn't add, plus the cocktail, plus another bucket-sized glass of wine.

'Max, eh? Is he a friend, or . . .?' He held a hand up. 'Sorry, that was inappropriate. I have no filter – that's my problem. It's absolutely none of my business.' He wobbled his head. 'Obviously.'

I laughed. 'Max Larson is a very good friend of mine.' I leaned on the word *friend*, then wondered why Aaron had asked. Surely he didn't have ideas about us outside our working relationship? I gave myself a shake. Of course he didn't. He'd told me about his girlfriend when we first met. And, Jesus, did I think I was that irresistible? 'He's an ophthalmologist too. He works at Moorfields and has his own practice.'

Aaron nodded, as if he knew who Max was. 'Looks like he's a bad influence.' His lips rose on one side in an amused smile. 'Best steer clear of Max Larson in future.'

'Ha, yes! This is all Max Larson's fault.' I shook my head. 'Not really. He's a very lovely man and I was asking for his professional advice.' A wave of exhaustion engulfed me. 'He was the one who asked me to take on the case we were researching, actually. He's as puzzled as we are by Rachel Cartwright.'

'Really? So this case has got two eminent doctors flummoxed?' Aaron's eyes were large and questioning through his round glasses. Evidently, it wasn't just me who'd been sucked right in by this mysterious case. He looked as interested as I was.

'I don't know about eminent, in my case, at least, but yes. It's got us all foxed.' I was sorry I didn't have time to discuss it further. Margaret Dawson, MP, was my first patient, and she was always early. She acted as if I were wasting precious time she could be spending saving the country even when I saw her at exactly the appointed time. I needed caffeine and sugar, and I needed them fast. 'Can you dump a sugar in that coffee, please?'

He opened his mouth and hesitated, as if he wanted to say more, but after a moment he said, 'Will do,' and made his way out of the room.

I fell on to my sofa when I got home, too tired to think about anything other than my bed. I'd been mainlining carbs at every opportunity during the day, Aaron acting like my enabler. When he brought a greasy bacon sandwich and family-sized Galaxy in for me at lunchtime, he earned the award for best employee ever. Now, though, it felt like the thick white bread and sugary chocolate were pushing their way back up my gullet. I searched through the bag of various medications I kept in the bathroom cupboard but didn't have anything for acid reflux. Fuck my life.

I turned on the TV and scrolled the channels. Nothing appealed to me, so I tuned into *Selling Sunset* on Netflix, massaging my bloated stomach as I mindlessly watched the impossibly thin woman in tiny clothes teetering around ultra-expensive LA properties in ankle-threatening heels. The absurdity of women with dangerously low BMIs using their surface beauty to sell homes valued for what they looked like above comfort or homeliness made me question the evolution of the human race. Surely we should have realised that appearances were only skin deep, and homes were made up of the people who lived in them by now?

Glancing around my lonely flat, the thought made my mood plummet lower. It then occurred to me that many of the beautiful homes featured would have been razed to the ground in the recent wildfires anyway and tears pressed at the back of my eyes. I gave myself a talking-to. If I was going to cry at anything, it should be the people suffering in the Middle East, not myself or a bunch of wealthy Americans who probably had a house on every continent. Then I couldn't shake the images of lost and injured children, and the tears came. I brushed them away, furious at myself for being an emotional wreck. I was always like this when I needed to sleep. I pulled the blue-and-white wool throw from the back of the sofa and draped it over myself.

I'd have a quick nap, then get something nutritious to eat, if I had space.

A buzzing sound woke me. I opened my eyes to darkness. I lifted my head, my skin prickling with the fear of knowing I wasn't in my own bed. I blinked as my eyes adjusted to the dim light and became aware of the lights from barges on Regent's Canal through the patio window at the far end of the room. I was in my sitting room. I was safe. I picked my phone up from the coffee table where it buzzed against the wood. The digits on the screen told me it was 1 a.m. Every hair on my body stood on end.

I slid the green icon to accept the call. 'Hello?' I said, my dry voice rasping on the word.

'Beth.' Rachel's voice on the end of the line whispered. 'There's someone here.'

I sat up, alert. 'Where are you?'

Her breath came down the line, fast and ragged. 'I'm at home. There's someone in the house. I can hear them moving around.'

'Are your eyes open?' I tried to calculate whether it was an open-eye day, but my brain wouldn't click into gear. I blinked around my dark room. The shadows on the walls were ominous enough with my eyes wide open. I stood and flicked on the overhead light, the sudden brightness making me flinch.

'No. I can't see. I can't open my eyes. I'm frightened, Beth. I don't know what to do.' Tears bubbled in her voice.

'I'm going to call the police,' I said. 'I'll tell them what you've told me, and explain your condition, then I'll come over straight away. Okay?' The muffled sound of her crying made my chest contract. 'Okay?' I repeated. 'I need to end this call, so I can ring the police. Can you hear me, Rachel?' My heart thundered when she didn't reply. 'Rachel?'

'Yes. Please hurry,' she whispered, 'I'm so scared,' then the line went dead.

I thanked the Lord I was still fully dressed. Throat tight with dread, I grabbed my coat and my car keys and punched 999 into my phone.

Chapter Fifteen

Adrenalin made my hands shake on the steering wheel. I pulled up behind a police car parked on Thomas More Street near the entrance to St Katharine Docks' East Basin and dragged on the handbrake. A beeping sound broke the silence when I opened the passenger door. I hadn't switched the headlights off. Cursing, I flicked the switch, and the road ahead went dark, before being briefly illuminated in a burst of orange when the indicators flashed as the car locked. I glanced around me, the feeling of eyes on my back from yesterday returning. The street was empty. No one was following me. I was just on high alert.

I dragged my puffa jacket tighter against the freezing air and rushed into the dock towards the water, then turned left towards Rachel's house. I paused at the sight. In the middle of the row, hers was like a glowing beacon against the dark, every window blazing with light. The turret stood out against the blue-black sky like a lighthouse. Dark figures moved around inside. My heart leaped, then settled when I remembered they were police officers, not intruders. There was only one police car in the street: no van, no blue lights, no yellow crime-scene tape being strung around Rachel's home. These were all good signs.

I rushed along the terrace to the back of her house, knocking hard on the door. A young female police officer opened it. 'Can I help you?'

'I was the one who rang the police. Beth Sanderson. I'm, erm, Rachel's doctor.' I wasn't surprised to see the woman's thickly drawn eyebrows dip in confusion. Very few people would ring their doctor first in a time of non-medical crisis.

A voice came from further inside the house. 'Beth, is that you?'

'Yes,' I shouted. The police officer stood aside, and I rushed in. Rachel was sitting on the sofa facing away from the windows.

'Thank you for calling the police, and for coming over. It's a lot to ask, I know,' she said, when I sat next to her. 'I can't tell you how scared I was.'

I took her hand to reassure her I was there. It was cold and clammy. 'You okay?'

'I think so.'

I raised my head at the sound of heavy footsteps on the stairs behind us. A thick-set male police officer with a goatee beard that extended over his several chins reached the bottom and wandered over to the patio doors, staring out at the lights of the boats moored on the water. He took an audible breath and turned to us. 'We've done a thorough search, and there's no one here, Ms Cartwright.' The way he said 'Ms' sounded deliberate. I wondered if he'd called her 'Mrs' initially and she'd corrected him. Pronounced marionette lines deepened his scowl, and he exuded an air of disdain. 'And there's no evidence of a break-in.'

Rachel held my hand tighter. 'I heard someone moving about. I know I did.'

The female police officer came to stand nearer. There was sympathy in her eyes, at least. 'I imagine you feel quite vulnerable when you can't open your eyes,' she said. 'Maybe the noises were' – she shrugged – 'just normal, and you thought it was an intruder.' Her south-east London accent was strong, the 'l' at the end of the words pronounced as a 'w' and the 'th' an 'f'. I'd said 'fink' instead of 'think' once in front of my mother and got a sharp slap across the face for my slattern voice. I could still feel the sting now.

'I . . . I don't think . . .' Rachel let go of my hands and raked through her hair with shaking fingers. 'I don't know. Maybe.' She exhaled. 'I suppose there's no other explanation.'

'You haven't given a key to anyone else?' asked the man, brusquely. 'No ex-boyfriends?'

Rachel's expression soured. She turned her head in the man's direction. 'No. No ex-boyfriends,' she said, her tone icy. I could imagine her then, in court, disassembling a witness's statement, and felt a shiver of pride.

The male officer seemed to shrink. 'All right, only asking.' He glanced at the female officer as if looking for an ally, but her eyes were still on Rachel.

'If you're scared again, give us a call, yeah? And I hope your eyes get better soon.'

The male officer's jaw tightened as his colleague spoke and I could imagine the effort it took him not to roll his eyes. It made me feel even more protective of Rachel. How were women meant to feel safe when we were sneered at for asking for help?

'Right, you ready?' he said. The female officer followed him to the door. I stood and saw them out, offering my thanks directly to the woman, avoiding the eyes of the man, who clearly thought Rachel was wasting his precious time. If he'd heard her voice when she first called me, he would be in no doubt she was genuinely frightened. When they reached the last red brick step, I closed the door, turned the latch and pulled the handle to make sure it was locked.

'I've checked the door,' I said, moving back to the sofa. 'It's locked properly.'

'Will you stay for a bit?' Rachel said, then hung her head. 'Sorry, that's not fair of me to ask. It's the middle of the night and you've already done more than—'

'I'll stay. It's okay.' I sat beside her, trying not to think about my NHS shift, which started at 8.30 a.m. at Moorfields. 'I think I might have parked on double yellow lines, though.'

'Oh, if you need to move the car . . .'

'No, it's fine.' I couldn't believe I was talking about parking when the woman in front of me was still trembling. A parking ticket wouldn't kill me. 'How are you doing?'

'I wasn't making it up,' she said, her voice urgent. 'I know there was someone here. I could feel them watching me.'

I tensed. Before, she'd said she could hear someone moving around. Watching was different. It was a feeling I knew all too well. 'What do you mean?'

She shuddered. 'I had that very specific sense that someone was staring at me. Do you know what I mean? It's like a sixth sense. You don't even have to be able to see them to know their eyes are following you. I felt that.' Her fingers clenched in and out of fists. 'I know they said everything looks normal, but that isn't how it feels. Appearances can be deceptive, can't they? Just because somewhere looks safe, it doesn't mean it is.'

'Just to be clear,' I said, as insects crawled over my skin again, 'could you hear someone in the house?'

'Yes,' she said, 'but it was more than that.' She put her hand across her heart as though swearing an oath. 'I don't expect you to believe me. The police were clonking around in their boots long enough for me to believe they did a thorough search. It must be in my head. There's no other explanation, is there?' She let her hand drop. 'But I felt it. I really did. I felt someone watching me.'

'I believe you,' I said.

Her expression lightened. 'Do you? Really?'

'Yes,' I said. 'Because, not too long ago, it happened to me.'

Chapter Sixteen

We went up to Rachel's kitchen on the first floor. It was an enviably sleek space, at the back, away from the windows, with dark green-grey fitted units with chrome handles. A granite island with low-backed leather stools at either side stood near the front, in the semicircle where the first portion of the black-clad turret protruded out over the water. I told Rachel to sit while I made us both a cup of chamomile tea, carefully following her instructions about where to find everything.

'Your cupboards are so organised,' I said. 'I'm jealous.'

'I can't stand clutter,' she said. 'It clogs up my thinking. I try to keep things as streamlined as I can.'

Another thing to admire about this woman. I put the mug down in front of her.

'Give it a minute. It's hot.'

'I'm excited about having a hot drink,' she said. 'I hardly dare use the kettle when my eyes are closed.'

'I can imagine.' Again, I enjoyed the freedom to take in my surroundings, when, ordinarily, I would have focused on the person I was with. I gazed out of the first window across the dock from the entrance on Thomas More Street, then turned to see a full ninety degrees round to the Dickens Inn on the other side of the basin, the bright tip of the Shard piercing the night sky. As I did, I considered all the things that are impaired by loss of sight and felt a moment's pride at my choice of career. I was glad I was here to help Rachel. I think Moira would have been proud of me, even if Mum wasn't. I turned back to the room. It was so neat and tidy. Rachel must've finished unpacking when her eyes were open over the weekend because there wasn't a thing out of place. I envied her the ability to live in such an ordered way. I'd never managed it myself. Then I felt guilty for the thought. Of course Rachel had to create order. She couldn't clutter the place up if she wanted to. A left-out hoover or washing piled on the stairs could kill her if she tripped over them when her eyes were closed.

I caught my reflection in the window. It was unavoidable in this place. It seemed like this house with all its glass was determined to hold up a mirror to me, and it was unnerving. I didn't like what I saw. Deep shadows ringed my eyes and my face appeared gaunt and sad. Looking past my reflection at the dock outside made me feel exposed. I shuddered at the thought of anyone being able to see us sitting at the island, her with her eyes closed, me with my haunted appearance.

'Are you sure you wouldn't prefer to sit downstairs, where there aren't as many windows?' I said. 'I know I avoided being anywhere near glass when . . . when I felt vulnerable.'

'It's okay. It's a pretty view, when you can see it.'

She wasn't wrong. When I peered again beyond the image of myself in the glass, the reflection of the lights strung across the bows of the boats glittered on the black water and the Georgian-style streetlamps gave off a soft yellow glow.

Rachel took a sip of her drink, her lips twitching when the hot liquid touched them. She put the mug down carefully. 'I hope you don't think I'm prying, but what did you mean before, when you said it happened to you?'

I curled my hands round my mug. 'I'm one of the twenty per cent.'

'Twenty per cent?'

'Or fifteen, or twenty-five, depending on which reports you believe. The percentage of women who've been stalked.'

'Christ. I'm sorry you've had that experience.' She reached her hand across the island, and I took it and squeezed before letting go. 'What happened?'

'Are you sure you want to know, given what's happened this evening?' It was stupid of me to mention it. The last thing a frightened woman needed was to be told scary true-life stories.

'Beth' – her voice was firm – 'you know what I do for a living. There's nothing you can tell me that I haven't heard far too many times before. If it happened to you, then I want to know, because you're my friend.' She paused. 'I hope I'm not overstepping by saying that.'

I smiled, surprised at how lifted I was by her words. More than lifted, hopeful, as if she were offering me a layer of warmth when I was cold. A tiny voice in my head reminded me to consider professional boundaries, but I didn't want to listen. I'd been so lonely for so long. 'You're not overstepping.'

'Good.' She smiled for the first time that night. 'Who was it? Do you know?'

'A patient,' I said, glad she couldn't see my face. 'He was a little older than me. He was kind and interesting at first, and he seemed vulnerable, like he really needed my help. He was intensely grateful, made me feel like I was changing his life, not just helping his eyesight. I suppose my vanity got the better of me. We got close.' Simon's traditionally handsome face appeared in my mind's eye. I saw his dark blond hair, grey at the temples, his perfect teeth when he smiled. How easily he'd hooked me in. How naïve I'd been not to see his obsessive behaviour for what it was. 'It was all perfectly normal at the beginning. I treated his eyesight, then he kept coming back with more issues. He acted like I'd completely changed his life, like I was his saviour, and it made me feel good – needed, I suppose.'

I didn't add that I always experienced a trill of excitement when his name appeared on my appointment list. There was an undeniable chemistry between us. Mine and Joel's relationship was floundering. Mum was demanding more of my time as she slowly recovered her speech and movement, and the cost of her care was spiralling. I was love-starved and lonely and the attention Simon gave me quenched a thirst I hadn't acknowledged I had. When he told me he couldn't make it to Bath Street for one appointment and asked me for a home visit, somewhere deep inside me I knew what it would lead to. I should have said no, but I didn't. I pretended it was just work, and when I got there I was impressed by his flat in Mayfair, with its uniformed doorman and birdcage elevator. I'd only ever seen them in movies before. It all seemed like a film: unreal somehow. Maybe that's why I let things happen the way they did: I pretended I was someone else, having an experience I would never allow myself in my true reality.

I examined him, and he persuaded me I was doing something extraordinary, that I was special and gifted. For a short while, I felt like I was the person he seemed to think I was, like I could replace my mother's voice in my head with his, that I could believe I was worthy of the life I had. I should have stopped him when he leaned in to kiss me, but I didn't. I got carried away in feeling like I was a film star, and we ended up moving to his bedroom and having sex. I regretted it immediately. I left straight afterwards, unable to believe I had broken both my marriage vows and my medical ones at once. I tried telling myself that he wasn't really a patient. There was nothing wrong with his eyesight, after all. But I had gone there in a professional capacity, so lying to myself didn't work. The self-loathing was intense. It grew inside me like a tumour.

Maybe Joel sensed something was going on, because he suggested we talked, and when we sat down, face to face, he told me how much he missed me, and that he'd come to terms with what I needed to do for Mum, and understood why. We were in this for better or worse and shouldn't let money get between us. He wanted us to sort out our schedules so we could spend quality time together. He said he loved me and wanted us to start a family. I realised how much I still loved my husband and the magnitude of the mistake I had made. I discharged Simon and told him I could never see him again.

Even though the scenes were playing out in my head, I couldn't bring myself to tell Rachel I'd slept with Simon. I was still warmed by the fact she'd called me a friend. If she knew the details of the last couple of years, I was sure she'd rethink, and I didn't want her to. I wanted her friendship very much indeed.

'When I realised he had an unhealthy view of me, of our relationship, I said I couldn't treat him any more and tried to cut off contact. He took it badly. He started to call, a lot. When I blocked him, he rang reception and asked to be put through to me. When I put a stop to that, he started to ask to be put through to my husband. My ex-husband,' I corrected myself. The memories clogged my throat. 'He didn't say anything in the calls. I think it was just a tactic to get me to acknowledge him.' I swallowed. 'He would use different numbers to call me at all hours of the day and night. Then I would see him sitting in his car on Bath Street.' I was meant to see him. I knew that. He was certainly the only man I knew who drove a Bentley. 'Then he would drive around the square where we lived, always slowing down outside our house.'

'I'm sorry that happened to you. It sounds very disturbing.'

'It got worse,' I said, shame at not disclosing my part

in the proceedings, at least, burning in my gut. 'He would stand in the square, staring up at our flat. I got scared to go near the windows.' I glanced out at the thick blackness of the sky, then down at the dock, feeling that familiar terror reverberate through me.

'What did the police do?'

I closed my eyes, acid burning in my stomach as I recalled the day Joel insisted we went to the police. I had no choice then but to tell him the truth about what had happened between me and Simon.

'I'm so, so sorry,' I'd said. 'I don't know why I did it. I've never regretted anything so much in my life. You have to believe me.' He'd slumped on to the sofa as if I'd punched him. I could still hear the sound of the air escaping from the cushions.

When he'd eventually looked up at me, there was disgust in his eyes. 'You did this.' He gestured to the windows. 'This stalking, all the phone calls, that weirdo frightening our staff, is your fault. You started it. Jesus. You were his doctor, for fuck's sake. You know how wrong that is, before we even start on what you've done to our marriage. I would've trusted you with my life, Beth. And you've brought this psycho into our lives.' He'd covered his eyes with both hands and rocked forward. 'What have you done? This can't be happening. You've destroyed everything.'

I ended up going to the police station alone.

'The police did about as much as the two who were here earlier.' I sighed. 'Someone with about as much empathy as the male officer took a statement. Simon must've been questioned, though, because a few days later I got a letter from a lawyer accusing me of defamation and threatening to sue me.'

'Jesus.'

'Yep.' I didn't add that I spent at least the following month waiting for a letter from the General Medical Council telling me I'd been struck off. I still found it hard to believe no one reported me, not Simon, the police, Joel or any of our old friends. I only found out later that Joel was about to report me, but Max persuaded him not to. I lost everyone, though. In many ways, that was probably harder than losing my job.

'Did he stop?'

I nodded, then remembered Rachel couldn't see me. 'I think so. As far as I'm aware, anyway. I sometimes feel vulnerable, though, as if someone could still be watching me. But I'm sure that's all in my head.' I took a drink to try to dislodge the blockage the memories of Joel trying to forgive me, then admitting he couldn't and asking for a divorce, formed in my throat. 'Is there anyone you can think of that might hold something against you? Someone you prosecuted, maybe?'

'I doubt it,' she said. 'I'm not saying there's no one out there with a grudge, but I deal with organised crime at work and I'm a very small fish when it comes to that kind of set-up.' She emphasised the word *very.* 'They wouldn't target me. There's nothing to achieve by it. Hard to believe, but they're run like any other business: resources spent where they're most needed, if you know what I mean. And before I had to take the time off I wasn't even involved in any cases where someone might want to intimidate me into behaving how they want. I've been thinking about it, and I've come up blank.'

'Maybe it was just the unfamiliar sounds around here.' I tried to tune in to the noises of the house as I gazed out across the basin, listening for the hum of the fridge, the hiss of water through the central heating pipes. The conversation I had with Max when he asked me to treat Rachel came back to me. 'And you can't think of anyone from your past who might want to . . .' The words *hurt you* came to mind, but I didn't want to say that.

'No.' Rachel spoke quickly. 'No one.'

'You can't think of anyone who—'

'Can we talk about something else?' Rachel said abruptly. 'I'm sorry, but I'm still feeling pretty shaken. I need to settle my nerves if I'm going to get any sleep at all.'

I watched her roll her shoulders, then move her neck from side to side, with the keen sense that the movements were designed to distract me. Rachel clearly didn't want to talk about her past and I couldn't help wondering why.

Chapter Seventeen

The Watcher

You're wearing that awful puffa jacket when you scurry out of St Katharine Docks at 6 a.m. I watch you pull the hood up against the rain and hurry to your car. You're lucky you didn't get a ticket, parking on double yellow lines like that. But you weren't thinking about that when you arrived last night, were you? You were thinking about your new friend, poor Rachel, with her clamped-shut eyes and fear of things that go bump in the night. It's going to get a lot worse for her, bless her. And you. This is just the start.

You stayed longer than you should, and now you don't have long to get ready before your shift at Moorfields. I know your schedule off by heart, and I'm shocked at you, Beth. A good girl like you would usually get a decent night's sleep before treating vulnerable patients. Eyesight is so precious, wouldn't you agree?

But you're not such a good girl, are you? You've made mistakes and you've tried to hide them. But I know everything. That's why I'm here, watching you, biding my time, waiting to make my next move.

Chapter Eighteen

I was in a complete daze the following morning as I walked along the corridor leading from the waiting room to the examination cubicles at Moorfields. I had one more patient to see before I could grab a coffee and, as usual, I needed caffeine very badly indeed.

I jumped when someone touched my elbow. I turned to see Max. The stubble was gone and he looked well rested. I envied him that. 'I called your name three times,' he said. 'I was starting to think you were ignoring me.'

'Sorry, I'm away with the fairies this morning,' I said, unable to hold in a yawn. I covered my mouth with my hand. ''Scuse me.'

He narrowed his eyes. 'What's up? You look exhausted.' He pulled a face. 'Sorry. I'm not supposed to say that, am I? Obviously, you look as radiant as ever.' He raised his eyes to the ceiling's polystyrene tiles. 'Now I sound insincere. I should have stopped at hello.'

I laughed. His face became blurry as another yawn made

my eyes water. 'Don't overthink it. You're good. I know I look knackered. I'm just tired.'

'Sure you're okay? You do look like you've been up all night.'

'Wow, way to make a girl feel good. I take it back: you should have stopped at hello.' The way he was scrutinising my face made me uncomfortable. I didn't want to lie to Max, but since he'd warned me not to get too emotionally invested in Rachel's case, I could hardly tell him about what happened last night, or that I'd stayed up talking with her until six this morning.

He glanced down at the case notes he was carrying, 'Well, if you tell me you weren't a dirty stop-out, I'll just have to believe you.'

'All right, Mum.' I nudged him with my elbow, covering my guilt with what I hoped was a playful smile. He didn't smile back, and I realised I was an idiot for calling him that. He was the only person I was still close to who knew what my relationship with my mother was truly like. 'Mum' was a pretty damning insult coming from me. I felt worse when it registered then that he might suspect me of having spent the night with a new lover. That would account for the way he was avoiding my gaze.

'I don't know why I said that. You're the opposite of my mum. And I don't know why I'm so tired either,' I said in a rush. 'I was in bed by ten thirty . . . on my own.' I blushed, hating myself for adding the last part. Now I'd made it a thing. A nurse guiding a patient tapping a white stick on the linoleum ahead of him approached and we stepped close to the wall to allow them to pass.

'You don't have to . . .' His Adam's apple bobbed as he swallowed. 'You don't owe me an explanation, or anything.'

That wasn't true. I probably owed him for me still having a career. I definitely owed him a debt of gratitude for always being there for me when no one else was. 'I know. I just thought . . .' I trailed off, my brain too fuzzy to find the right words.

'Any more thoughts on that blepharospasm case?' he said after an awkward beat.

'Rachel Cartwright?' I said, as if her name just came to me, despite the fact I'd been sitting across from her, putting the world to rights, until a couple of hours before sunrise. 'I'm going to run more neurological tests. I thought I'd get Sardia Abassi to take a look at her.' I'd trained with Sardia, and when I went down the ophthalmology route, she continued to specialise in neurology. 'See if she can find anything I've missed.'

'Good idea,' Max said. He took a step, as if he was about to carry on his way, then stopped. 'You're sure you're okay?'

'I'm fine, honestly. Just tired. I'll get an early night tonight, promise.'

'You'd tell me if there was anything wrong?'

''Course I would.'

He nodded, tapped a knuckle against his notes and said, 'Okay. Best get on, then.' He turned and walked away down the corridor, his soles squeaking on the shiny floor.

* * *

I checked in on Rachel daily by text, and she seemed to be doing okay. When she started to send me funny memes that made me smile, I did the same in return. Soon, her messages were the brightest parts of my day. I was disappointed not to have uncovered the root cause of her eyelid spasms, but she'd agreed to undergo neurological tests, so that Friday I met Sardia in London Bridge after work, primarily for a long-overdue catch up, but I also planned to discuss the case. She arrived looking as cool as ever in a black-and-white-checked coat over a black rollneck and voluminous flares. I always felt parochial in comparison to her. She was one of the popular gang at uni, always surrounded by other impossibly trendy, overtly confident people. I was one of the smaller, duller stars orbiting her sun.

These days she was extremely difficult to pin down. We'd rearranged this evening three times. I was always the one to message first, suggesting dates, which she invariably couldn't make, then offering others until we finally found one we could both do. Despite that, she would often cancel and reschedule, leaving me sure she'd had a better offer. I never complained. She was the only one of our university friends that hadn't entirely disappeared along with Joel. I often wondered if that was only because I sent so many patients her way.

Her face was rounder than the last time I saw her. 'You look well,' I said.

'You mean fat?' She shoulder-barged me and I was suddenly back at medical school, walking through the quad with Sardia on our way to some lecture or other, me shrinking in embarrassment as she ranted about a topic on which she had strong and vocal opinions. She was a force of nature. I had no idea how she managed a frantic social schedule as well as two small children and a cardiologist husband who seemed to need as much tending as the kids.

'I meant you look well.' We left the station concourse and headed along St Thomas Street.

'Okay, but I admit I am plumping up, because . . .' She put her hand on her stomach and grinned.

I stopped, almost bumping into a man rushing in the opposite direction towards the station. 'You're not?'

'Yep. Abbasi number three is in the house.' She stuck out her abdomen. 'I already feel as big as a house, actually.'

'Oh my God. Congratulations.' I hugged her. 'When are you due?' I fought the image of Joel's hopeful face when he told me he wanted us to try for a baby.

'I'm only seventeen weeks, so there's a way to go yet.'

'How have the girls taken the news?' We continued past St Thomas's towards Borough Market. 'Are they looking forward to being big sisters?'

'Ha. They're excited, but only if it's another girl, apparently. If it's a boy, they're going to put him in the bin.'

'Oh. Seems a bit harsh.'

She laughed. 'I see where they're coming from, to be fair. I know what I'm doing with girls now. I'm kind of hoping for another. I shouldn't say that, should I? Obviously, we're just hoping for a healthy baby.'

'Yeah. Boys are smelly.' I laughed. 'You can tell the girls I said that, unless you're having a boy. Then boys are as good as girls . . . or nearly as good. Wait, don't say anything. I'm digging myself a hole I can't get out of.' We waited for the crossing sign to turn green, then marched across the road with the hordes of other people surging towards the market. 'Do you have a preference for where we eat? I suppose you're avoiding certain foods now?'

'I take all the advice with a pinch of salt,' she said. 'Low-sodium salt, these days.' She sighed. 'We could try Elliot's? I'd kill for their cheese puffs.'

We bagged the last table at Elliot's and after she filled me in on life with a growing family, I told her about employing Aaron, then more about Rachel's case, trying not to notice that all I had to talk about was work, while she had an endless stream of personal anecdotes to share. The cheese puffs arrived, crispy on the outside with oozing, molten cheese on the inside. Sardia brushed the dusting of Parmesan off one and popped it into her mouth, chewing thoughtfully. 'So, this patient's still adamant it's not psychological?'

'Yep. That's what she says.' I felt oddly disloyal by even thinking it could have a different cause to the one Rachel was so sure about. 'Max told me there's some kind of trauma in her past, but this condition is recent. It started in November.'

'That means nothing. Trauma can resurface at any time.' Sardia's warm brown eyes stayed on mine. 'You know that.'

She was right – I did know that. Sardia had been the one who insisted I saw a counsellor after an eight-year-old girl who'd had undiagnosed congenital heart disease died during my early training in pediatrics. The counsellor told me the trauma of finding my aunt dead when I was fourteen resurfaced when I couldn't help save the little girl. One small mercy was that it had happened just before our summer break, so I could go home and spend the months convalescing. Sardia didn't know how ill I became that summer. No one did. I couldn't eat. I barely left my room. I even considered not going back in the autumn term. Everything seemed hopeless. What was the point in becoming a doctor when you couldn't stop a child from losing their life, when people you loved could still drop down dead and leave you to face this brutal world alone?

It was only the constant sniping from my mother, telling me that she knew I'd never amount to anything, that got me to haul my bony body back on the train in late September. That and the fact Moira had always told me I'd make a brilliant doctor. I told Sardia and my university friends I'd lost weight intentionally and I was feeling perfectly well again. A couple of months later, I met Joel, and soon I stopped having to fake it: I was almost back to my old self. I decided to specialise in ophthalmology, that year. Blindness is a dreadful affliction, but even my patients who are suffering from eye cancer have an eighty per cent survival rate.

'You're right. I did try to get her to open up about her past when I was round there, but she closed me down.'

'You did a home visit?' Sardia speared another cheese puff with her fork.

'Well, yes. Then I went around because she thought someone had broken in, so she called me.'

'And was someone there?' She stopped chewing.

'No, thank God.'

Her nose wrinkled. 'Why you?'

'What do you mean?' I knew exactly what she meant.

'A home appointment is one thing, but why did she call you, of all people, when she thought someone was in her house?'

'I don't know. I was probably the last person on her call log or something. She was frightened and she couldn't open her eyes. I didn't ask why she was ringing me. I just called the police and went around there to make sure she was okay, like any normal person would.'

'All right, no need to be so defensive.'

Sweat prickled in my armpits. Sardia never pulled her punches, and she was right – I was tense, and my voice had risen in pitch. I shook my head. 'Sorry.' I took a sip of water, irritated with myself for getting so uptight. 'I'm just trying to help the woman. That's my job. And I like her. We get on.'

Sardia shrugged. 'Fair enough.'

I tried to smile, knowing that my overreaction was because my fall from grace and the end of my marriage had been the talk of every medic in London. I didn't want her to think I wasn't capable of making good decisions. I poked the last cheese puff in the dish. 'I want her to have these last tests to rule out something physical before I step back. So, are you going to win the last savoury delight by agreeing to help, or do I have to eat it myself?'

'When you put it like that,' said Sardia, circling her fork over the dish, 'send over the notes and consider it done.'

Chapter Nineteen

January dragged on for ever. It started to feel like the icy, gunmetal weather, punctuated by the odd gusty storm, was the permanent state of affairs. My mood was equally miserable. On Thursday I had an urgent call from the care home to say Mum had had a fall. I cancelled my last patient of the day and drove through the rush-hour traffic and sleet to Chelmsford, only to find her fast asleep in her bed.

'I tried ringing to tell you the on-call doctor gave her the all-clear,' said Marie, wringing her hands, 'but there was no reply.'

I took my phone from my bag and saw three missed calls. 'Sorry. I must've had it on silent by mistake.' I pressed the button on the side and felt it give a buzz of recognition. It occurred to me that I could have missed a call from Rachel too, and that thought sent chills through me. Mum had Marie and all the other staff to watch out for her. Rachel only had me. I scrolled down, ignoring the mild disappointment that there were no new messages from her. Deciding it was best to let Mum sleep on, I got back in the car and drove along the slippery roads home.

The following morning was brighter, but the weather did nothing to lift my spirits. I had a new patient with the worst halitosis I'd come across yet, and that was saying something. He was a sweet man in his seventies and I could see the questions in his eyes when I kept turning away to breathe. If he'd seemed less vulnerable I might have said something, but he told me he was widowed and was desperately worried about losing his sight now he was alone in the world. Telling him about his bad breath would have been like kicking a kitten. The smell lingered in my nostrils long after he'd gone, and my room still stank of rotting gums an hour later.

A message from Rachel at lunchtime was a welcome distraction. We'd been exchanging messages every day, much like my old friends and I used to before I was cut off, and they were often the only thing that improved my state of mind. Even her choice of gifs seemed effortlessly perfect. Whenever one popped into my inbox, it took me an age to find anything half as funny, or pertinent, to send in reply. I'd grown to admire her, and knowing that she was thinking of me enough to keep up regular communication made my chest lift. She chose me to be friends with, so perhaps I wasn't a lost cause after all?

Her message was a gif of a panda slumped against a wall looking bored, with the message *#mood* underneath. I replied with, *Hard relate.* So when another message pinged on to my phone later, when I was sitting at my desk in a blue funk, to ask whether she could take me for a drink that evening to say thank you for all my help, and for referring her to Sardia, I was sorely tempted. More than that, it felt like being invited out, one on one, by the most popular girl in school.

Yes, Max was concerned about me getting too close to another patient, but this was completely different. She was a woman, for a start, and, having kissed a couple of my female friends at uni without any urges to go further, I knew I wasn't likely to fall for Rachel. And what Max didn't know was this was the only social invitation I'd had all month that wasn't from him. The fact that it was a Friday night at the end of the longest month ever, and that an empty weekend gaped ahead of me, made it very hard to refuse. Rachel suggesting a pub within walking distance of where I lived made my impulse to accept stronger. After a few minutes' deliberation, I texted back to say yes, and immediately felt lighter and more able to dictate the last of my week's referrals for Aaron to type up later.

That evening I asked Alexa to play the Kaiser Chiefs at high volume and sang along to 'Everyday I Love You Less and Less' as I carefully applied winged eyeliner. I assessed myself in the bathroom mirror, decided it looked too bold and wiped it off. Then I put it on again, thinking, what the hell. It was Friday night, and I was going out. My blood fizzed with anticipation when I finally closed the door of my flat behind me.

The Palm Tree stood right next to Regent's Canal, and if it had been a light summer evening I would have walked there along the towpath beside my apartment block. But it was bitterly cold and as dark as this relatively well-lit, densely populated area of London got, so I took the long way round, down the main road and past the row of pretty Georgian terraces, then into Mile End Park, where the pub had sat for almost a century, all the time checking behind me. The only downside to having met Rachel was the reawakening of those unsettling feelings. No one was following me. I knew that.

I pushed open the pub door and instantly felt like I'd gone back in time. Red lighting gave the room a cabaret feel, and the claret velvet frill round the top of the oval gold chintz bar added to the old-time ambiance. A group of thin young men in brightly coloured trousers sat on the bench to the left. I presumed they'd come for a drink after a session at Mile End climbing wall. Beyond them, an older couple sat, silently sipping their drinks. The woman's sagging cheeks were rouged pink and her voluminous bleached hair appeared to be solid with hairspray. The gold bracelet the man opposite her wore looked so heavy I was surprised he could lift his pint.

That's what I'd always loved about this place: it was pure old-style East End, and it wasn't changing for anyone. Once, when Joel and I had recently moved to the area, I'd asked what wine they had by the glass. The man behind the bar lifted two small bottles to show me, and said, 'Red or white.' I chose white. The next time I chose red, but neither made me want to go back for more.

In the enormous mirror emblazoned with 'Trueman's',

I saw the door behind me open and was relieved when Rachel walked through. I turned to greet her, hesitating because I wasn't sure whether to embrace her, air kiss or shake hands. She took the decision away by pulling me in for a hug. She held me to her like an old friend. I'd almost forgotten what it felt like to be hugged like that. Her hair smelled of coconut and, when I stood back, feeling woozy from the unfamiliar affection, I could hardly believe the change in her from the cowering woman I'd seen a couple of weeks ago. The red lipstick was back and her blue eyes glowed when she smiled.

'So good to see you.' She blinked heavily mascaraed lids. 'I mean actually see you.' She held on to my hands as she assessed me with a look of approval. 'You look gorgeous.'

'Thank you.' I was glad of the eyeliner now. The compliment made me stand a little taller and suck in my abs. 'Good to see you looking so well,' I said. She looked beautiful, but I didn't feel right saying that. *Well* felt weak in comparison to her *gorgeous*. I was reminded of Antony and Cleopatra. I'd studied it at A-level and had once acted out the scene where Cleopatra is furious when a messenger tells her Antony is well. She replies, 'We use to say the dead are well.' Why did that occur to me? I shook the thought away as we went to the bar and waited for our turn to be served.

'I put loads of slap on.' Rachel touched her face. 'I feel like I've got to make the most of the days when I can actually live my life. Do you know what I mean? If I can only go out half the time, I've got to make those days count.' I thought back to dancing around my flat to the

Kaiser Chiefs and knew exactly what she meant. She held my forearm. 'That's why I'm so glad you agreed to meet up tonight.' She seemed to think I was doing her the favour, rather than the other way round. She surveyed the bar. 'Isn't this place wonderful? There's nowhere else like it in London. They have a jazz band that plays in that raised section over there sometimes and they always seem to have a late licence.'

'Yes,' I said. 'I've been in a few times when they've been playing.'

She turned to me. 'You've been here before?'

I laughed. 'It's practically my local. I live just off the Roman Road.' I didn't tell her I used to live a little further away, but my ex-husband and I loved this place from the moment we set foot inside. It occurred to me that if Joel and I had prioritised date nights instead of work, it could have been him and me standing here now.

Her jaw dropped. 'No way?' She shook her head. 'Here's me thinking I was introducing you to a little-known gem. You said you were in east London, but I'd imagined somewhere a bit more . . . doctory, if that's a word, like a fancy house in Shoreditch or something.'

'Nope. This is my manor, guv.' I coloured at my misguided attempt at a cockney accent when the dark-haired barman approached.

'What can I get you, ladies?' he said, in the genuine voice of someone born and bred in Mile End. He smiled and crossed his arms.

'I'll have a gin and tonic, please,' I said, not able to meet his eye in case he'd overheard me, although the easy look on his face suggested he hadn't.

'Same for me,' said Rachel. 'Thanks.'

'Doubles or singles?'

Before we could answer, a voice shouted from the snug, across the other side of the bar. 'Rachel Cartwright!'

Rachel leaned forward and peered across the bar. 'Billy?'

'Doubles it is,' said the man behind the bar, tucking his chin into his neck, as though hearing from the man in the snug gave him the information he needed.

'They're on me, Tone,' the man yelled at the barman. He disappeared from sight and reappeared through the door behind us. He was short and muscular, like a bull terrier, and wore a Harrington jacket over a tight polo shirt that showed off pronounced pectorals. 'Well, as I live and breathe, Rachel bloody Cartwright.' His phrasing was straight out of *EastEnders*, and I found myself wondering if he was for real as he took Rachel's hand and clapped her hard on the back. 'What are you doing in my neck of the woods?'

'I'm with my friend, Beth. She's a local.' She turned to me and grinned.

There was that word again: *friend*. The man took my hand in both of his, his grip so tight my knuckles ground together. 'Nice to meet you.'

'And you. Any friend of Rachel's is a friend of mine.'

He turned back to Rachel. 'I owe you more than a couple of drinks, mate.'

'You paid for my services,' she said. 'That's how business

works.' There was a flirtatiousness to her I hadn't seen before, and Billy was clearly receptive to it. His small dark eyes flashed bright when he looked at her.

Billy banged his fist on the bar, making everyone turn towards us, including Tone the barman. 'Whatever these ladies want, it's on me, all night, right?'

Tone saluted. 'Got it.'

'You really don't have to,' purred Rachel.

Billy held her by the shoulders and stared into her eyes. 'Darling, it's the very least I can do. I owe you. We both know it.' He leaned closer and spoke so quietly I had to strain to hear. 'I can't thank you enough for what you did for my girl. Anything you need help with, and I mean anything, you know where I am.' He stood back and raised his bristly eyebrows. 'Understood?'

Rachel put a hand on his thick arm. 'Thank you.'

'Nice to meet you, Beth.' He winked. 'You two enjoy your night.' He gave Rachel a kiss on the cheek, then disappeared back through the door.

We took our drinks over to a pocked copper table near the area reserved for the band. 'He seems nice,' I said.

Rachel laughed. 'Looks can be deceptive. *Nice* is not the first word most people would use to describe that man.'

'Well, he seems to like you. What did you do for him to deserve that kind of reception?' I said. 'I've only ever got a greeting like that when I've saved someone's eyesight.' I pinched my lips. 'Actually, not even then.'

She laughed and took a sip of gin. Her lipstick left a red

smudge on the rim of the glass. 'I defended his daughter last year and she got off.'

'Got off? That sounds like you thought she was guilty?'

'No, no.' She waved her hand. 'That's just the phrase.'

'What was she accused of?' I said, intrigued.

Rachel gave her head a quick shake. 'It was really sad, actually. She was in a coercively controlling relationship, bless her. She was only eighteen, still a kid really.'

'Oh. How did she end up being the one charged?' I paused. 'If you're allowed to tell me.'

'Her boyfriend, and believe me, that word does not accurately describe that young man, forced her to do some pretty unpleasant things. She ended up on a drugs charge. It should never have been brought. If she wasn't part of Billy's family, I doubt it would have even got to court. But she was who she was, and so the police believed that scum of a boyfriend over her, just because he was from a nice, respectable, middle-class family. Like I said before, you can't always believe what your eyes tell you. She was a vulnerable young woman, possibly more so because she's been cosseted by Billy all her life. But because of her name she was treated very badly by the system. It was prejudice, plain and simple.'

I listened, enthralled. This was so far beyond my realm of experience. 'Billy's family?' I felt my eyes widening. Of course, I knew the history of the East End, and its infamous historic inhabitants. I'd even drunk in the Blind Beggar, where Ronnie Kray shot George Cornell. I'd heard rumours some of the Krays' relatives used to frequent the Palm Tree back in the day, but I'd naïvely thought the old families who used to rule this part of London had lost their power and significance.

'Look at you, all goggle-eyed.' She laughed. 'There's still a romance about the old East End gangster scene, isn't there? But this was nothing to do with that. And it couldn't be less romantic. Billy's from a long line of rogues, for want of a better word, and anyone connected to him is more likely to be suspected of wrongdoing than your average member of the public. There are certain jumped-up law-makers who would like to put a stop to his line, if you know what I mean, and it's not fair. I help him because it's the right thing to do. He's no angel, but he's no master criminal either, and his daughter's a sweet kid who got herself mixed up with a bad man. Same old story: girl meets boy, boy treats girl badly, so girl falls even more in love, then boy uses girl as drug mule without her knowledge. It was him and his gang that should have been on trial.'

'Oh, that's such a sad story.'

'Right? Good job she had an excellent advocate.' She raised her glass, and I clinked mine against it.

'Indeed.' I drank, feeling more than a little bit proud of my new friend for saving a young girl from injustice. 'It must feel good to put wrongs right.'

Rachel nodded slowly, a wide smile growing on her lips. 'Do you know what, it really does.' She nudged my foot with hers. 'I bet it feels better to save someone's eyesight, though.'

For a moment, I'd forgotten about Rachel's problem. How insensitive. If I couldn't help her, then her law career might be over, and innocent people like Billy's daughter would suffer too. 'How did it go with Sardia?'

'Dr Abbasi?'

'Yes.'

She scrunched up her face. 'That wasn't my favourite afternoon ever.'

'Yeah, I can imagine.' Neurological tests were sometimes what we doctors called *uncomfortable*, which everyone knows is code for *hurts like hell*.

'Bloody expensive as well, but if it helps me get to the bottom of whatever is causing these spasms, I don't care what I have to go through.' She picked at the beer mat under her drink, all sense of the cheerful woman from minutes ago gone. She was the scared, blind woman I'd found quaking on her sofa almost two weeks ago again. 'I'm already dreading waking up tomorrow morning. It's so weird that I expect my eyes to be clamped shut. I try to be hopeful, honestly.' She glanced up, then back down at the paper coming away from the edge of the mat. 'But it happens anyway. And' – she dug her nail into another edge of the beer mat – 'I know the police didn't find any evidence, and there was no one there when you came over, but somehow I can't shake the feeling I'm being watched.'

My skin tingled. 'Still?'

'Yes. It started just before Christmas and now, at night, when my lids are closed and I couldn't open them if I tried, I can feel someone else's eyes on me. I'm not imagining it. I'm being watched, Beth. I know I am. And it's scaring me to death.'

Chapter Twenty

The barman, Tone, brought two more glasses over to our table. 'I've been told to keep you two topped up,' he said. He stood with his hands on his hips, and I felt strangely obliged to drain what was left of my previous drink. Ice cubes clinked against my teeth, the acid of the slice of lime sharp against my tongue. I handed the empty glass to him, and Rachel did the same. As he wandered back to the bar, I scanned the framed photographs of old-time celebrities displayed above the red velvet frill. If any of those stars were still alive, they'd be at least ninety by now. This place really was a throwback to an age gone by.

'I can't keep this up,' I said. 'I'm already feeling it. I'm such a lightweight.'

'Don't feel you have to drink it,' said Rachel. 'Shall I get you some water?'

'Maybe in a minute.' I lowered my voice. 'If you still think someone is watching you . . . and you've had dealings with people in gangs, then perhaps they could be the ones who—'

'It won't be anything to do with that,' she said, her tone

confident. 'That's not how it works. They're really not interested in the lawyers. We're irrelevant after the case. It would be too risky too, if they were shown to have a motive. And I haven't even got anything ongoing because of this.' She pointed at her eyes. The brightness had dulled, and I missed it. 'If it's not gone by the end of February, that dick Reece will make partner, and that wouldn't just be bad for me.'

'What do you mean?'

She glanced around, then leaned in. 'I'm worried about the other women in chambers, especially the younger ones. I've seen him watching them. I have this awful feeling that he's a predator.'

'Sexually?'

She tightened her lips and nodded. 'As far as I know, he's stuck to leering and the odd inappropriate remark, but that could change if he gets more power. I've seen it so many times. A slightly dodgy bloke can turn into a very dangerous man when the restraints are taken off. Chambers is already a completely fucked-up old boys' network. Women like me are breaking through, but it's slower than any right-minded person would like.' A perfect ringlet fell over her face. She pushed it back and it lodged in her curls. 'I thought this was my chance to make a difference, to do something good, you know? But unless I'm back at the end of next month, it's game over.'

I hated hearing the resignation in her voice. 'Let's not look at it as only a month. Let's reframe it as having a full month ahead to sort you out.'

She smiled weakly. 'I like your optimism.'

Another thought occurred to me. 'You don't think Reece could be the one watching you, trying to throw you off balance?'

'Oh, God, don't say that. It hadn't occurred to me.' She visibly shuddered. 'That's terrifying.'

I cringed. Me and my stupid mouth. 'Ignore me. I'm being an idiot. Even if he's a creep, he's still in law, so he'd know what the consequences were for stalking. Not that I'm saying he's stalking you.' I rushed out the last words, furious with myself for making it worse.

'Yeah, they're not as significant as they should be – we both know that.' She widened her eyes and gave me a knowing look. I was glad I'd shared what happened to me. It was another connection between us. She sipped her drink, looking off to the other side of the bar thoughtfully. 'You've got me thinking now. Even if he's not exactly stalking me, he might be trying to find something to give him an advantage over me. He's a risktaker, I know that much, and I don't know how far he'd go to get what he wants. He could be paying someone to do his dirty work, but it's not as if I could accuse him. He has many faults, but he knows the law inside out, and the thing the law demands above all else is evidence.'

I nodded. Science and medicine were the same. 'Have you called the police again?'

She rolled a piece of torn beer mat between her fingers. 'I can't, can I? You saw how they responded last time.'

'Only the male one.' I watched the man with the heavy bracelet stand and lumber to the bar. Before he got there,

Tone placed a pint of lager and what appeared to be a glass of sherry on the polished wood. They didn't exchange any words, even when the man placed a ten-pound note on the bar. They nodded at each other, then the man took the drinks back to the woman with the rouged cheeks.

Rachel pulled at a curl and stared at me. 'You know how many police officers I come across in my daily life?'

'Surely they're not all like that?' I thought about the patients I worked with at Moorfields. There were plenty of men who treated me as if I were dirt simply because I was a woman. I was called *love* in a patronising way almost daily, and that was the least offensive I could recall. Sardia regularly had to deal with racist behaviour, and the single reason we were there was to help people, but that didn't stop the prejudice.

She dropped the ball of cardboard on the table and rolled it under her finger. 'No, they're not. I've worked with plenty of good ones, but I can't choose who comes around to my house, and you were there.' She glanced at me, then back at the table. 'There's nothing to find. Whoever's doing this is clever. They know a way in and out that I haven't figured out yet, and they know how to make it appear like I'm making it up.'

I examined her face. She looked deadly serious. 'You really think someone is getting into your house?'

'I know it sounds ludicrous, but I honestly do.'

'Okay,' I said. 'If you don't feel like you can call the police, maybe you should stay somewhere else for a while, just until we get to the bottom of your condition.'

'I've thought about that, but I don't want to be a burden to anyone.'

'It would only be temporary,' I said, hoping it was true and that Sardia's tests would come back with something more illuminating than I'd managed to find.

'I know, but . . . The only friends I could conceivably ask are lawyers, and I'm desperate to stop anyone from work finding out what's going on. I really think it could end my career.'

The tip of her tongue appeared, tapping on her top lip a couple of times, before she carried on. 'I'm about to over-share, but I feel like I can trust you. I can, can't I?'

I nodded, flattered, but trying to hide how eager I was to hear what she was about to confide. 'Of course.'

She leaned in closer. 'At the start of my career I made friends with a group of women I worked alongside, and I thought we were close. I would have said we were good friends, but I learned the hard way that, in my line of work, you can't afford to put your complete trust in anyone. I was seeing this guy from our chambers. I really liked him and I thought it was going somewhere, but we kept it quiet because it's frowned upon. We were both single, and there was no power imbalance or anything like that, but the head honchos worry things could get messy, you know, if things don't work out?' She took a drink, then continued. 'Anyway, I told my so-called friends everything, and one of them let it slip to the senior partner.'

'What happened?'

'We were both hauled in and given an ultimatum. One of us had to tender their resignation.'

'Shit.' I couldn't stop my mind equating what she described with what my old friends could have done after they found out about my indiscretion. And what I did was wrong. Rachel's relationship might have been disapproved of, but it didn't sound unethical.

Rachel sat back. 'Yep. I was devastated. I mean, if you can't trust your friends, who can you trust? Anyway, because I thought I had a future with this guy, I took the hit and left, then the bastard dumped me anyway and, to add insult to injury, he was promoted six months later when I was still struggling to get a foothold in a new job. So you can see why I don't feel like letting anyone know that I'm compromised now. Sad as it sounds, I don't trust anyone not to use it against me, even people I think of as friends.'

'I get it,' I said. 'I'm sorry that happened to you. Do you still come across the man you were seeing? If London lawyers are anything like doctors, it can be hard to avoid each other.' I took a gulp of gin to quell the memories of the times I'd bumped into Joel in the busy corridors of Moorfields.

'No, actually, he died in a hit and run a couple of years ago, and I hadn't seen him for years before that.'

'Oh, I'm sorry.' I didn't know what I was apologising for.

'Yeah ... And this is going to sound stupid.' Rachel tugged a ringlet straight then let it bounce back up.

'Go on,' I said.

She took a sharp breath in. 'Not trusting anyone from

work isn't the only reason I feel like I should keep what's going on to myself. I've thought long and hard about it, and I've decided I don't want to put anyone else in danger.'

I'd feared she was going to say that.

She watched a man carry an enormous case on to the raised area behind us, unclip it and take out a double bass, before continuing, 'You think I'm being dramatic. I'm not surprised. It sounds ridiculous when I say it out loud.' I opened my mouth to speak, but before I could, she said, 'I need to stay where I am, anyway, because I've rearranged the house so I don't inadvertently kill myself by tripping over anything. I know where everything is, so at least I can get through the closed-eye days on my own. I think I'm better off in my own house. I'm sure I am.'

'Okay.' I could see she wasn't going to be swayed on that.

'Thank you for listening and for taking me seriously, though. I know not many people would.' She picked up her drink and threw half of it back. 'I don't blame them, I suppose. It's easier to believe what you can see with your own eyes, isn't it?'

'Looks can be deceptive.' I wanted her to know that I truly understood. I was moved by her gratitude. I took a deep drink too. I was already fuzzy from the gin, but it was starting to feel nice, relaxing. I shifted in my seat, working out how to ask what I really wanted to know without being too overt. I knew there was something in her past she wasn't disclosing. 'Why do you think you would be putting someone else in danger if you stayed with them?'

She rolled her head back. 'I don't know that I would, if

I'm honest. My gut tells me it's only me they're interested in, but I don't know for sure, and I couldn't bear to think I'd put anyone I cared about in harm's way.' She rubbed her forehead and gave a short laugh. 'I'm probably being completely paranoid, anyway. Maybe it's all tied up with me not being able to see half the time. I could be linking the anxiety I have when my eyes are closed to the fear that—' She stopped abruptly, then spoke again. 'It's probably all in my head.'

I was tempted to agree, but didn't want to sound dismissive. I had an idea. 'Why don't I come over one night when your eyes are closed? Then I can keep an eye on you and maybe that would put your mind at rest.' The words were out of my mouth before I'd really thought them through.

She shook her head. 'No way. Absolutely not.' The deep timbre of the double bass sounded behind us.

Now I'd voiced the idea, it made perfect sense. 'Think about it. I can see. I can watch to make sure no one else is in the house.' I'd kept vigil myself when things were at their worst with Simon. I knew the feeling of hyper-vigilance and fear and was ready to defend my friend. 'If anyone even attempts to get in, I could call the police straight away. We'd have evidence, then they'd have to take it seriously, escalate it.' I was warming to the idea. 'If it is this Reece character, you'd be knocking out the competition by exposing him. Win–win.' Despite what I said, I couldn't imagine that anyone who practised law would be injudicious enough to take risks like that. I was convinced no one was in Rachel's house on those nights, and I could help her know that for sure. I would have given anything to have had the support when I really was being stalked. 'And if nothing happens then it will help to put your mind at rest.' It didn't feel like I would be taking a risk, because I was sure it was all tied up with not being able to open her eyes.

'I don't know.' She clutched her hands together. 'I can't ask you to spend half your time at my house.'

That was a good point. I didn't want that either, but I did want to help. 'Not half the time, but any night you feel vulnerable.' The double bass had been joined by keyboards and the smooth tones of a saxophone played the melody of a jazz number I vaguely recognised. 'I mean it: you have to promise me that whenever you're frightened you'll call me. Agreed?' I had to almost shout to be heard.

Her face broke into a wide smile, and she held out her hand. 'Agreed.'

Chapter Twenty-One
The Watcher

I watch you walk home from the Palm Tree on your own in the dark. How naïve you are. You should have shared a cab with your new friend when she offered. She clearly is your friend now. Anyone could see that from the way you hugged goodnight in the car park. You two might be besties now, but you still don't want a ride home with her, do you? Don't you want her to know exactly where you live? Is that it? Is the memory of what happened last time you got too close to a patient still niggling away at the back of your mind? It's something I think about a lot, believe me.

And what were you doing, accepting strong spirits from a complete stranger all night? Have you never heard of drink spiking? Men like Billy Galvin don't play by the same rules you do. He wasn't brought up by good old Aunty Moira, with her rights and wrongs and cream-rises-to-the-top optimism, God rest her soul. He had a very different education to yours. He's a dangerous man.

But I shouldn't be surprised that you are blind to the

signs. You're not great at spotting dangerous people, are you? I'm proof of that.

As I watch you walk out of the park and along Haverfield Road, your limbs are loose. You stumble over a cracked paving stone and giggle. You shouldn't be laughing. Not when you're on your own late at night in the dark and you've been drinking. Not when you're vulnerable. Because you are vulnerable, Beth. That's what makes you a target for people like me.

Chapter Twenty-Two

I expected a call from Rachel at the weekend, but it didn't come, and I found myself disappointed at not being needed. I composed a few texts to check on her, but deleted them without sending, feeling bashful about our nascent friendship: nervous about looking too keen. I'd had such a good night on Friday. It felt like the old days, when I used to have true friends and a social life. I'd forgotten what it was like to wake up, groggy and hungover but with the feeling that it was worth every sting of the head to have spent the evening with someone you really connected with. I experienced that with Rachel. Despite only having known her for a matter of weeks, we'd formed a bond. I could see us remaining friends long after this eye situation was a distant memory.

One thing preoccupied me, though. I pondered it on my way into work on Monday morning. Max had told me about a traumatic event in Rachel's past, but she was clearly reticent to share what it was. I'd told her about Simon, well, most of it, so it hurt a little she wasn't ready to confide in me. It was none of my business, but, still, I found myself more and more curious. At my first appointment on Monday morning, I made the mistake of thinking about that instead of Angela Sutherland's cataracts.

'I haven't been wearing my contact lenses,' she said, when she arrived. 'And I'd forgotten how annoying glasses are. I keep taking them off and putting them down, then forgetting where I've left the blasted things.'

'Why aren't you wearing your lenses?' I gestured for her to sit in the examination chair.

She tucked in her chin and looked at me as though I'd gone mad. 'Because you told me not to for three weeks before surgery. I'm booked in next week. This is my pre-op appointment.'

'Oh, of course,' I said. 'Sorry. I don't know what I was thinking.' I did. I was thinking about Rachel, and that wasn't fair on my other patients. I needed to get a grip.

In an attempt to clear my thoughts, when I had a gap between patients I decided to do a little gentle research to see if I could find out what had happened to the woman I felt myself growing close to.

Annoyingly, I found her social media profiles, but they were set to private. I supposed that was a prudent move on her part, considering what she did for a living. I thought about sending friend requests, but decided I should wait until I was no longer her doctor and the lines between friendship and professional relationship were less blurred. On further inspection, I found her LinkedIn profile. It listed her work trajectory, and it looked pretty impressive. She hadn't updated it for a while, though, so I clicked off and did a Google search. Aaron knocked on my door just as I was huffing about not being able to find anything useful. His part-time contract meant he hadn't been in at the back end of last week, and I'd missed his presence and his ability to know exactly when I needed a shot of caffeine.

'Coffee?' he said. 'I expect you need one after Mrs Sutherland. She had a face like a slapped bum when she left.' He bit his lip. 'Sorry, that was unprofessional. She looked a mite disgruntled.'

'Ha! I can imagine.' I made myself sound amused, despite the guilt at knowing Angela Sutherland had every right to be annoyed. On top of forgetting why she was here, I couldn't find her file when I looked on the system, and it was an age until I realised I'd typed Southgate as her surname instead of Sutherland and was looking in the wrong place. All in all, I hadn't exactly come across as the consummate professional. If you're trusting someone with your eyesight, you need them to be doing better than I was that morning. 'Coffee would be perfect, thank you.'

He regarded me for a moment, then pouted. His full lips and large eyes, magnified through the lenses of his glasses, made him look like a cutesy cartoon character. As a tall man in his thirties, I wasn't sure he'd like the comparison. 'You look a bit gloomy,' he said. 'Anything I can help with?'

I hesitated, wondering what he'd think of me doing an internet search on a patient. I checked the time on the bottom of the screen. I was seeing Mr Anderson to check on his glaucoma in ten minutes and then I had a full list for the rest of the day, so I decided to enlist Aaron's help; I employed him as a researcher after all, and even if he did think it was strange, he wasn't likely to say so. 'I'm still trying to get to the bottom of the Rachel Cartwright case,' I said. 'Nothing physical has turned up yet, so I was wondering if there was something in her background that might give me a clue about whether the spasms could have a psychological rather than a medical root.'

If he thought that was beyond my remit as an eye specialist, he didn't say so. He came further into the room and peered over my shoulder at the Google search open on my computer. His citrus scent reached my nostrils, and I almost told him he smelled nice, but stopped myself in time. Now that really wouldn't be professional. 'What have you found so far?'

'Nothing,' I said. 'This is all there is.' I limply gestured to the screen.

'Have you checked her socials?'

'I haven't,' I lied. 'That might be overstepping?' I made it sound like a question.

Aaron stood tall. 'Oh, right, sorry. I just thought that might give you some insight into her life, but I can see why you might not want to. Clinical boundaries, and all that.'

I nodded, my eyes still on the screen. 'I suppose she's paying me to get to the bottom of her condition . . .' I let the words hang in the air.

'I could have a look, if you like,' he said. 'Just to see if there's anything that might be relevant to the case?' His voice had a similar tone to mine: casual, questioning. I got the impression he thought it might not be entirely warranted, but he clearly thought it could throw up something useful.

I swivelled in my chair to face him. 'Do you have time?'

He lifted his shoulders. 'You're the boss. I could do it while I'm on reception this afternoon, if you think it might help.'

'Go on, then,' I said. Giving him the task allowed me some distance. It made it feel more like research than snooping. Which it was.

'No problemo. I'll grab that coffee and send Mr Anderson up when he gets here. And I'll let you know if I find anything helpful at the end of play today.'

At six thirty, Aaron knocked on my consulting-room door. 'Do you have time to talk about the Rachel Cartwright stuff now, or do you want to wait until my next shift?'

'Come in,' I said. I fell into one of the blue Conran chairs and gestured for him to sit in the other. 'That felt like a long day,' I said. 'How are you doing? Still enjoying the work?'

'Yep,' he said, crossing his legs. 'Suits me down to the ground. I'm a nosey sod by nature.'

I laughed. 'We call it research, Aaron.'

'Absolutely,' he said, pretending to straighten an invisible tie. 'Research.'

I massaged the tight muscles at the base of my neck. Too much desk work meant my neck and shoulders screamed to be released at the end of each day.

'In pain?' he said, wrinkling his nose.

'No more than every other person who sits at a desk for most of their working life. Now, what have you got for me?'

'Well,' he said, with obvious relish, 'from what I can gather, she lives alone.'

I nodded, keeping my face neutral. I didn't want him to know this wasn't new information to me.

'She's got a fairly active social life.'

'How do you know that?' I'd sat forward, and made myself relax back into the chair.

'Her accounts are private, but she's been tagged in a few posts on most social media.' He took his phone with its black-and-white case from his pocket and tapped on the screen, then turned it towards me. A picture of Rachel in the middle of a group of women, most of them in floaty dresses, denim jackets and white trainers. She stood out in a sleek red shift dress, black tights and chunky boots. She looked like the cool one, and the way the others were gathered around her suggested they thought so too. They were all laughing, and I felt a prick of envy. It wasn't just that my new friend was clearly a popular woman, it was more that it reminded me of my and Joel's group from our university days. I was never in the middle of that group. I would be on the edges, but at least I would have been included. I missed that enormously. I remembered Rachel saying she'd lost touch with most of her friends who weren't in the same field as her. 'Are these posts recent?'

'Actually, there's nothing for over a year.'

I told myself the relief I felt was because it added credence to what Rachel told me about feeling isolated recently. Not that I hadn't believed her – it was just good to have it confirmed.

Aaron turned the phone back to himself and touched the screen again. 'And I found an old Facebook account she hasn't used in a while. Maybe that's why she hasn't made it private – she might have forgotten it existed. No one uses Facebook any more, do they?' He twisted the screen back to me, and Rachel's face was smiling out from a photograph. Her hair was shorter and a shade redder than I'd seen it. Her face seemed fuller, the cheekbones less defined, but it was definitely her. It seemed typical Rachel to have improved with age. 'When did she last post on there?'

'About three years ago.'

I resisted the urge to reach for the phone and scroll through. 'And did you learn anything . . . enlightening?'

He examined the picture, sucking in air through his teeth. 'I'm not sure.'

'Not sure?'

'It's probably nothing.' He lowered the phone. 'It's probably not worth mentioning.'

'Go on,' I said, leaning forward.

'Well, something just struck me as a bit odd.'

I waited, willing him on.

After a pause in which he seemed to be choosing his words, he continued, 'There's lots of posts about holidays and friends, there's the odd boyfriend, and then a few things about work . . . but there's nothing about family. No parents, no siblings, no trips home to wherever she comes from. I went right through to when she started the account, and there's not a single hint at anything . . . difficult. There's no mention of anything before she was about twenty-four.'

'That's still over a decade and she told me her mother died five years ago.'

He turned the phone over in his fingers. 'Did she?' He uncrossed his legs and leaned forward, his elbows on his knees, mirroring me. 'Right. I could be seeing things that aren't there because I'm looking for anything that might give us a clue to her state of mind, but does it seem odd to you that she doesn't mention any family at all in her posts? It's all very surface-level stuff.'

I thought about my own socials. I didn't post about anything difficult either. I secretly judged the people who put their trials and tribulations out there for the inevitable *you all right, hun?* replies. I hadn't posted a thing since the split from Joel, and even before that I never said anything about my parents, and I certainly didn't mention what happened to Moira or Mum. I saw friends posting about loved ones dying or wishing them heavenly birthdays. I never did anything like that. The memories of finding Moira dead were still too painful, and what could I possibly say about my mother that was fit for social media? 'Perhaps she had a reason to reinvent herself.' That's what I'd tried to do. I wanted nothing more than to put the pain of my past behind me and move on.

'It's possible, I suppose,' said Aaron. 'But why would she want to do that? Again, it might just be because I'm trying to find a problem, but I can't help thinking she's trying to hide something.'

I observed his soft, round face and was glad this sweet man had never known what it was to feel like every nerve ending was exposed on the surface of your skin. If he'd ever felt utterly alone, unloved and hopeless about the future, then maybe he would choose to create an entirely new persona for himself too. 'Maybe she went through something she would prefer to forget,' I said. 'She must have her reasons.'

I felt even more empathy, then, for the woman who was my patient and who had become my friend. I was more curious too.

Chapter Twenty-Three

On Tuesday I was examining a young woman with unusually dry eyes when my concentration wandered and I lost my grip on my ophthalmoscope. It slipped from my hand and hit her kneecap. She shouted in pain and I swore, partly because I was appalled by my mistake and also because it bounced off her knee and the lens shattered on the tiled floor. It was part of an expensive diagnostic set and I could have done without the expense of buying another. I made copious apologies, but the set of the patient's jaw when she left told me she was unlikely to make a follow-up appointment.

Aaron helped me clear up the splinters of glass with a dustpan and brush he borrowed from a practice on the lower floor. 'Forgive me if I'm prying, but are you all right?' he said. 'I can't help thinking you seem a bit distracted.'

I was both annoyed it was that obvious and moved that he was bothered enough to ask. 'I'm just tired.' I bent to pick up a shard of glass glinting near the examination chair, wincing when the sharp edge pierced my thumb. 'Shit.' I tried to pick it out, but the thickest end broke off, leaving a sliver in the flesh.

Aaron put down the brush and came to peer at my thumb. 'Have you got any tweezers?'

I opened the bottom drawer of my filing cabinet where I kept a small make-up bag for when I wanted to reapply before going out after work. I couldn't remember when I last opened it other than to use the tweezers to pluck out the single dark chin-hair that seemed to appear from nowhere every couple of months. Not that I was going to mention that to Aaron. I fumbled with the bag's zip, trying not to use my thumb since blood was now seeping from the cut.

'Let me.' He opened it and rummaged around, finally drawing out the tweezers. 'Can I have a look?' He drew my hand towards him. I could feel his breath on my palm as he examined the small puncture wound. 'Hold still.'

The gentleness with which he extracted the glass made tears well in my eyes. I couldn't remember when I was last touched with such care.

'All done.' He held the offending shard aloft at the end of the tweezers and I forced myself to smile.

'Thank you. You'd make an excellent doctor.'

He laughed. 'I don't know about that. I wouldn't have the stomach for anything more gory than a splinter. Why don't you go and wash your hands and get a plaster from the first-aid kit, and I'll finish clearing up in here?' He dropped the offending shard in the bin, handed the tweezers to me, then got down on his hands and knees with the dustpan and brush as I went downstairs to the bathroom.

The day didn't really improve, and when 6 p.m. arrived, along with a message from Rachel, I was enormously relieved

Are you in work? I'm outside. Pressed the bell but no answer.

I thought Aaron was still in the building, but clearly not. I tapped out a quick reply telling her I'd come and let her in, then rushed down the stairs. She was standing outside the glass door under a black umbrella. 'Hiya.' I pulled the door wide. 'Come in.'

'So sorry to call around unannounced.' She shook the water from the umbrella out into the street then folded it. 'You're not with a patient, are you? I thought someone on reception might know whether you were free or not.'

'Don't worry. I've seen my last patient, so it's good timing.' I examined her face. Dark circles ringed her eyes. 'You okay?'

She exhaled loudly. 'Not great, to be honest.'

'Come up,' I said. I pressed the button for the lift, too exhausted to climb back up three flights myself. When the door closed and we started to ascend I became hyper-aware of the mirrors lining the enclosed space. I could see the back of Rachel's head, and her profile, and she would be able to see mine. I resisted the urge to smooth down the back of my hair. Made too self-conscious by the multiple sides of each of us reflected in the glass, I focused on the real Rachel who stood in front of me and examined her more closely. Her sclera was more pink than white and her eyelids were swollen. Maybe my presumption that this was a psychological condition was wrong. 'Can I do a quick eye exam when we get upstairs?'

'That's not why I came,' she said. 'I don't expect preferential or free treatment because we're friends.'

'I know,' I said. 'But I'd like to just check everything's okay. You look tired.' The lift jolted as it came to a stop. When the door swooshed open, we went into my consulting room and I gestured for her to sit in the examination chair.

'I don't think there's anything different with my eyes,' she said, resting her chin and forehead on the machine as I moved the slit lamp closer. 'I'm just not sleeping.'

After a close inspection, I couldn't see any change, so shifted the lamp back and waited for her to blink away the brightness. 'How are things when your eyes are closed?' I moved to one of the blue chairs and she joined me, slumping into the other. It was only weeks since we'd first sat there together, but it felt far longer. I'd become so invested in Rachel's case, and in her as a person.

'Shit,' she said abruptly, then laughed. 'I believe that's the Latin term for it, the correct medical terminology, right? Or is it shitus?'

'Shitus completus,' I said.

'Exactly that.' She wound a dark curl round her finger. 'They taught you that at medical school, didn't they?'

'Among other things,' I said. I took a breath. 'I thought, since you didn't call over the weekend, things were . . . calmer.'

'I wish that was the case. But no. I didn't want to bother you. You've been so supportive.' She sighed. 'Honestly, it's got worse. A lot worse.'

I wanted to say she should've called me, but was afraid that would have been making it about me. 'What happened?'

'It's like I'm being purposely tormented, like someone is trying to make me go mad with fear.' She fiddled with the hem of her black sweater, a gesture I'd only seen her do when her eyes were closed before. She was clearly anxious.

The hairs on my arms stood to attention. 'What do you mean?'

'I heard footsteps. Actual footsteps. Before, the noises were' – she lifted her hands and moved her fingers – 'kind of nebulous. I couldn't have said exactly what they were, but this weekend there were definite footsteps.'

'And they couldn't have been from outside?'

'I tried to tell myself they were, then, when I could open my eyes again, I noticed things had been moved around.'

My breath stalled. 'What things?'

Rachel swallowed hard. 'When I opened my eyes on Monday morning, the things on the console table under the mirror weren't where I left them. One book had been placed on top of the others. I know I didn't do that.'

That didn't seem as bad as I was expecting. I wanted to ask if she was certain she hadn't simply moved the book while dusting or something and forgotten, but I didn't want to sound dismissive. 'Anything else?'

'My desk chair was by the window, as if someone had been sitting in it, looking out across the dock.'

That sent a shiver through me. I could visualise the chair she meant. When I was there, it had been tucked under a desk underneath the stairs. Her words conjured an image of a man, dressed all in black, staring out across the dark water, as she sat on the sofa, blinded, vulnerable and terrified. In my imagination the face turned and I saw Billy, who we'd met at the Palm Tree. She had said he was from a long line of rogues, which I translated as a notorious crime family. Now I thought of it, he'd been overly friendly that night. Could all that flattery and insistence on buying our drinks be an indication that he'd developed feelings for her? Dangerous feelings? Was he another Simon? I didn't know how to ask about this theory without adding to her fears. I reminded myself that what she felt was most likely a manifestation of her anxiety, not a real threat. 'I can see why that would be frightening.'

'And I know my eyes are going to be clamped again when I wake up tomorrow. I tried to stay awake all night on Sunday, to see if I could change the pattern. I thought that if I could not sleep at all, then it might reset whatever's making these bloody spasms happen, but I fell asleep on the sofa. It's a lot harder staying awake when your eyelids won't open. It wasn't like I could watch TV or read. I listened to an audiobook, then when I found myself drifting off I put loud music on, but that still didn't work. It must've been late by then, though, and it didn't stop whoever it was getting in and moving things around. I woke up on the sofa, freezing cold, to see the chair in front of the window.' She shuddered.

'And you're sure you didn't just forget moving it? The mind can play tricks, especially when we're already on high alert.'

'I'm not making it up.' The hurt on her face made me regret opening my mouth.

'No, that's not what I meant.' I wanted to suck my clumsy words back in. 'I really hope we get some answers when the neurological tests come back.' It felt like a feeble attempt to win back her trust. I wanted to ask again why she thought someone would want to torment her like this, but she'd already made it clear she couldn't answer that and her stern expression told me I'd already disappointed her

'Yeah,' she said. 'Me too.' She stood. 'Anyway, thank you for letting me offload.' It felt like she was leaving so quickly to punish me. I should have kept my thoughts to myself.

'Any time,' I said, then rushed out, 'I'm finished for the day, if you fancy a drink?'

To my relief, her face softened. 'Oh, that would have been lovely, but I'm meeting a friend for dinner. She's over from the States and this was the only time we could meet when I was sure my eyes would be open.' She made fists. 'I can't believe my life has been reduced to this. I see few enough people already, and now I have to timetable the rare occasions I do have plans to fit in around this bloody condition.' She released her fingers and sighed. 'Anyway, that's why I'm in the area; she's staying nearby. I was early, so I thought I'd pop in and say hello.'

My heart dropped when I heard she hadn't come specifically to see me, and that made me feel needy and pathetic. Aaron had told me her socials showed she had an active social life, even if it had tailed off over the last year, and just because she was my only friend right now, it didn't follow that I was hers. 'I'm glad you did.'

She pulled her lips back. 'If I'm honest, I'd rather be going out with you. You're the only one who truly understands what I'm going through. I can't tell her what's going on with me, so it will all be pretty surface stuff this evening, and that's not very satisfying, is it?' She let her shoulders rise and fall. 'But she's only in town briefly, so I didn't feel like I could say no.'

I was buoyed by the inference that our interactions weren't surface level. 'Well, you can talk to me any time.'

'That's kind. You are so kind, Beth,' she said. 'I wish more people were like you.'

'I mean it. I hate to think of you being frightened. That offer to come around one night and keep watch still stands.' I stood and looked her directly in the eye so she could see the offer was sincere.

She stepped forward and hugged me. 'You're a star, do you know that?' When she let me go, her eyes were watery. She composed herself, smiling at me. 'Right, I'd better get off. I'll see myself out.'

The room felt empty without her. I gathered my things and prepared to go back to my flat alone.

Chapter Twenty-Four

When I took the lift down to the ground floor ten minutes later, reception was still empty. I yanked my coat tight around me when I stepped out on to the dark pavement. Buildings loomed from each side and the pockets of light from the streetlamps seemed too far apart. I rushed from one to the next.

'Beth.' I jumped at the sound of a deep voice coming from the shadows ahead.

I stopped, clutching the top of my coat tight. A man stepped into the pool of light below a streetlamp and my pulse hammered harder when the glow fell across familiar features.

'Joel. You frightened me.' The sentence sounded stupid as soon as it was out of my mouth. This was the man I'd stood across from in the registry office, vowing to love and cherish until the end of our days. Even in our darkest times, when I knew his feelings for me resembled hatred more than love, he'd never made me afraid. But that was what I felt in that deserted street in the dark. It must've been my imagination, but his shadow seemed to creep forward towards me.

'Sorry.' He closed his eyes and shook his head. 'I shouldn't have ... I was surprised to see you. I shouted out instinctively.'

'You were surprised to see me on Bath Street?' I released my grip on my collar and cold air curled round my neck. That seemed implausible since he knew where I worked better than anyone. We'd bumped into each other a couple of times at Moorfields since the divorce. It was impossible not to, and we'd maintained a professional, courteous front. He didn't mean me any harm, as far as I knew.

'Yeah.' He hung his head. 'Sorry, that sounds stupid, doesn't it? I suppose I thought it would be a massive coincidence if you came out at exactly the time I arrived, but here you are.'

'Here I am.' I wished I wasn't. I was too tired and overwrought for a random interaction with the man whose heart I'd trampled on. 'How are you?'

'Good, thanks.' A door slammed further along the street and he turned at the sound of heels on tarmac. A slender figure in a long coat tied at the waist approached, and as it passed under a light I recognised Chloe, a nurse from one of the other practices near Moorfields. She didn't appear to see me in my position in the dark. Her face broke into a smile when she looked at Joel. He glanced over his shoulder at me and I read guilt in his expression.

'I found it,' Chloe said, holding a folded umbrella aloft. She reached Joel and threaded her arm through his. 'Sardia and Adam are already at the restaurant, so we need to get a move on.' She looked puzzled at Joel's stillness, then followed his gaze to me. 'Oh, Beth. Hi.'

'Hi,' I said. My mind floundered for something to say to make this less excruciating. 'Actually, you've just reminded me that I've left my umbrella at work. Can't afford not to have one handy in this weather.' I turned and started to move away. 'Say hi to Sardia and Adam,' I said over my shoulder. 'Have a good evening.'

I fumbled my way back into reception and sat on the stairs as minutes ticked by, trying to regulate my emotions. I had no idea Joel was dating again, and certainly not someone we both knew. Why would I? We were divorced; it was none of my business. From what I knew of her, Chloe was nice enough, and they made an attractive couple, her with her bleached pixie cut and round apple cheeks, and him willowy and slightly scruffy in a way that made people want to mother him. She must be a good eight years younger than Joel and me. I pressed on the cut under the plaster on my thumb as my mind conjured a future for them with a house and two sandy-haired toddlers playing with a puppy in the garden. I pressed harder until the pain filled my mind. Joel deserved to live happily ever after. He wasn't the villain in our story.

Sitting on the cold step in the stark space, I was surprised to find that my imaginings didn't cause me the kind of agony they would have done when we first separated. As if my subconscious thought I was getting away too lightly, it presented me with an alternative image of Max waiting on the street outside for Chloe. That thought caused an ache in my heart even worse than the throbbing of my hand.

I jumped as the door suddenly opened, then stood as an exhausted-looking woman in a tabard with the office cleaning logo on the front pushed her way inside, arms laden with bags.

'Evening,' I said, rushing forward to hold the door open for her, then I put a stop to my wayward thoughts and stepped back out on to the pavement. It was eerily quiet. I hurried towards Old Street, unease making me glance behind at the shadowy road more than once. Rachel's words had clearly got to me because, once again, I had the uneasy feeling I was being followed. I knew it was ridiculous, but even when I joined the throngs of people marching towards Old Street tube station, I couldn't shake the prickling sensation of someone's eyes on my back.

Chapter Twenty-Five

The following day, I was brushing my teeth before bed when my phone rang. The buzz was drowned out by the sound of my electric toothbrush at first, but when I spat into the sink the sound continued and I rushed from the tiny en suite and caught it just before the voicemail kicked in.

'Beth?'

'Hi, Rachel?'

'I'm so, so sorry to ring you so late.'

I glanced at the screen. Ten thirty. 'It's not that late. What's up?'

'I don't know if I can do another night like this.' Her voice was breathy. 'I feel like I should check myself into a unit or something.'

'What do you mean?' Was she admitting her spasms could be a trauma response?

'A psychiatric unit. I'm going mad, aren't I? Nothing's happened yet tonight, but I'm literally sitting here shaking, jumping at every sound. It's not even chucking-out time yet, so God knows what I'll be like by the time everyone's on their way home from the Dickens Inn.'

It was the anxiety caused by not being able to open her eyes that made her think she needed psychiatric help then, not the symptom itself. I imagined her curled into the corner of her cream sofa and my heart gave a squeeze. 'You're not going mad. What you're experiencing would spook anyone.'

'I'm being completely irrational, though. I keep thinking about that man who stalked you.'

'Simon?'

'Yes. I know it sounds mad, but my brain keeps telling me he's watching me because he doesn't like us getting close.'

The hairs on my arms stirred. 'He wouldn't take the risk after I went to the police,' I said, hoping I sounded more convinced than I felt. I remembered how blatant he'd been, standing in the road, staring up at our flat, sitting in his ostentatious car on Bath Street. Could I really put anything past him? 'And this isn't his style. He likes to be seen.'

'But, like you said, he went quiet after you went to the police. He could have changed his tactic, adopted a new MO so he was less likely to be arrested, but still got his twisted kicks.'

'I honestly don't think it's him.' I pushed away the memories of feeling like I was being watched recently too. 'I haven't heard from him in months. I think he's moved on.' Why did I say that? She thinks he's moved on to her. I regretted ever telling Rachel about him. It was stupid and selfish, driven by my desperation for connection. I was an idiot.

'But you said he was unhinged.'

'I honestly don't think you need to worry about Simon.' I tried to reassure her, though part of me feared it *was* him. If so, then her association with me had brought him to her door. And now I had added to her distress by mentioning him. I needed to make it right. 'Do you want me to come around?' I glanced at myself in the mirror built into my wardrobe door. What I saw was the at-home version of me, my unhappy face clean of make-up and hair scraped into a messy bun on top of my head. Hardly the well-presented doctor, but that didn't matter under the circumstances, especially since she couldn't even see me.

'No . . . I don't know.' The words were shaky, and that made my mind up for me.

'I'm coming over. I'll stay tonight and keep watch, then at least you can get some sleep.'

'But what about you? You need to sleep too.'

'I'll sleep on the sofa, then, if I do hear a noise, at least I can open my eyes and do something about it.' I couldn't imagine sleeping a wink with the threat of an intruder, even one I was fairly sure was imaginary, but I didn't want her to know that. Hopefully, her mind would be put at rest after one night and she could stop worrying and concentrate on her recovery going forward. I convinced myself it wasn't about me making her safe, because I didn't see myself as physically capable of that. No, it was about the illusion of safety, and that I felt I could provide. If me being there made her believe she was safe, that might be enough.

'You really don't have to. I shouldn't have called.'

'Rachel.' My voice was firm. 'I am coming to yours. I'll be there in half an hour.' I thought about what I'd need for my clinic tomorrow. 'Forty-five minutes, tops. Okay?'

Chapter Twenty-Six

The haunted expression on Rachel's face when she opened the door convinced me I'd done the right thing in coming over. 'Hiya. It's only me.' Her eyes were closed and her skin was pale. She stood back from the door to let me in. The living room was in darkness. 'Okay if I switch the light on?'

'I should have turned them on, sorry,' she said, groping along the wall for the switch. 'There's no point when I'm here on my own. I wish I'd thought to get it all set up automatically before this happened. You can do everything by voice activation these days, can't you? There's only so much you can do in a rental house, though.'

She pressed the switch and the overhead light came on. The glow illuminated a sheen of sweat on her top lip and forehead. It wasn't overly warm. She must be in quite a state to be sweating like that.

'Thank you so much for coming. I've been feeling pretty foolish for calling, to be honest. I haven't heard or felt anything strange tonight, so far. Sod's law, isn't it? It's like your rash disappearing the day you go to the doctor's.' She wiped the sweat from her top lip. 'Although, these spasms haven't buggered off yet, so . . . anyway, come in. Make yourself at home.'

'Thanks.' I dropped my bag out of the way, so she didn't trip over it.

'I keep thinking about how tired you're going to be tomorrow.' Her thumb and forefinger fiddled nervously with the hem of her top.

'Don't worry about that. It will be worth it to put your mind at rest. What do you want to do, go straight to bed, or . . .'

She rubbed a hand over her face. 'I wanted to get the quilt and pillows down from the spare room, but I was scared I'd trip on the stairs and break my neck. Would you mind helping me make up the sofa?' She grimaced. 'I mean, you could sleep in the spare room, but—'

'The sofa's fine. I'm here to make sure there's no one getting in, so it's best if I'm near the door and those windows.' I glanced over at the windows and the dark water beyond, not relishing the idea of spending the night in this room at all.

'If you're sure?'

I wasn't, but I couldn't exactly say that. I followed her up the first flight of stairs. The kitchen was dark. Through the turret's windows at the far end, reflections of a boat's lights shimmered on the black water. 'All right if I put the lights on up here too?'

'Yes, of course. Do whatever you need.'

I put my finger on the cold aluminium button and pressed.

The overhead light sprang into life and when I next glanced towards the windows my own reflection stared back at me, wide-eyed and frightened. It told the truth about how I really felt. I looked away. I turned on the lights to illuminate the next narrow stairwell and the tiny landing at the top of the steps. I planned to keep all of them burning all night. Surely that would deter an intruder?

'My room is up on the right. The spare room is in the top turret.' She half laughed. '*Turret* sounds so grand, doesn't it, like I live in a castle or something. I wish. I won't be able to afford this place unless I can get back to work. Anyway, I could only fit a single bed in there. You okay to gather up the quilt and pillows?'

'No problem. It might take a couple of trips. Why don't I see you downstairs, so I don't accidentally knock you over when I'm carrying everything?'

She hesitated before heading down. It was natural, I supposed, not to relish leaving a relative stranger to go up to the place where you slept alone. When the sound of her slow footsteps receded, I was tempted to peek into her bedroom, but I resisted. I wouldn't want someone invading my privacy, especially when I was in a vulnerable state. That's why I was there, after all, to keep her safe from intruders, not to be one.

She wasn't wrong: the spare room was tiny, with only enough space for a narrow single bed in the centre of the hexagon. There were five windows up there, but no curtains or blinds. Feeling exposed in the bright light against the black sky, I quickly bundled up the quilt and made my way down the stairs. Rachel was perched on the sofa facing away from the windows, so I put it down on the other. 'I'm just going to collect the pillows,' I said, making sure she knew what my movements were.

I returned a minute later. 'This will be comfy,' I said. 'Like a sleepover.'

'Ha.' She smiled for the first time since I arrived. 'I remember my mum complaining when me and my friends started to call staying at each other's houses sleepovers. She said it was an Americanism.'

That was the first time I'd heard her mention her mother when she was alive. 'Did you have a lot of sleepovers?' I sat on the sofa and pulled the quilt over my lap.

'Yeah, loads,' said Rachel. 'Did you?'

'My mum didn't like the noise or the mess,' I said, 'so I'd go to other people's houses more than they came to mine.' That sounded a bit sad. It was also untrue. I stopped staying out overnight after the time I came home early one morning and couldn't wake Mum. It wasn't long after Moira died and I thought I'd lost her too. Eventually, she came round, groggy and furious that I'd called an ambulance. I was too scared to leave her again, sure she'd drink herself to death and I'd end up in care.

I lifted my tone. 'Did you ever camp out when you were a kid? My aunt was a lot younger than my mum and I spent most of my time with her when I was growing up, especially in the school holidays. We used to put up a tent in the back garden when I was little and pretend we were in Spain or France.' The memory was bittersweet.

Moira and I would have midnight feasts and read books to each other by torchlight. A hole opened up inside me every time I thought of her. I didn't allow myself to often, but for some reason I wanted to mention her name to my new friend.

'That sounds brilliant.' The corners of her mouth lifted. 'In summer we used to take our sleeping bags to this place by Windmill Hill. We always said we'd stay there all night, but we'd end up spooking each other out and rushing home before it was even fully dark.'

'We?'

Rachel turned her head to me. 'Sorry?'

'Who were you with?'

'Oh, right. My best friend. Now I come to think of it, I bet our parents knew we'd never have the nerve to stay out all night. That's probably why they allowed us out in the first place.'

'Probably,' I said.

'And, after what I saw, I wasn't exactly in a hurry to go out after dark again.'

I stilled, waiting for her to continue. When it became clear she wasn't about to say more, I said, 'What was it you saw?'

She pulled a curl to her mouth and rubbed it across her lips. 'Nothing. Forget I said that.' She let the hair fall. 'Fancy a hot chocolate or something before bed?'

'I'm fine, thanks.' I waited a beat then said, 'You said you saw something after dark.'

'I'd rather not talk about it, if that's okay.' She scratched the back of her head. 'I don't mean to be rude. I know you're only here to help, but—'

'I am here to help,' I said. 'You initially came to me for help with your eye condition, and it's not impossible that—'

'What happened back then has nothing to do with this.'

I spoke gently, aware her interruption was an attempt to shut me down. 'It could have, though. I think we need to keep our minds open. It's possible a repressed trauma could have caused a physical response.'

'I knew it.' Rachel slammed her hand on the cushion beside her. 'I knew you thought I was making this up.'

'That's not what I'm saying at all. Psychological responses are as real as physical ones – very often they're co-morbid; they present simultaneously.' I vividly remembered the heaviness of my own limbs and the way my throat closed at the thought of food during my own breakdown. There was no doubt that psychological symptoms and physical symptoms were closely linked, and I certainly wasn't judging her one way or the other.

Tears seeped from Rachel's eyes. 'I'm not choosing not to open my eyes. I totally get that loads of people have physical responses to anxiety and mental health issues, but I don't have a mental health issue. I have an eye issue, eyelid spasms. What's it called?'

'Blepharospasm,' I said quietly. I wished she could accept what I was saying, but she was too distressed to listen at the moment, so I decided not to push my point.

'It's a medical condition, isn't it?' Tears dripped off her chin. 'And you said the timings weren't that unusual, didn't you, when you take into account things like circadian rhythm and the way our periods work?'

'Yes, but . . .' I stopped. This wasn't the time. And what did I know, anyway? I wasn't a psychologist. I was an ophthalmologist, and the tests I had done showed she could not open her eyes if she wanted to. 'Yes, it's a medical condition.'

I went to pluck a tissue from a box on the coffee table and held it close until it touched her hand. 'Here's a tissue.'

She took it with a weak smile and wiped it over her face and blew her nose. 'Sorry I'm so emotional.'

'It's fine. It's no surprise, really. You're going through a lot, and you're tired.'

'I'm so tired.' She let her chin rest on her chest. 'In fact, I think I might go up, if that's okay with you?'

'Yes, of course. That's why I'm here.' I didn't want to leave the evening on this note, but didn't know how to rescue it.

'Do you need anything?' she said as she stood, playing with the hem of her top again. 'I mean, you'll keep your phone by your side, won't you? It's charged, right?'

I took my phone from my pocket and checked the screen. 'Yep. Ninety per cent.'

'There's a charger in the kitchen if you need it,' she said. She hesitated. 'And if you need anything else from the kitchen . . .' Her voice was serious.

Goosebumps rose on my arms when I understood what she was implying. She was asking if I wanted a knife? Did I? 'I'm good, I think. I can always go up if I . . . if I need anything. And remember, if you hear someone moving around, it's only me, okay?'

New tears rolled down the side of her nose. 'I can't tell you how much this means to me,' she said. She held her arms wide, and I walked into them. She hugged me for a moment, then let go. 'Thank you, Beth. You are an incredible friend. Goodnight.'

'Sleep well,' I said, watching her trail her fingers along the back of the sofa, then feel for the banister. Soon, the sound of her footsteps disappeared, and I was left downstairs all alone.

Chapter Twenty-Seven

An hour later, when my eyelids scratched across my dry eyes, I realised I'd been trying not to blink. How ridiculous. It was deeply unhealthy too; I, of all people, should know that. I dragged my tired limbs off the sofa, keeping my gaze averted from the patio doors and the dark water beyond. I kept my tread light on the stairs, determined not to give Rachel any more cause for concern. I hoped she was sleeping soundly, knowing I was downstairs keeping watch.

Once in the brightly lit kitchen, I opened cupboards, searching for a glass. Everything matched. There were six heavy-bottomed tumblers, six wine glasses, six champagne flutes. I thought of my own kitchen cupboards with their hotchpotch of miscellaneous glasses and mugs. Mine had been accumulated over the years with Joel. He'd bought me mugs with funny slogans on; I'd bought him two crystal brandy glasses, partly as a joke, when he'd started to have a nightcap like some rich old man.

All our possessions had been divided in the split and, through guilt, I'd accepted the crappy half. Rachel had always lived alone, as far as I was aware. She clearly preferred an ordered life. Until the spasms began, she had her shit together. I wanted to be the kind of person who had their shit together. I would start by organising the tat in my kitchen. I yawned as I ran the tap, held my finger in the water stream until it was ice cold, then filled the glass and forced myself to drink half of it then refill it. I was going to be exhausted enough tomorrow; I didn't need to be dehydrated too.

Back downstairs, I switched on the small lamp on the console table by the mirror, then turned off the overhead light. My breathing slowed in the calmer atmosphere. Pulling the quilt over me and resting on the soft pillow, I opened my Kindle and tried to focus on the type, but my eyes were heavy, and my brain wouldn't absorb the words. The quilt was warm and heavy over my legs and my eyes began to close.

In my dream, a thousand black-feathered birds flocked towards me, their sharp beaks trained on my eyes. I jolted awake, but the noise like the flapping of wings was still audible. My pulse galloped when I didn't recognise the room. I turned towards the noise, awareness of being in Rachel's house growing along with the terror at the sound that was coming from directly outside the windows. I kicked off the quilt and stood on shaking legs, eyes darting around for any sign of threat. I shivered. The house had grown cold, and I felt alone and exposed. I took my phone in one hand and my glass of water in the other, wishing I had a more effective means of defending myself.

My ears buzzed with static as I moved towards the tall windows at the far side of the room. The lamp's reflection shone at my back, and my image grew larger as I approached, the expression of fear on my face clearer with every step. My breath fogged the glass as I peered out at the basin, straining my eyes to see if I could locate the origin of the weird noise. I whipped around at a creaking sound behind me. The lamp's glow cast shadows across the room; dark places for people to hide. I stayed still, shoulders tense, phone gripped in my hand, but the room remained still.

I forced myself to turn back to the window, using my forearm to clear the condensation of my breath from the glass. My shoulders released at the sight of the tarpaulin covering the rear end of a boat moored close by flapping in the wind. That was what was making the noise. Of course it was. And the creaking was just the central heating pipes. My reflection half smiled back at me as my heart rate slowed. I moved back to the sofa and dropped on to the cushions. My phone screen told me it was 3 a.m. My head thumped with exhaustion, but when I closed my eyes again, I knew with absolute certainty that sleep wouldn't come.

I was dozing when I heard Rachel's footsteps on the stairs. I half sat and watched her take careful steps, her hand firmly on the banister. She was wearing blue cotton pyjamas, and her feet were bare. It was oddly intimate to see her still in her nightclothes, and at such an early hour. As an adult, I'd only ever seen my closest friends like this. Our friendship had advanced at pace, but I was fine with that. 'Morning,' I said when she reached the bottom. 'Sleep okay?'

'Oh, my God, yes,' she said, with more energy in her voice than I'd heard in some time. 'You are a bloody legend. Honestly, I can't remember when I last had a sleep like that, even when my eyes aren't doing this.' She circled her finger in front of her closed lids. 'I'm not kidding. Having you here changed absolutely everything.' She moved further into the room. 'I don't know how I can thank you. I'd forgotten what it was like not to be rigid with fear. I feel like I've been to a spa, not just had eight hours' uninterrupted sleep.'

'That's great,' I said, trying to muffle the sound of a yawn that crept out with the words.

She felt her way along the back then the arm of the sofa and sat next to me. She held out a hand and, when I took it, she held it in both of hers. 'Did you manage to get any sleep?'

I couldn't help but smile at the care in the gesture. She smelled of laundry detergent, and the skin-to-skin contact was comforting. 'Not bad,' I lied. 'This sofa is comfier than it looks.'

She squeezed my hand. 'What a relief. I was worried sick you'd be down here tossing and turning, jumping at every sound.'

'Nah, not me. I'm hard as nails.' My terrified face in the reflection of the window came back to me. It seemed absurd now to have been so petrified by the sound of flapping tarpaulin. I thought about mentioning it, but didn't want her to know I'd been frightened. 'There was nothing to be worried about. It's all good.'

'Thank God for that.' She let my hand go and held on to her pyjama top. 'And you really were okay? Comfortable enough, I mean?'

'I was fine.' I forced a smile into my voice.

'Then' – she put her thumb nail between her teeth – 'I absolutely hate asking this, and of course you should say no if you're too tired, or you were just being nice, and you can't really sleep on this thing' – she tapped her hand on the cushion – 'but I don't suppose you'd consider coming back again tonight?'

Chapter Twenty-Eight

The Watcher

Oh dear, Beth, how tired you look when you walk from St Katharine Docks back to your car. Your face is slack, your shoulders rounded like a woman twice your age. Is it any surprise when you stay up all night like that? You can't expect to hold down a job like yours and burn the candle at both ends, now, can you? You're making such silly mistakes, the kind you can't afford to. You need to be alert, otherwise how will you recognise the threat when it shows its face?

It could come in the form of that man with the baseball cap pulled down low over his brow, for example. He almost walked into you as you stumbled over a cobble in your hurry to get out of the wind. He could be tracking you, ready to lunge and tip you into the frozen water of the dock. What about the woman pushing her pram towards Waitrose? She looks innocuous enough, doesn't she? But how can you really know what's nestled under those pink blankets? It could be a baby, or it could be a machete. Think about it. Any one of the people you're passing on the short walk from your new friend's house to the supposed safety of your car could be intent on harming you.

Even when you get inside your car, are you truly safe then? Do you always check the back seat to see if some malevolent creature has found their way in and is lurking, ready to put a blade to your throat and press, ever so gently? I can hear them now, describing what's about to happen to you in sickening detail, as their other hand reaches for your breast.

But look at me, getting all carried away. There's no one in your car. The man with the baseball cap isn't going to hurt you, and there is a pink-cheeked baby in that woman's pram. It's crying now and kicking little pink booties in the cold air.

The lesson I'm trying to teach you is that you should be looking beyond what you first see. I suppose trusting sight comes along with the job. If you didn't value sight, why do everything you can to save it? But you need to scratch the surface more, to get to what's underneath. That's where the truth lies. Open your eyes and really look, Beth, because there is a dangerous person in your life right now – and that person is me.

Chapter Twenty-Nine

I'd never needed coffee more than when I arrived at work that morning. I was grateful to be at my private practice, at least, with comfortable chairs I could sink into between clients. And Aaron was in that day, so at least the caffeine stream was constant.

Mid-morning, Sardia messaged asking me to call her when I had a chance. My hand shook as I held my phone; I didn't know if it was because of how exhausted I was or because of too much caffeine. I pressed Sardia's number and waited.

'Hi,' I said when she answered. I wanted to ask how her evening with Joel and Chloe had been, but didn't know how to broach it without sounding nosy or bitter. I decided to wait and see if she brought it up. 'How's the bump?'

'Pressing on my bladder,' she said. 'Constantly.'

'Good to know,' I said. 'And don't pretend you haven't always had a weak bladder. It's not fair to blame it on the baby. Remember that messy time in the queue for the chemical toilets at that gig in Finsbury Park?' Just after we'd bought our flat, Joel and I had bumped into Sardia and her husband at an open-air concert, and we'd spent a glorious afternoon drinking and dancing in the sunshine. That life was so alien to me now that it seemed as if I were accessing someone else's memories when I thought of that carefree time.

'Don't,' Sardia said. 'Even the thought of those toilets is enough to make me gag at the moment.'

'Ah, the joys of pregnancy.'

'Ha! This will be you one day, then you'll understand.'

I was caught off guard by a sudden sense of grief. I didn't believe that would be me one day. I couldn't see a partner or children in my future. I remembered my vision of Joel and Chloe's perfect family and my eyes filled with tears.

'Sorry, I don't have long before my next patient. What was it—'

'I've got the results from the tests on your pet patient.'

My jaw dropped. 'She's not my pet patient.'

'Keep telling yourself that. Anyway, they're all clear. Every last one of them. There's nothing I could find. Zero neurological indicators for her condition. Nada.'

There was a self-satisfaction in her voice I didn't like, as if she'd like to say *I told you so*. I wondered if she'd discussed me with Joel over dinner. Had they talked about my weakness when it came to boundaries with my patients, and how much better off he was without me? The thought made my shoulders tighten. 'Interesting. Thank you.'

'I'm not sure she'll be thanking me when she realises the money she's spent on these tests should have gone to a psychiatrist.'

I didn't like her tone. She sounded almost derisive, as if it were obvious Rachel had mental health problems instead of physical ones. I fought the urge to remind her Rachel was suffering and she should have more sympathy. She was a doctor, for God's sake. Where was her empathy?

Her voice lightened when she added, 'I'll email the full findings over to you. You didn't uncover anything else that might be causing the spasms at your end, did you?'

I reluctantly admitted I hadn't.

I heard her exhale. 'Okay. Do you want me to go through the results with her in a follow-up appointment, like I'm supposed to, or do you want to save her the cash and discuss them at your next appointment?'

'I'll do it,' I said.

'Good. I'm happy to have a follow-up with her if she has any questions, obviously, but she'd be wasting her money if we're both just going to tell her there's nothing wrong, physically.'

'Leave it with me,' I said. 'Sorry, I'd better get off. Thanks for this. Take care of yourself and that bump, and see you soon, yeah?' Despite what I said, I was in no hurry to see Sardia any time soon. She and Joel were welcome to their cosy dinners with their other halves.

I ended the call and slumped back in my chair. I'd been hoping there was a neurological explanation for Rachel's condition, since I couldn't find an ophthalmic one. After the appointment to go through Sardia's report, the right thing to do would be to discharge her, and I didn't want to do that. I gave my head a shake. I shouldn't want to prolong someone's care just so I could still spend time with them. I was pathetic.

At lunchtime, I ordered in sandwiches and more coffee for myself and Aaron. We'd fallen into the habit of eating together on the days he was in, and I'd begun to look forward to it, which added to my sense of neediness.

'What's happening with that patient we were cyber-stalking?' he said, retrieving a piece of cheese that had fallen from his sandwich on to his trousers and tucking it between his lips.

'We were not cyber-stalking her,' I said. 'We were . . . looking into different avenues of care.' He grinned at me, and I smiled back, trying to front out my bullshit.

'Did you find any other . . . avenues of care?'

'Sadly not. The neurological tests were all clear. I'm a bit at a loss, to be honest.'

Aaron placed his crust back in the wrapper. 'Don't suppose there's anything else you can do, is there, since it's not her eyes or . . . or whatever neurologists deal with?'

'Brain, spinal cord and nerve disorders.'

'Gotcha. Maybe a therapist can get to the bottom of it. Want me to send out a letter of discharge?'

I chewed my mouthful, wishing I hadn't ordered feta cheese and rocket. I was too fragile for such strong flavours. 'Not yet. Wait a bit.'

'But why?' He tore a piece off his crust and squidged it between his fingers. 'There's nothing else you can do.'

'Maybe,' I said, 'but I don't want to give up on her yet.'

He dropped the flattened bread into the wrapper and tore off another piece. 'It's what you lot do, though, isn't it? You deal with one case, then move on to the next. It's not giving up. It's just part of the job.'

'Yeah, but . . .' I poked my tongue at a globule of food lodged between my molars. 'She's become sort of a friend.'

'Oh, okay.' He continued to play with the bread, looking down at his fingers.

I could sense he didn't like the idea of Rachel and me being friends. 'Becoming friends with your patients isn't unethical,' I said. The knowledge that I could easily have been struck off after what happened with Simon presented itself in my mind, as it often did. If Joel, or anyone else, had contacted the GMC I might not be here now. The facts hadn't changed, so the threat hadn't completely disappeared. But this was different. Very different. Friendship wasn't unethical and I was not about to embark on a romantic relationship with Rachel. Still, Aaron's silence was unnerving. 'And it's not as if she'll be my patient for much longer, is it?'

He glanced up, then back at his hands. 'I worry that, well . . . you can't find anything physically wrong, can you?'

'No, but that doesn't mean there isn't anything to find, just that it needs more investigation.'

He crossed his legs in the other direction, looking uncomfortable. 'I don't want to sound judgemental, but if she's got mental health problems, then maybe it would be best to, I don't know, keep a bit of space between you?'

His words hung in the air, and disappointment flooded

me. I expected better of Aaron. 'Having mental health problems doesn't make her any less of a person, and it certainly doesn't make her a high-risk friend, if that's what you're implying. One in four adults will experience some kind of mental health problem, Aaron. Are you suggesting we should avoid all of them?' I could have disclosed my own struggles with mental health then, but shame stopped me, and I hated myself for it.

'No, of course not.' He shifted again in his seat.

'Good, because I run an inclusive practice here, and it's important to me that my staff don't propagate the stigma that already exists around mental health.'

He crushed his sandwich packet in his fist. 'Understood. I was only . . . Never mind.' He viewed me, his face unreadable. 'Forget I said anything.' He rolled his lips over his teeth. 'I'd better get back to work.'

He stood and left my room, and a chill lingered in the air behind him.

Chapter Thirty

When Aaron left, I only had ten minutes to finish my lunch and prepare for my next patient. I threw away the rest of the sandwich, downed the last of the coffee, then peeled two extra-strong mints from the packet I kept in my drawer. The fiery cool of the mints hit the back of my throat and burned up my nose. Even that wasn't enough to invigorate me, so when Aaron called in to say my next patient was stuck on a faulty train and was going to miss their appointment, I could have sobbed with gratitude.

I set the alarm on my phone and sat back with my eyes closed. A nap would do me the world of good. Ten minutes later, thoughts about Rachel's condition, and what might have happened in her past, wouldn't stop pinging around my brain. Huffing, I opened my eyes and gave up all hope of sleep. Maybe if I found the answers to some of the questions I had, I'd be able to switch off and rest.

As I opened the search engine on my computer, I tried to recall what Rachel had said last night before shutting me down. We'd talked about sleepovers, and she mentioned somewhere called Windmill Hill. I typed that in the search bar. There were more places in the UK called Windmill Hill than I'd expected. Already frustrated, I scrolled through information on a city farm, a school in Luton, then a place in Sussex with an actual windmill. I wished I'd asked exactly where she was talking about. I carried on scrolling, scanning the English Heritage site, moving on to details of an activity camp, then a hill in Hitchin. None of them gave me a clue.

I tried *crime, Windmill Hill* and horrifying statistics for the various places appeared on the screen. Exasperation added to the tension in my head. I scoured my mind for how to narrow down the search. We were talking about when we were growing up, and whatever it was made her wary of the dark. A new surge of energy made me lean forward and tap on the keys, grimly typing, *Rape, Windmill Hill*. A BBC report of a teenage girl being raped in woodland in 2015 came up, but Rachel would have been around twenty-six then, and I'd got the impression that whatever happened took place when she was a teenager.

Hoping I was stretching the realms of reality, I typed in *Murder, Windmill Hill*. There were a depressing number of results, but, scrolling through, one link made my finger still on the mouse. I clicked on it, and a picture of a green space with a path snaking through it appeared. I enlarged it, and a saw path to the left had been cordoned off by yellow police tape. The date of the piece was 2005. Rachel would have been sixteen or seventeen. The headline said: *Suspect in Teenage Girl's Murder Case Released*. I read on.

'The man held on suspicion of murdering schoolgirl Becky O'Gorman was released earlier today after being eliminated from our inquiries,' said Police Chief Brian Philby. 'After thorough investigation, we have ascertained that the young man in question was not at the scene when Becky lost her life.' He went on to ask anyone who'd witnessed anything unusual on the night of 6 March at the Dell, in the Windmill Hill area of Hitchin, to come forward. 'We are very keen to apprehend the perpetrator of this terrible crime,' he said, adding, 'We are supporting Becky's family and the girl who witnessed her friend's death, and appeal to the local community to do everything they can to help us take this dangerous man off our streets.'

There was a murder, and a witness. I reread the article, desperate to find the name of the witness, but there were no more details. I started a new search, including the date and the victim's name, and combed everything I found for new details. Finally, I discovered that a nineteen-year-old man had been apprehended after being named by the only witness to the crime, a seventeen-year-old girl called Kate Simpson. Kate Simpson. Not Rachel Cartwright. Drained by the disappointment of another fruitless search, I sat back and let my eyes close, but was jolted awake minutes later by the arrival of my next patient.

Max popped in to see me after his shift at Moorfields. Aaron had left at the end of his contracted hours without saying goodbye, which was unusual for him. I regretted being sharp with him. We'd formed a good working relationship, and I'd thought it was turning into a friendship. Now I'd gone and ruined it, just like always. I would try to smooth things over next time he was in and be extra vigilant not to cock things up with Rachel.

'How's tricks?' said Max, sitting down and crossing his legs. His trousers rode up, showing off striped socks. That was one of the reasons I loved him . . . liked him, I corrected myself; he always wore socks with some kind of pattern and I was sure they were designed to show the world that he was more than just a boring old medic. He liked bright, colourful things.

Simon only ever wore black socks – socks that didn't announce his personality to the room. Or perhaps they did. His persona matched his socks: dark. I just hadn't recognised it. Max's socks were cheerful, like him. That was why I had to keep him at arm's length, so I didn't cast a shadow over his natural brightness. Despite my best efforts, my imagination conjured an alternative reality where I stood and crossed the room. In my mind's eye I saw myself sit on Max's lap and felt his arms curl around me. I lifted my chin and he slowly lowered his head until his lips touched mine.

'Oh, you know,' I said, shaking my head to rid myself of the fantasy. 'Busy, tired. You?'

'Same.' If that were true, his clear eyes and the healthy glow of his skin were covering it well.

'I bumped into Joel. He was outside, meeting Chloe, the nurse with the short bleached hair. Do you know the one I mean?'

'Yes.' He blew out his lips. 'I'd heard they were an item.'

'Oh.' *An item* sounded more serious than dating. 'I had no idea.'

'I thought about mentioning it, but wasn't sure you'd want to know.' He pinched the crease in his trouser leg between his thumb and forefinger. 'Sorry. Perhaps I should have. I'd have said something if I'd known you might come across them like that. Was it uncomfortable, seeing them together, I mean?'

The subtext was clear. Was I over my ex-husband now? I'd allowed Max to believe that it was my feelings for Joel that prevented us from being together. If he was a less principled man, he might have told me about Joel and Chloe as soon as he heard, but, typically, he'd prioritised my feelings and didn't use it to his advantage. I thought back to sitting on the stairs, the image of Max with someone else making my heart ache. 'It was a surprise, but I'm okay. I want him to be happy. He deserves it.'

'So do you,' he said, gently.

How I wished he was right. 'If you say so.'

He looked crestfallen and I wished I hadn't been so glib. 'Did you get any further with the Rachel Cartwright case?'

'It's ongoing.' I powered off my computer and tidied my desk.

'Did Sardia turn anything up?'

'Unfortunately not.'

'And your tests were all normal?'

'So far.' I went to unhook my coat from the back of the door. I didn't want to talk to anyone else about this case or, more accurately, my new friend. No one else's opinion mattered. I knew what I was doing.

'I think you've probably done all you can, then. Time to hand over to a mental health specialist, I think.'

I turned to face him. 'You thought it was psychosomatic all along, didn't you?'

He lifted his hands. 'I've never met her, so I couldn't give a clinical opinion, but the way the spasms come and go like clockwork suggests to me there's more going on.'

I went to the other chair and sat, laying my coat over my lap. 'But that case reported in the *Sun*, where the man's eyes closed for days at a time. That had been happening to him for fifteen years.'

'And who's to say that wasn't psychosomatic?' His tongue flicked over his lips.

'He had surgery to remove the muscles. Surely they wouldn't have done that if there was doubt?' I wrapped the belt of my coat round my hand. 'Anyway, I just don't think I should discharge her yet. Even if it does have a psychological cause, it's presenting in her eyes, so that means she needs to be under the care of an ophthalmologist.'

'So you agree it's probably not a physical issue?'

I felt cornered. I dragged the belt until my knuckles ground together. 'Truly, I don't know. It might help if you could go back to the doctor who sent the referral to see if they've got any more information on the reason she's wary of men?' I thought back to the time Rachel and I were in the Palm Tree. Rachel hadn't seemed nervous of men then, but the only men we interacted with were the barman and that Billy character, and she already knew him. I thought again about the possibility that he might be stalking Rachel. I still hadn't mentioned it to her, and I sure as hell wasn't going to tell Max about him. I didn't think he'd respond too well to the knowledge I'd accepted drinks from a known criminal.

Max shook his head. 'Let it go, Beth. It's not our place to go digging into patients' pasts. That's not in our professional remit. Leave that to the people who are qualified.'

I released the belt and looked down at the red marks it had left on my skin. 'I feel a duty of care.'

'Don't do this, Beth.'

'What?' I knew what he meant, and I didn't want to hear it. 'I'm not getting too close. Jesus, I'm sorry for caring about my patients. I'm sorry for trying to do the best I can for the people I'm supposed to be helping.'

Max sighed, then stood. 'I'm trying to help you. You have a history of getting . . . too emotionally invested.'

I raised my eyes to the ceiling. 'I'm a big girl, Max, and I learned my lesson. Don't you think the price I paid was enough to stop me doing the same thing again?' My brain asked me what I had left to lose if I did. Other than work, nothing.

'I hope so.' He turned when he got to the door. 'Look after yourself, all right?'

'I will,' I said. 'I promise.' He smiled and nodded, then turned and walked away. As I heard his tread on the stairs, I held back the urge to ask him to stay, to have dinner with me, to come home with me and fill the gaping void in my life. I wondered if he'd seen that girl from New Zealand again, whether they'd had a second date. I hoped so. That's the lie I told myself as I tidied my desk and prepared to return to my empty flat alone.

Chapter Thirty-One

The Watcher

Back so soon?

Staying at St Katharine Docks for the second night in a row seems like poor decision-making to me, Beth. You should have refused. You're too nice for your own good – that's your problem. You care to the extent that it makes you weak. I have more respect for people with healthy boundaries than pathetic saps who spend their lives trying to make everyone else happy.

Unlike you, I'm in charge of my life, and I'm enjoying playing puppet master with yours. The stakes are high, but it's basically a game of cat and mouse. And I'm excellent at games, even if I do say so myself. It helps that I have a ruthless streak when it comes to self-preservation. A lot like a cat, now I come to think of it. A big-game cat.

Yes, I like that. I'm the hunter, Beth, my lamb, and you're the prey.

Chapter Thirty-Two

I thanked the parking gods that there was a bay free on Thomas More Street. I parked up and turned off the engine. The temperature immediately dropped, and I wished I'd dried my hair more thoroughly. I hadn't had time. When I got back from work, I'd sat down for a quick rest and must've fallen asleep, because I woke up in the dark on my sofa at half past nine, then I only had time for toast and a quick shower. I'd promised Rachel I'd be with her by 10.30 p.m. and didn't want to let her down.

The road was deserted, which wasn't a surprise since it was a freezing Thursday night in February. A movement behind my car drew my gaze to my rear-view mirror. I peered into the darkness, but whatever had caught my eye had gone. I gritted my teeth and told myself it was probably a fox. I jerked my keys from the ignition and the car's lights extinguished. To the left something stirred in my peripheral vision. I swivelled my head, but couldn't detect anything other than the tall wall and the road leading to the shops behind other parked cars. I was jumpy because I was tired –

that was all. I was the only person on the street. Being alone, outside in the dark, always unnerved me. Me and every other woman on the planet. Of course my brain was on high alert. It would be insane for it not to be.

I grabbed my bag and opened the car door, pausing to listen for any unusual sounds. There was nothing but the distant growl of traffic, so I stood, slammed the door and rushed across the street, throwing my arm back and pressing the key fob. The indicators slashed orange across the tarmac and the car bleeped. I hurried up the street, past the boxy flats, feeling exposed as I crossed the dark mouth of an underground car park. When I reached the entrance leading to the East Dock, the sound of footsteps behind me made the fine hairs all over my body rise. I glanced behind me. A shadow dipped into the car park's entrance. Heart thundering, I upped my speed, almost running between the two blocks of flats and on to the redbrick path. The footsteps got louder. I ran towards Rachel's house, cornering hard, leaping up the steps and arriving at her door, my lungs screaming for air. I rang the bell, then banged with the flat of my hand, my legs suddenly weak. When the door opened, I paused to gulp in huge breaths, glanced behind me to the empty alley, and gratefully stepped inside.

'You're breathing hard. What's wrong?' The panic in Rachel's voice made me suck in a breath, then force it out in a measured stream. The last thing she needed to know was that I'd felt like I was being followed. Now I was inside the warm house, where the air was calm and still, I began to question whether I had actually heard footsteps. I was jittery before I'd even got out of the car. It was probably just my mind playing tricks on me.

'It's bloody cold out there. I practically ran from the car so I didn't get frostbite.' I forced amusement into my voice.

'I'm so sorry for making you come out in this weather,' she said, opening her arms for a hug. I moved in and enjoyed the feeling of being held close by another human being. It was worth the exhaustion and that silly attack of nerves to experience this level of connection again. I heard her take in a breath. 'You smell lovely.' She put her hand to the back of my head then stood back. 'Your hair's wet.'

There was a furrow between her eyebrows. 'I always leave it to dry,' I lied. I usually dried it then straightened it to cut down on how long it would take to look presentable in the morning.

'Very wise. Much better for your hair, electricity bills and the environment. I do the same. This mop needs tons of product to stop it turning into a frizzy mess.' She touched the ringlets at the side of her face. 'That's one of the things that kills me about this bloody eye thing. I can't see to do my hair. I probably look like Barbara Streisand in *A Star is Born*, don't I? Did you see that film? My mum loved it. She must've watched it about a hundred times. I don't want that hairdo, though.'

She was rambling. I took it as a clear sign of how nervous she was. 'You don't look like Babara Streisand,' I said, using my toes to dislodge the trainer from my other foot. 'You have the kind of hair that always looks good.' I made my voice light and breezy to try to calm the anxious energy in the air around us.

'Don't be fooled,' she said. 'It takes a lot of effort to get effortless curls. It could certainly do with a good comb with something other than my fingers. In fact, I've got a wide-toothed comb around her somewhere, but I have no idea what I've done with it.'

I tucked my trainers near the door where she wouldn't trip over them. 'Want me to try to find it?'

She flapped her hand. 'No, don't bother. Hopefully, I'll wake up tomorrow with eyelids that actually open. Imagine that.' She crossed the fingers on both hands and held them in front of her face. 'Then I'll have a whole forty-eight hours to look for the stupid comb and turn from Barbara Streisand back into Shirley Temple.' She laughed, but it sounded forced. 'Get me and my current social references, not.' She walked, trailing her hand along the back of the sofa, then along the arm, and took a seat. She patted the cushion next to her. 'Come and tell me all about what's happening in the real world while I'm trapped inside like Rapunzel in the tower.' She shook her head. 'I'm stuck on hair, aren't I? I'm clearly going stir crazy in here.'

It sounded like she was. 'There's not much to tell,' I said. The conversations I'd had with Aaron and Max came back to me, but I wasn't about to tell her they both thought I should hand her over to mental health specialists. 'Not much happened today.' I wanted to ask her about Windmill Hill, but didn't think I could jump straight in with that. 'How have you been?'

'Other than bored out of my head, you mean? Actually, I can't complain,' she said, grinning. 'I've felt better than I have in ages. I've been able to concentrate on true crime podcasts, at least, and the legals' aspects, so my brain isn't actually atrophying through lack of use. Amazing what a peaceful night's sleep can do. Really, I'm so grateful, Beth. I feel like you're my guardian angel, sent exactly when I needed you. Does that sound weird?'

I laughed. 'I like it. It's what people go into medicine for, isn't it? We've probably all got massive saviour complexes.'

'Is that the same as the Messiah Complex?'

'Yep.'

'Then, if you have got it, I wholeheartedly approve.'

I felt bad about joking about mental health conditions, especially since I would soon have to tell the woman sitting next to me that it was more than likely she was suffering from one herself. Not now, though. It was too late, and it was too nice to be sitting on a sofa with a friend. 'I'm just glad you're feeling better.'

'I am,' she said. 'And I was thinking, earlier today, I don't know much about you at all. Here you are, giving up your time, sleeping on a makeshift bed on a sofa, all so that I feel safe, and I don't think I've asked much about you or your life. I'm so sorry. It's rude and selfish of me. They say that illness makes you selfish, don't they? I'm living proof.'

'Not at all,' I said.

'Don't be nice. I insist tonight is all about you. I want to know everything.' She paused. 'Unless you want to go straight to sleep, of course. I realise I probably got more hours in last night than you did, and you've been at work all day.'

I was so very tired. 'I could do with turning in before too long,' I said reluctantly.

'Okay. But, before that, quickly tell me about that aunt you mentioned; Moira, was it? She sounded like a lot of fun.'

No one had ever asked about Moira like that. Once I got talking, I found I wanted to tell her everything about my bold and charismatic aunt. Soon Rachel was laughing with me as I told her about how Moira would belt out soft-rock ballads as she drove me to school in the mornings and insist I joined in. Then she cried with me when I relived the desperation of trying to bring her body back to life when I found her dead when I was at such a tender age.

Sharing the memories brought the woman who had been my favourite person in the world for all my formative years back to me in a way I hadn't experienced for too long. I could hear her laugh again, see the mischief in her eyes. When Rachel eventually went off to bed, I replayed the recollections, hoping Moira would stay with me in my dreams and keep the bogeyman away.

Chapter Thirty-Three

There were no dreams. Sleep would not come. No matter how much I shifted around on the sofa cushions and pummelled the pillow into shape, I couldn't get comfortable. I was grateful, at least, that the terror from last night didn't return. But even though I wasn't waiting, quivering in fear in case of an intruder, every noise still made me start. My muscles were tense. A low-level feeling of dread sat heavy in my abdomen.

At 2 a.m. I gave up and peeled myself up to sitting. Rubbing my eyes, I peered around the room, still softly lit by the lamp, wondering how to pass the time until morning. I stood and wandered over to the window. The glass was spattered with raindrops, which sparkled with light reflected from the Georgian streetlamps along the path to the right of the basin. I put my forehead to the cold pane and peered out. The tarpaulin that had flapped like a thousand wings in last night's wind was firmly secured to the boat. What had seemed terrifying yesterday appeared pretty through the speckled raindrops. Funny how the same view could change depending on how I looked at it. The rest of the dock was eerily still. The sound of the footsteps I thought I'd heard earlier came back to me and once again my feelings about the dock beyond the glass shifted. I shivered, scanning the path and trying to detect any movement at the far side of the water.

What was I doing? I lifted my head. Nothing good could come from staring out into the dead of night looking for . . . for what? A man who I was sure I'd heard following me earlier? That was all in my head, and, anyway, surely lightning didn't strike twice?

The fact I couldn't close blinds or shutters against the dark night made me feel exposed. I would have given anything to pull curtains across every window in this house. That would make me feel safer, although it would be a false security: hiding from the dark, that's all. We often closed our eyes when we were frightened, I mused, like drawing down our own inbuilt blinds. It was possible, likely even, that Rachel's eyelids had chosen to close as a fear response. Perhaps her brain could only handle seeing the real world for half of the time and was doing what it could to protect her. I'd read about a woman whose eyes closed for weeks following a trauma. There was no recurrence, though, after she was able to open them.

I glanced ruefully up at the bare curtain rails. I understood Rachel's reluctance to spend the money on them if she wasn't able to afford to stay. I remembered how little time she had to recover before her chance of becoming partner dissolved and that awful man she told me about took her place. It wasn't beyond the realms of possibility that her condition could improve significantly if she was well rested. Sleep genuinely was a great healer. In that moment, I was even more convinced me staying over was the right thing to do, even medically beneficial. Yes, my own sleep was severely compromised, but I didn't have a condition that lack of sleep could possibly exacerbate. I could catch up in the coming week.

I turned back to the room, thinking of the comb Rachel mentioned earlier. She said it was here somewhere. I could help her out by locating it. I started by lifting the sofa cushions. Whenever I lost my phone or the TV remote control in my flat, that's where it would be. The underside of Rachel's sofa cushions were unusually crumb free. Typical Rachel, I thought, then smiled at myself for thinking I knew her so well. I didn't. How could I, after a matter of weeks? I wanted to, though.

I crossed to the narrow console table against the wall, admiring the railway-line bookends again. They were quirky. If I ever got my flat sorted, I might buy a pair for myself. I avoided looking up at my reflection in the mirror on the wall above the table because, however much I told myself I was looking for Rachel's comb, I knew I was also searching for more information on this woman I'd formed such a close bond with, but who refused to open up about her past. I opened the table's long drawer quietly. A few takeaway menus sat on the right-hand side, next to a packet of AA batteries and an assortment of pens and pencils. The side of one pencil was inscribed with the words *Twattington Arsecandle*. I burst into laughter, then covered my mouth, hoping I hadn't woken Rachel with my outburst. I closed the drawer and listened out for the sound of movement upstairs.

When I was reassured Rachel was still asleep, I moved around the room, looking for other places a comb might be hiding. Eventually, I came to the desk tucked underneath the stairs, next to the patio doors. On top was a desk tidy with more stationery. I lifted a pencil and read *Holy Shitbiscuits* on the side. I needed to get some of those pencils for Max. It was the kind of thing he'd love to keep in the pocket of his jacket to amuse a patient he knew well. I couldn't ask Rachel where she'd got them, though, otherwise she'd know I'd been going through her things. I'd google them.

The room was colder by the window. I quickly scanned the top of the desk, but other than a closed laptop there wasn't much of note. The temptation to open the laptop and see if I could get in to take a look at her browsing history was strong. My fingers itched to touch the silver lid, but I didn't. I couldn't begin to excuse that as searching for a lost comb. I could take a look in the drawer, though. How many times had I absent-mindedly put something away in a place it didn't belong, only to find it weeks later? Loads. I was sure of it. Everyone did.

After glancing back at the stairs, I pinched the drawer handle between my fingers and thumb and quietly dragged it towards me. It slid silently along its glides. A page torn from a newspaper lay on the base of the drawer on top of a ream of photocopier paper. My head became light. I shouldn't be doing this. I should close the drawer, go back to the sofa and try to get some sleep. But I'd already seen the headline on the report, and it was too late to look away.

Chapter Thirty-Four

I turned on the ceiling light and put my Kindle on the desk next to the newspaper page, thinking that if Rachel did come down, I could say I was sitting at the desk reading my book. The palms of my hands were slippery. I wiped them on my pyjama bottoms, lifted the article entitled 'A Mother's Dying Wish' and started to read.

Maureen O'Gorman, the mother of Becky O'Gorman, the seventeen-year-old girl murdered near Windmill Hill in the spring of 2005, says her dying wish is for Becky's killer to be brought to justice.

Mrs O'Gorman, who was diagnosed with terminal cancer eight months ago, says, 'I can't bear to go to my grave knowing that the monster who murdered my precious girl never paid the price for taking her from us.' She, along with family and friends, are calling for the case to be reopened. Hertfordshire Police declined to give a statement, but a source close to the family told our reporter that conversations with the authorities have been fruitful and they're hoping to hear positive news soon.

We've spoken to many people in the area who would welcome a renewed investigation into this horrendous crime. Nigel James, a local business owner, said, 'It's awful that that poor girl's killer has never been caught. There was an eyewitness. It should have been solved twenty years ago.' Another local, Bibi Abara, said, 'I think we'll all sleep safer in our beds if this case is reopened and that girl's murderer is found and locked up for what he did.'

My mind raced. So, this *was* the traumatic event Rachel had alluded to. But what was her connection? The eyewitness was called Kate, as far as I could remember. Maybe Rachel was a schoolfriend of both girls. The murder of someone close to you could still be traumatic, even if you didn't witness the crime itself, although she had said she'd seen something – I was sure of it. I opened the drawer further, hoping to find more information, but it was bare. My mind spun with questions. I would never be able to sleep now.

Letting out a disappointed lungful of air, I started to put the newspaper page back where I found it. I shifted the ream of paper aside and, as I did, I noticed something pale at the very back of the dark drawer. I opened it further and a strip of shiny paper came into view. When I lifted it out, my pulse drummed in my ears. I was holding a row of four photographs, each with the faces of two teenage girls, one with huge eyes and white-blonde hair, the other with a straight nose, cornflower-blue eyes and dark curls. The second girl was unmistakably a younger Rachel.

In the first picture, the girls stared at the lens, fixed smiles on their faces. In the second, both were pouting. Their arms were wound round each other in the third, cheeks squished close, their eyes scrunched, teeth bared in soppy grins. In the last picture they were pulling silly faces, the blonde girl dragging her mouth wide with her index fingers, Rachel sticking out her tongue. I couldn't help but smile at the familiar photographs. I was sure almost every girl in the country had at least one of those strips of themselves and a childhood friend somewhere in the back of a drawer, or in a box of special memories. I had one with myself and Moira somewhere. Panic gripped me when I realised I didn't know where those photographs were. They'd lived in my bedside cabinet in the flat in Tredegar Square, but I didn't know what I'd done with them in the move. I resolved to look for them that evening, as soon as I got home from work.

In my reverie, I turned the photographs over in my fingers, stopping at the sight of curled handwriting on the rear of the pictures. I swivelled in the chair so I could see the pencil marking more clearly under the light. My mouth went dry when I read the words *Becky and Kate, April 2005*.

Rachel was Kate. And Kate had witnessed Becky's murder.

Chapter Thirty-Five
The Watcher

Couldn't you sleep? I saw all the lights come on in the middle of the night. That was a foolish thing to do in a house that's like a goldfish bowl, now, wasn't it? The glow spread halfway across the basin.

Still, I'm not complaining. It was all the better to see you with.

Chapter Thirty-Six

My pulse beat in my throat as I put the photographs and the page from the newspaper carefully back in the drawer. I tried to remember the angle it was at when I found it, turned it a little to the left, then pushed the drawer closed. My mind sprinted as I turned off the ceiling light and sat back on the sofa, holding the pillow to my chest, trying to get my somersaulting thoughts in order. I thought back to the research I'd done at the start of this case. I recalled the woman who didn't open her eyes for an entire month in response to severe trauma. Witnessing a murder could definitely be catagorised as severe trauma. There was no doubt in my mind now that Rachel was Kate, and Kate's eyes had seen the death of her friend. Was it any wonder Rachel's trauma had come back to affect her sight?

The article said the murdered girl's mother was fighting to reopen the case. It seemed highly possible this new development could have been the trigger for Rachel's symptoms beginning when they did. Sweat sprang up on my skin when I realised what else it could mean: Becky's killer was still out there, and Rachel was the only witness. If that person knew Kate was now Rachel and had tracked her down, she could be in very real danger. The shadows in the room seemed to deepen, and once again the air was too thick to breathe.

When the grey light of dawn crept through the patio doors and across the oak floorboards, I was still sitting upright, searching the internet for more information about the killing on my phone. There was frustratingly little to discover. I wanted to know more about the man who had been arrested, then freed, despite him being named by the only witness, Rachel. I wanted to ask her about Becky's death, and the reason behind her name change, but if I did, I'd have to admit I'd been snooping in her drawers, and she'd probably never trust me again. If I discharged her from my care and suggested she needed to see a psychiatrist when she was so adamant her symptoms had a physical cause, she might also see that as a betrayal, and I didn't want to let her down. My job was to help her. I could go to the police and tell them what I thought, but there was no evidence of an intruder, and nothing concrete to explain why Rachel might be at risk. The police wouldn't be interested in my speculation. Nothing had actually happened. That didn't stop me from being terrified it might.

By the time Rachel's slow footsteps sounded on the stairs at 7 a.m., I'd hatched a plan to visit Hitchin that weekend. Since the internet was little help, I would visit the scene of the crime myself and try to find out more about the case besides what I'd read. Then, when I had enough information, I would tell Rachel that I decided to do some research after her mention of Windmill Hill piqued my interest. I wouldn't mention the newspaper article I'd found in her drawer unless I could source it somewhere else. That way, she needn't find out I'd poked around in her personal things.

I hoped that, if I could convince her I was doing it out of a duty of care, she might agree to us going to the police together and explaining why she was at risk. I would collate as much information as I could so they could see she was under real threat, and they wouldn't be able to fob her off. They'd guard her, then, and if she felt safe maybe her symptoms would disappear and she'd be able to go back to work. My whole body was leaden with exhaustion, but at least I had a plan. If I got this right, I'd be able to save my friendship with Rachel and sleep soundly in my own bed too.

Chapter Thirty-Seven

When I woke at home on Saturday morning, I had very little recollection of the day before. I'd been so sleep-deprived when I got to work that I'd conducted all my examinations on autopilot. Thank goodness I didn't have to perform surgery. I wouldn't have trusted myself with a scalpel. I'd fallen straight to sleep when I went to bed at 9 p.m. and was disappointed I didn't feel more refreshed as I got ready for the trip I'd planned to Hitchin and Windmill Hill that day.

I had a moment's doubt as I sat in my car. Maybe I should tell Rachel what I'd learned about her and ask her to go to the police. As I drew to where the car park of my apartment block opened on to the Roman Road, I was still undecided whether I would turn right in the direction of Rachel's flat, or left towards the road that would lead me to the motorway. I snapped the indicator down and turned left. If I was going to help Rachel, I should do it armed with as much knowledge as possible.

I regretted drinking the enormous coffee I'd taken with me in the car when the traffic on the motorway slowed to a stop. The hold-up added over half an hour to my journey to Hitchin and my bladder was screaming in pain by the time I found a space in a car park near a church with three enormous arched windows. I paid the parking fee on my phone, then leapt out and rushed towards the exit in search of somewhere with a toilet.

After ten excruciating minutes, I'd found a café, emptied my bladder and bought another probably ill-advised flat white. After that, I followed the map on my phone to Hitchin library. I knew from my internet scrolling that copies of the *Hitchin Comet* from 1971 to December 2010 weren't available online but could be viewed on microfilm there. Eventually, I found myself on the outskirts of the old market town, in front of a blocky white building with a panel on the side depicting what looked like mosaics of ancient warriors and various scenes from the town's past.

Inside, I approached a round-faced woman in a bright smock and leggings with a library lanyard hanging round her neck.

'Hello,' I said. 'I wonder if you can help me. I was hoping to view the microfilms of the *Comet* from spring 2005.'

The woman rubbed her hands together. 'You've come to the right place,' she said. 'My name's Judith, and local history is my area of expertise, if that doesn't sound boastful.' She smiled and her cheeks flushed.

'Not at all,' I reassured her. 'You're exactly the person I'm looking for.'

'Is it anything in particular you're after?'

I hesitated, wondering whether to show my hand. I

decided I would, since I'd already lost time sitting in traffic and wanted to visit Windmill Hill before it got dark. 'I was hoping to find some information on the murder of Becky Simpson.'

The woman's smile dropped, her jowls sagging below deep marionette lines. 'Awful business,' she said. 'I'd just started here when it happened.' She leaned in so closely I could smell her breath. I suspected she'd had tuna for lunch. 'Her mother used to come in sometimes. You wouldn't believe the change in her after that poor girl died.' She glanced behind her, as if ensuring she wasn't overheard, her eyes bright when she turned back to me. 'She was an accountant, worked in town. Quite la-di-da, if you know what I mean. But after what happened, well, she was never the same again.'

'I'm not surprised,' I said. 'I can't imagine how harrowing it must've been.'

Judith nodded so enthusiastically her lanyard bounced against her smock. 'And the poor woman's terminal now, of course. Cancer. Not sure how long she's got left.'

'Yes, I heard that. It's so sad.'

'I know. She's trying to get the case reopened.' She rubbed her palms together. 'But I don't know why I'm telling you that. You lot already know, don't you? That's why you're here, isn't it? You've started investigating again, and I, for one, am very glad you have.'

I wasn't certain who she thought I was, but decided to go with it. 'Yep. I'm gathering as much information as possible, no stone left unturned.'

'And I think you're right to come in plain clothes,' she said, stepping even closer, her voice low. 'If I were running the investigation, I'd keep it low key for now as well. I mean, it was a disaster last time, wasn't it, with that eyewitness being so sure, then getting it wrong and then the police arresting an innocent man . . . if that's what he was?' She crossed her arms over her vast chest and sucked her cheeks.

So she thought I was with the police. Surely I would have introduced myself and shown a warrant card if I were? Still, this could work in my favour. It was also fairly clear she wasn't so sure the arrested man should have been let go. That was worrying. 'I'm glad I found you. You're clearly a woman in the know.'

She gave a coy smile. 'I like to keep abreast of local news.'

'I can see that.' I let my head drop to the side. 'I suppose you knew the other girl, the one who witnessed the . . . the awful event?'

Judith shook her head. 'Only by sight. The family kept themselves to themselves, especially after what happened. I mean, you would, if you saw something as terrible as that, wouldn't you? I'd never leave the house again, I'm sure, especially if I'd said I saw someone kill someone else, then they got off scott free. You'd be scared for your life, wouldn't you? I think the family moved away soon after, and I can't say I blame them. They were probably afraid their girl might be next.' She ran her thick fingers up and down the ribbon of her lanyard and stared off into the distance. 'What I'd really like to know is who they arrested, you know, after that girl said she witnessed him do it.' She sidled closer. 'I don't suppose you could give me a hint?'

I pursed my lips and lifted one eyebrow. She definitely thought the man who was released without charge was still of interest. I wished I had all the information she thought I did.

She smiled. 'Worth a go.'

'But if you could help me find all the old press about the case, we might happen upon something that could point in the right direction . . .' I let my voice drift off, and excitement glinted in Judith's eyes.

'Give me half an hour,' she said. 'It'll be quicker if I do it, because I know my way around the system. I'll gather everything I can find, scan it and put it all in one file. Why don't you wait in the library office? I'll stick the kettle on.'

I swallowed down my guilt at deceiving poor Judith, along with a weak cup of tea and the two Hobnobs she pressed on me. When she blustered back into the office a short while later, she carried an iPad, which she thrust into my hands.

'It's all on there,' she said triumphantly.

'You absolute star,' I said, staring at the newsprint on the screen. The headline read *Police Appeal for Witnesses in Windmill Hill Killing*.

'Just slide across to see the rest,' said Judith. 'I'll be back when I've opened up the back room for the little ones. It's Monkey Music in ten minutes. I love hearing the toddlers singing. She did a little shimmy and left the room.

I gazed at the iPad, hardly able to believe how easy it had

been to get my hands on all the local press from that time. I flicked through to assess how many pieces there were to get through. There were six articles, all written by a journalist called Vic Townsend. I scanned them quickly, frustration building when none of them mentioned the name of the man who was arrested, or even a clue to his identity. There didn't seem to be much more information than I'd found myself online.

I paused on the last item in the folder. It was a class photograph of a group of teenagers, all in the same school uniform: white shirts and blue blazers with a crest on the breast pocket. I searched for the curly hair I knew I would find. There Rachel was at the end of the second row, a broad smile on her face, back when she was seventeen-year-old Kate Simpson. Becky Sanderson sat next to her, straight blonde hair a direct contrast to that of her best friend.

My heart went out to that poor girl, smiling for the camera, looking like she didn't have a care beyond A-levels and teenage crushes. It was hard to believe that within months of this picture being taken she'd be dead. I exhaled, my gaze trailing the rest of the photograph, wondering who was friends with whom, which of these innocent souls were experiencing their first loves, their first heartbreaks.

A figure in the back row caught my eye. Static crackled in my ears. I knew that face. I knew it very well indeed.

Chapter Thirty-Eight
The Watcher

I can't pretend I wasn't surprised when the tracker I put on your car showed you travelling north. I had to break the speed limit all the way here to arrive at around the same time as you, but then I suppose that's not the worst of my crimes.

I admit I was mildly irritated when I realised you were heading for Hitchin. You really are a little snoop, aren't you? I wonder what your agenda is. I don't like not knowing. I prefer to be in control. But then perhaps I should thank you, because I find it's good to be back here. I have a lot of happy memories of the time I spent in this old market town.

When you walk through the sliding doors of the library I realise you're probably trying to find out more about what happened to poor Becky O'Gorman. Bless you. Don't you think that if there was even the hint of a clue, I'd be behind bars by now?

Reassured you're on a fruitless quest, I go on a little pilgrimage of my own, back to the scene of the crime. It's a bright winter's day and the walk up Windmill Hill then down to the Dell leaves me breathless and invigorated. I sit on the cold stone at the edge of the raised area sometimes used as a stage and raise my face to the sun. I'm replaying the memories of the last time I was here when I'm disturbed by the sound of my phone.

Chapter Thirty-Nine

My wet palms slid on the steering wheel as I exited the car park. After the shock of seeing that picture, I'd lost all desire to visit Windmill Hill. I didn't want to be anywhere near the scene of that horrific crime – a crime which had swollen in significance in my mind since it seemed like I was now somehow connected with everyone involved except the victim.

At the library I'd asked Judith if I could email the photograph to myself, so I could scrutinise it more closely in private, but she said she wasn't allowed to share a picture of minors without a warrant. She'd smiled coyly and said if I showed her my warrant card, she could make an exception. I didn't want to be arrested for impersonating a police officer, so I said I'd get proper authority to ensure she wasn't put in a compromising position and left. I wished I'd had the presence of mind to take a picture of the photograph on my phone. For now, at least, that face was imprinted in my memory. The soft features, the dimples, even the same-shaped round glasses he still favoured. Aaron had been in the same sixth-form class as Rachel and Becky. He had helped me research Rachel, without ever mentioning his association. Why didn't he disclose that deeply relevant information? What was he hiding?

My thoughts galloped, desperate to make sense of what I'd learned. Aaron must've recognised Rachel's face when I asked him to research her. I thought back. Had I asked him, or had he offered when he looked over my shoulder and saw the search on my screen? I tried to remember if her image was on the computer at the time, or just her name? It certainly wasn't Kate Simpson because I didn't know they were the same person at that point. He definitely saw her face during the research he did after that, and I knew from the photobooth shots she hadn't changed that much. But why did he offer if he had something he didn't want me to know? Questions tumbled over themselves in my mind.

I was finding it hard to concentrate on the road as I tried to put things in order. He was the one who found her Facebook profile. She might have a few more lines now, and her face was thinner, but there was no mistaking the photograph was of her, especially with that distinctive hair. He must've known Rachel was Kate. Why did he pretend otherwise, and why didn't he tell me they had some shared history?

I remembered how he'd tried to put questions in my mind, painting her as someone with an unreliable history, someone potentially mentally unstable. Did he have an agenda? I recalled our last conversation, when he'd suggested I discharge her. The sharp words that followed. He'd left without saying goodbye that evening. I hadn't seen him since.

I thought back to when Aaron first applied for the job at my practice. Where did he say he lived? I couldn't remember exactly, but I remembered him mentioning a girlfriend. He'd never mentioned her again. Was that significant? Did she even exist, or was everything I witnessed a ruse to get into my workspace while I was treating Rachel, a false front to make me believe what he presented to me? He applied for the job around the time I started to treat Rachel. I was sure of that. That couldn't be a coincidence. His background check and references had all been fine, so I hadn't questioned why he was applying to work with me any more than the brief exchange in his interview. I'd been too trusting, my poor character judgement at play again.

My thoughts were mangled. I shouted at Siri to call Aaron Fletcher. As soon as the dial tone started, I changed my mind. 'Siri, end the call,' I said. I needed a clearer head before I spoke to him, and I needed to make sure Rachel was safe in case he was pushed into action by me revealing what I'd learned.

I swerved at the sound of a car horn. I'd veered into the next lane. I needed to keep my wits about me, or I'd end up dead myself. The thought brought me out of my head and into the present. I had no doubt now that Rachel really was being watched. Her fear about an intruder wasn't unfounded, and none of what was happening to her was a figment of her imagination.

Tomorrow her eyes would close, and I needed to tell her

what I knew before she was vulnerable again. This wasn't a conversation I could have over the phone.

'Hey, Siri,' I said. 'Open messages.' I waited a moment then said, 'Send a message to Rachel Cartwright.' I pulled into the inside lane and decelerated behind a slow-moving lorry so I could concentrate on what I wanted to say. 'Hi, Rachel. I think I have an idea about who might be behind everything that's been happening to you. Call me when you get this. I think we should discuss it face to face.'

Chapter Forty

I called Rachel as soon as I parked up in my space outside my flat, but the ring tone just reverberated around the interior, seeming to get louder with every unanswered tone. Eventually pressing the button to end the call, I dragged myself out of the driver's seat, wishing I'd asked her what her plans for the day were. I knew she tried to fit in as much as possible on her open-eye days, so she could be out with friends, or at the theatre or cinema – somewhere her phone would need to be silent. There were any number of reasons she wasn't answering. I shouldn't panic. There was probably some kind of logical explanation to all of this.

Forcing myself to replay that thought, I went inside, made a cup of tea and sat on my sofa, taking calming breaths in through my nose and out through my mouth. There were two people who could make this make sense, and since I couldn't get hold of Rachel, and the lack of action was killing me, I decided to call Aaron again. With my heart thumping against my ribs, I found his number and dialled. The phone rang and rang. I switched it to speaker and laid it on the coffee table, watching it vibrate against the glass as the dial tone continued. It was weird and frustrating that neither Rachel nor Aaron had a voicemail option.

I switched the call off and tried to compose a text, but nothing I wrote seemed right. If Aaron was a threat to Rachel, then messaging him could be a mistake. I was glad then that he didn't have voicemail. What would I have said? *I suspect you were involved in the murder of Becky Simpson, and now I think you're trying to scare off the only witness, or worse?* I realised that was what I thought, and the truth of it made the skin on my scalp shrink in fear. I'd become friendly with a man who might be a killer. He had access to my consulting room, my computer, my life. How could I be certain he hadn't been into my bag and taken an imprint of my keys like I'd seen criminals do on TV?

I rushed to the door of my flat and checked it was locked. I slid the chain across, then undid it when I realised someone could already be inside and, if the chain was on, I'd find it harder to escape. I grabbed a knife from the kitchen and rushed through the apartment, opening cupboard doors and looking first under my bed, then the one in the spare room. Satisfied there was no one hiding in the shower cubicle, I went back to the door and secured the chain. Only when I returned to the sofa did I feel how hard I was gripping the handle of the knife. I looked down at my hand and let go. The knife fell on to the cushion beside me. My hand throbbed. Red marks in the shape of the handle marked my palm. This was insane. I was actually going mad. I hadn't even been this frightened when Simon was stalking me.

But, as far as I knew, Simon had never committed murder. My petrified brain was telling me Aaron had, and he might know that I was the only person other than Rachel who suspected him.

I was spiralling. I needed someone to talk me down. I reached for my phone and dialled Max. My heart leaped when, after three rings, I heard his soft New Zealand accent. 'Hi, Beth. How's things?'

Tears gathered behind my eyes at the familiar warmth of his voice. 'Yeah, not feeling great, actually.'

'Oh, why's that?'

I started to cry. 'I'm scared.' I tried to go on, but sobs bubbled over my words.

'You at home?' His voice was urgent.

I managed a strangled 'yes'.

'Stay where you are. I'll be there in twenty minutes.'

I finished the call, tucked myself into the corner of the sofa and waited for him to arrive.

Chapter Forty-One

I peered into the door's spyhole, despite having heard Max's distinctive voice on the intercom before buzzing him up. His face was distorted through the glass, his nose huge and his body cartoonishly small, but it was him. Relief flooded through me as I opened up and let him in. He stepped over the threshold and gathered me in a hug. I allowed myself to melt into him, resting my head against his chest. His heart beat against my ear and I felt safe for the first time in as long as I could remember. His arms tightened around me and his head began to lower. It took all my strength to pull away.

'What's all this about?' he said, sighing quietly before following me through to the kitchen.

I'd calmed a little in the time it took him to arrive, and put the knife back in the drawer, but there was still a tremor in my hands as I filled the kettle. 'Let me get us a drink, then I'll tell you everything.'

He reached into the black leather bag he carried over his shoulder. 'I brought a proper drink. You sounded like you needed it.' He pulled out a bottle of red wine. 'Malbec?' He raised his brows with the upward inflection. The dark shadow on his chin was back and I felt a tug of affection for this man who had interrupted his weekend to rush around here as soon as he heard my distress.

'Good idea.' I put the kettle down and opened the cupboard that held my wine glasses instead. I couldn't find two of the same size and was reminded again of Rachel's ordered kitchen. The thought of her made a lump appear in my throat. 'I'm really worried about Rachel.'

Max let out an audible breath. He slumped against the sink and put the bottle on the draining board with a heavy clunk. 'That again?'

I was bewildered by the strength of his reaction. 'I've found out something that's pretty troubling, actually.'

'Found out?' He shook his head as he screwed the top off the wine. 'You've been digging?'

'Don't be like that.' He poured huge measures of wine into both glasses.

He tutted. He was acting completely out of character, and that was the last thing I needed. I wanted the soft, gentle, caring Max I was used to, not this cross, judgemental one.

'I'm not being like anything,' he said. 'I don't understand you, Beth. It's like you're on self-destruct. You can't let things go. I wish I'd never referred that woman to you. She's clearly got psychological issues.' His voice was harder than I'd ever heard it.

Heat rushed to my face. 'I've had psychological issues, Max. Does that mean I don't deserve to be helped?'

He gripped his glass. The muscles in his jaw twitched. 'Of course not. You're deliberately twisting what I'm saying. Of course she should be helped, but as soon as the tests you and Sardia did came back clear, you should have discharged her and moved on.'

'Well, I didn't, and now I think she's in danger, so I can't just walk away.' When he put it like that, it seemed so logical. It certainly seemed professional. But I was emotionally invested whether he liked it or not, so it wasn't as cut and dried as he made it sound. Ashamed that he was probably in the right, I couldn't look at his face, so I picked up my glass, went through the arch to the sitting room and flopped on to the sofa.

'What kind of danger?' He followed me and stood, glowering down at me. From that angle he appeared large and almost threatening, like someone I didn't know, someone frightening.

That was preposterous. Max wasn't frightening in the least. He was my calm and gentle friend. 'Sit down. I don't know why you're angry,' I snapped. I was starting to regret calling him. He was meant to be here to comfort me, not have a go. 'I haven't done anything to you.'

He sighed and his shoulders dropped, and he looked like himself again. He sat on the edge of the cushion next to me, knees angled towards mine. 'I'm frustrated, not angry. You're my friend. I care about you.'

'I know, and I appreciate that.' I weighed up whether to tell him about the time I'd spent with Rachel. I had to, if I wanted him to understand why I couldn't give up on her. 'But Rachel is my friend, now.'

'She's not your friend.' The vehemence of his words shocked me. 'She's a patient. I don't understand why you're failing to draw the line, again.' He ran his hand over his scalp. 'Jesus, Beth. Wasn't it bad enough last time?' I followed his eyes as he scrutinised my miserable boxy room, imagining him thinking back to the beautiful high ceilings and original fireplaces in the flat I'd lost.

'She is my friend.' I sounded like a petulant toddler, even to my own ears. 'And even if she wasn't I'd still be worried about her after what I found out today.'

He took a gulp of wine, then put his glass down on the coffee table. 'What did you find out?' He sat back, knitted his fingers behind his head and stared at the ceiling.

This was my opportunity to make him understand why I couldn't walk away. I spoke fast. 'Last week, I discovered that Rachel changed her name from Kate Simpson to Rachel Cartwright.'

'What?' He shifted to face me, his eyes slits under his furrowed brow. 'Did she say why she changed her name?'

'I haven't asked her, but I presume it was because she was the only witness to the murder of her best friend, Becky O'Gorman, when she was seventeen.' Max's eyelids closed tight and his cheeks reddened. He looked like he was trying not to explode. My continued involvement was clearly making him angry, but I carried on, determined to clarify why I couldn't step away now. 'This all happened in Hitchin, in Hertfordshire, and I went up there today—'

His head snapped around. 'Are you kidding me?' His eyes glowed with fury. 'You're actively investigating what happened in this woman's past? Have you gone mad?' He held up a hand. 'You need to stop this, Beth, seriously. I can't believe you're stepping so far over the line again. God knows what you're getting yourself mixed up in.'

'Stop overreacting and listen,' I said, irritated that he was making this about me, when Rachel was the one at risk. 'Let me tell you what I found out, then you'll see why I'm so worried.' He rested his head back and closed his eyes again, taking in deep breaths through his nose. 'I looked up old local newspaper reports, but there wasn't anything I hadn't already found on the internet.' I ignored his loud exhalation. 'But there was a class photo on file, one from the year Becky was killed.' My mouth was dry as I recalled the face with the dimples and round glasses. I took a sip of wine, but the tannin was bitter on my tongue. 'There was a face I recognised in the picture, not just Rachel, or Kate as she was then, someone else.'

'Who was this mystery person?' His voice was full of cynicism. He opened his eyes and stared at me.

'Aaron.'

'Aaron?' He flung out his arms. 'Who's Aaron?'

I was surprised by the question at first, but then remembered Max probably hadn't met him since Aaron only worked part time and may not have been in on the days Max had visited my practice. 'My receptionist and research assistant. He's new . . . well, newish.'

Max let out a long breath. 'None of this makes any sense. What has this Aaron character got to do with Rachel?'

'He was in her class at school. The same class as the girl who was killed.'

He lifted his palms. 'So what?'

His voice was high with exasperation, but I didn't understand why he couldn't see the significance. 'Rachel started to feel like she was being watched when she couldn't open her eyes. She thought someone had got into her house and was trying to frighten her at exactly the same time Aaron began to work with me.'

'Thought she was being watched? What, like a sensation on her skin? And you believe this absolute bollocks, do you?'

I tensed. 'I've been stalked myself, remember? I know that feeling well enough.'

'But that was real. That bloke was actually there, sitting outside your work or on the street outside your home. You saw him with your own eyes. It's very different to thinking someone is watching you with fuck all evidence.'

'Spoken like a true man.'

'What do you mean by that?'

'You're in the privileged position of always being able to go about your business without fear that someone looks at you like . . . I don't know, like prey, or a body they can use at will, or their possession, just because they've decided that's the case.'

'Jesus.' He reached for his wine and took a gulp. 'I didn't know I was coming here to be told I was the problem.'

I closed my eyes, trying to contain my fury that now he'd made it about himself. I opened my lids and spoke slowly. 'That's not what I'm saying, and you know it. The very real problem is that I suspect my employee might be a dangerous man with an agenda and a threat to one of my patients.'

One side of his mouth lifted in a half-smile. 'Okay, I hear you, but surely you can see this is all sounding a bit far-fetched. You honestly think her old schoolmate has turned up to frighten her, and that someone has got into her house? Surely if she heard an intruder, she should call the police? I don't know how you've got yourself involved in this.'

'She did call the police . . . at least, I rang them for her.' I hardly dared say the words, now I could anticipate his reaction. 'But they were no help. That's why I've been staying there when her eyes are closed.'

Max's mouth formed an O. 'You've stayed at Rachel's house?'

I flushed. 'She's frightened out of her wits, Max.'

'So, you thought it was a good idea to sleep at a patient's house when they openly admitted they thought someone who wanted to harm them was breaking in?' He rubbed his hands over his face. 'Do you know how mad that sounds? I can't even begin to understand you. You've got some kind of . . . saviour complex. Like, a real one, not just something to joke about because you're a doctor. I think you might need to see someone, seriously. It's not Rachel who needs to see a psychiatrist, Beth. It's you.'

'Are you telling me you wouldn't do the same for a

terrified friend?' I almost jumped when I realised a way to make him understand. 'You did! That's exactly what you did this evening. It's why you're here. I was scared; you came over straight away. That's what people do for friends.'

'She is not your friend.' He spoke slowly and deliberately. 'It's not the same at all. I care about you, I . . .' He stopped speaking, but we both knew what he was about to say.

'Just listen,' I said, desperate to avoid the truth, that he still loved me and that was why he was acting so defensively. I needed to get back to the facts so he would understand. 'Now I know Aaron was in their class, things make more sense. I think Aaron is the person who Rachel saw kill her friend. I don't know how he got away with it before, but now Becky's mum has terminal cancer and she's pushing hard for the police to reopen the case. Aaron must know that, and so he's watching Rachel, waiting to pounce because she was the only witness to what he did.'

'Waiting to pounce? Can you hear yourself? I think you've got caught up in a drama, and I don't know if this Rachel person is feeding it,' he said, 'but it's time to stop.' He licked his lips and seemed to consider his next words carefully. 'And that's a lot of potentially dangerous conjecture. You're adding up dots that might not be there.' He reached for his glass and held it to his mouth, before lowering it again. 'How sure are you the person in the picture was this Aaron bloke?'

'I'm sure.'

'And your eyes couldn't be handing you what you wanted to see – providing what makes sense to you, rather than what's really there? Even we know that what we think we've seen isn't always reliable.'

'You're questioning my sight? You think I'm having visions, or making stuff up?'

'No, but . . .' He sipped, then narrowed his eyes, appearing a little calmer. 'How similar do you look now to when you were in sixth form?'

I thought back to myself at seventeen. I had dark, straggly hair and wore a man's overcoat I'd bought in a charity shop, heavy black eyeliner and clunky boots. The picture I conjured was a far cry from the chin-length highlighted bob, subtle make-up and tailored suits I wore these days. 'All right, I get your point, but it's generally different with men, isn't it?'

'Is it? I had long hair,' Max said.

'You did not.' I viewed his neat short back and sides, trying to imagine it flowing over his shoulders. I couldn't.

'I did. I was a rocker, with tight trousers and a leather biker jacket, until I was about twenty-one. I didn't get it cut until a consultant I was training with kept calling me Doris.'

An unexpected laugh gurgled from my throat. 'I don't believe you.'

'It's true. New Zealand fashion was a couple of years behind the UK,' he said. 'And it goes to show you can't necessarily rely on what you think you saw in that photograph.'

I visualised it again, and this time it blurred in my memory. 'I'm sure it was him.'

'You don't sound sure.'

I had to admit there was hesitancy in my voice. 'No, it

was him. I'm sure it was. The boy in the picture even had the same kind of round glasses.'

Max's laugh was like gunfire. 'Are you serious? You're going on his specs? Remind me what you do for a living again?' He shook his head. 'I don't know about you, but some of my patients pay for an appointment just because they want some new glasses they've seen in a magazine or on some celebrity. They want to justify spending extortionate amounts of money on designer eyewear by getting a new prescription. Fashions change, Beth – you know that. No one wears the same style of glasses they wore when they were teenagers. Come on.'

He was right. Of course he was. 'I was so sure.' I could hardly recall the boy's features now, but the sense of danger still swilled in my gut.

Max's voice became serious. 'You need to be careful, Beth. You can't go around accusing people of unsolved murders on the strength of an old photo, especially not when you're clearly not certain about who you actually saw in that picture.' He nudged me with his elbow. 'I want you to promise me you won't go around to Rachel's house any more. It's not professional, not when it's about more than her treatment.'

He probably didn't mean to patronise me, but that's how it felt. And surely it was unethical to be aware someone was frightened and possibly in danger and walk away? I was suddenly exhausted.

'Ignore me,' I said. 'I was overreacting.'

'You think?' A smile played on his lips.

I tried to swallow my irritation. 'I'm sorry for dragging you over here. I should have gone to bed and got some sleep. Things always look better in the morning – am I right?'

'I don't mind.' He shuffled on his seat, looking more relaxed.

He clearly wasn't getting the hint. I gritted my teeth. 'Please don't hate me, but I'm pretty drained after today. My bed is calling.'

He sat forward, a look of embarrassment on his face. 'Oh, right. Yeah, of course.'

'I'm so sorry.' I stood and went through to the kitchen and screwed the top back on what was left of the wine. 'I shouldn't have let you drive over when I was this knackered. It wasn't fair. Here, take this back with you.' I held out the bottle.

'No, you keep it.' He moved towards the door, arms tight to his sides, as though trying to make himself smaller. He slid the chain out of its fixing, then paused with his hand on the latch, focusing on me with his serious grey eyes. 'You be careful, okay?'

When the door closed behind him, those words hung in the air.

Chapter Forty-Two

I woke early the next morning and immediately reached for my phone. The screen was blank. There was still no reply from Rachel to the message I'd sent on my way back from Hitchin. That felt wrong. She always replied to my messages. Aaron hadn't rung back either. Despite what Max had said last night, dread still tightened my stomach into a ball. It might not have been Aaron in that picture, but it might. I'd only find out by asking one of them, and I was even less inclined to confront him now the idea of what he might have done had solidified in my mind.

I filled the interminable hours before ten o'clock by utilising my nervous energy to clean the bathroom, then decided it was a reasonable hour to visit Rachel at home. I should probably have called ahead, but it was a closed-eye day, so I anticipated she'd be in, and I wanted to see her in the flesh. If I could see her reaction when I told her my suspicion, I might be able to gauge how serious Aaron being on the scene was.

The wind sliced at my skin as I walked along the redbrick

path beside the moored boats on the approach to her house. The baby-blue sky and low winter sun reflected on the surface of the water rippled by the wind. I tried to see through Rachel's windows, but the rooms were all unlit apart from a faint yellowy light just visible in the sitting room. The lamp on the console table was on. That suggested she was home, as I'd hoped. I hurried round the back and rang the bell, tucking my frozen hands up my sleeves as I waited.

'Who is it?' her familiar voice called from behind the door.

'It's only me,' I said, adding, 'Beth.'

There was the sound of metal scraping, then the door opened a crack. Rachel stood behind it, eyes closed. 'Hi. Sorry, I, erm . . . I wasn't expecting you.'

'No, sorry. I . . .' I paused, embarrassed then for coming unannounced. 'I messaged yesterday, but I didn't hear back, so I was worried.'

She put her hand to her mouth. 'God, I'm so sorry.' I was childishly relieved by her reaction. I wasn't rude for coming here, I was a caring friend, and she saw that. She opened the door wide. 'I was out with friends, and it was late when I got in so I didn't look at my phone. And then this' – she waved at her face – 'happened when I woke up, so . . . I'm so sorry I worried you. That was really insensitive, especially after all you've done for me.'

I couldn't help but smile at her words. 'It's fine – don't worry. I'd forgotten you wouldn't be able to read messages this morning. My head's been all over the place.' Relief that there was a simple explanation, rather than any of the gruesome scenarios my dreams had offered, made my chest feel light as I stepped inside. I rubbed my hands together. 'It's good to be out of that wind. It's arctic out there.' My fingers stung as the warmth of the room thawed them. I kicked off my shoes. 'I'm glad you're okay, but that's not the only reason I'm here. I wanted to speak to you about something, if you've got a minute?'

'Sure,' she said. 'Coffee?'

'Great.' I followed her slow walk up the stairs to the kitchen. The room smelled of coffee and toast. 'Want me to make the drinks?'

'No, thanks,' she said. 'I'm managing all right now, as long as you don't mind instant? You sit down.'

'Instant's fine, thank you.' I sat on a stool at the granite island and gazed out across the dock as the kettle rumbled to a boil behind me. A couple strolled along the path to the right of the house, the man's arm slung casually over the woman's shoulder, her hand tucked into the back pocket of his jeans. They could have been Joel and I, from the back. We'd once meandered around St Katharine Docks, thinking our joint future was ahead of us. Loneliness assaulted me.

With a well of sadness at my centre, I watched the couple pause and kiss before going on their way. I missed having someone special in my life. I'd struggled with feelings of isolation since Moira died. Losing her had set me adrift, and trying to make Mum fill the gap had been a fruitless, endlessly painful exercise. I'd spent the years since catching on to people like driftwood, hoping they would be the one to pull me out of the cold, dark water.

I was shocked from my reverie by a shout. I twisted my head, jumping off the stool at the sight of Rachel, standing by a pool of water, vigorously shaking her hand. 'What happened?'

'I overshot with the kettle,' she said, moving to the sink and flailing about before finding the tap and turning on the cold water. She winced as she held her fingers under the stream. 'I thought I'd worked out how to pour boiling water safely, but clearly not.'

'Ouch,' I said. 'I should have insisted on making the drinks. Sorry.' I hovered behind her, watching her fingers turn pink under the flow. 'Do you think you need to get that looked at? I could take you to St Thomas's?'

'No, I don't think so,' she said. 'Thanks, but it was only a splash. Can you finish making the drinks, and mop up any spilled water so I don't skid and kill myself that way?'

'Of course.' I unspooled a wad of kitchen paper from the roll on the worktop and soaked up the water on the surface, then on the floor, realising as I did so that I still hadn't told her the reason for yesterday's message. Over the sound of the running tap, I said, 'I hope you don't mind, but . . . because you mentioned something had happened in your past and I thought that might be relevant to any ongoing treatment . . .' I tore off more kitchen roll and folded it into a pad, dropped it on to the pale wood floor and moved it under my foot. 'I went up to Hitchin yesterday.'

Rachel turned towards me, a deep V between her brows. Water thundered against the porcelain sink. 'What? Why?'

I swallowed. 'I couldn't stand seeing you so frightened.

I wanted to help. A couple of days ago, I did an internet search and found out about Becky . . . and what you saw.'

Rachel turned back to the sink and slammed off the tap. The room was silent. I could feel my pulse in my neck. After a moment, she spoke, her voice tight. 'What gave you the right to go digging around in my past?'

'I wasn't digging . . .' My voice came out weak. I lifted the damp paper from under my foot and held it. 'I was trying to get to the bottom of—'

'The bottom of what?' Her curls shook as her head moved slowly from side to side. 'I knew you didn't believe me. You think this is all in my head, don't you? You could have told me that and sent me off to a quack, instead of rooting around to see what dirt you could dig up from my past.' She sniffed. 'I thought you were my friend, Beth.'

'I am your friend.' I moved towards her, but the set of her shoulders made me stop. 'I only did it because I care about you. I want to help.'

'That doesn't help me.' Her voice was cold. 'I don't want to think about that part of my life. I changed my name for a reason. I needed to leave those memories behind for the good of my mental health, which, for the record, I think is pretty robust, considering.' Her jaw jutted out. 'I don't appreciate you bringing all that into my home. Don't you think I'm going through enough right now, without raking all that up? You clearly have no concept of how harrowing that experience was for me.' She turned and held on to the sink.

I glanced down at the wet tissue gripped in my fingers,

despair seeping through me. I always got it wrong. I alienated everyone I got close to. 'I'm sorry. Please, just hear me out.' If I could get her to listen to me, maybe she'd see everything I'd done was to help her.

'I've heard enough.'

'I think Aaron is behind what's happening to you. Aaron Fletcher.'

She spun around. 'What?' The colour drained from her face. Her fingers gripped on to the sink behind her, knees buckling, as though struggling to hold her up.

It was clear she knew his name and was as shocked as I was when I saw his face in the picture. I was right all along. I shouldn't have let Max make me question what I saw with my own eyes. The look on her face made my mouth dry. 'Let's go downstairs and sit,' I said gently. 'I'll tell you everything.'

Once on the sofas, I told Rachel about the photograph. 'It can't be a coincidence that someone who knew both you and Becky applied to work for me at the same time I started to treat you.'

'I didn't know he worked for you,' she said. 'I had no idea. I haven't heard his name for almost twenty years.' Her colour hadn't returned; her face looked like a death mask.

I was reminded of Max saying he'd never met Aaron either. Even though he only worked part time, it seemed odd that neither Max nor Rachel had come into contact with him at my practice. I was beginning to think that could have been deliberately orchestrated on his part, like he had a plan and I was some kind of unsuspecting pawn in it. 'I'm beginning to think he might have avoided being around when you were at Bath Street.'

'But why? It doesn't make any sense. Aaron was our friend. He loved Becky, adored her. They lived literally next door to each other. They grew up together; they were like family.'

I took a deep breath. 'But he's lied his way into this situation for some reason.' A lie by omission was still a lie. I swallowed, trying to work some saliva into my dry mouth. 'Is it possible Aaron was the man you witnessed hurt Becky?' *Hurt* seemed like a weak word, but I couldn't bring myself to say *murdered*.

Rachel shook her head. 'No. You've got this all wrong. It wasn't him.'

'Are you certain, though? It seems like too much of a coincidence, him turning up like that at the same time you felt like someone was watching you.'

She tugged at the hem of her sweater. 'It wasn't him. I know that for a fact. I don't know why he's here in London, but I do know he's likely to be helping Becky's mum try to make the police reopen the case. She's terminally ill. Like I said, he lived next door to her growing up. They were close, they probably still are.'

I couldn't let her know I'd been aware of that since I saw that newspaper article in her desk drawer. She was already angry I'd gone behind her back. A memory of Aaron's interview for the job came back to me. He told me he was a carer to an elderly woman who was unwell Could that be Becky's mum? If so, then maybe I'd got it wrong. 'If you're sure it wasn't him,' I said, 'then who was it?'

Chapter Forty-Three

Rachel sat, her spine straight, her face turned to me. Her eyes were closed, but the pain of recalling the night her best friend was murdered was evident in her clenched fists and the lines scoring her brow. 'I know exactly who I saw that night,' she said, her voice low. 'But he was given an alibi and the police believed it, so they let him go.'

I noted the word *given* and tried to keep my breath even as I waited for her to go on.

After a long minute, she continued. 'There is no doubt in my mind that I witnessed a man called Daniel Howard smash a rock into Becky's head.'

I'd read that Becky had a head injury caused by blunt-force trauma, but the way Rachel described it so viscerally made my stomach turn over. And Daniel Howard? I'd never heard that name before.

'Was Daniel Howard at your school?' I wondered if Aaron knew him. Maybe they were close friends and now he was acting on his behalf.

Rachel gave a brief head shake. 'No. I don't think they

ever met. There was no reason for them to because Aaron didn't do sciences. Aaron was studying business and economics, as far as I can remember.'

What did science have to do with it? Questions tripped up my throat and on to my tongue, but I grounded myself by pushing my feet into the floorboards and stayed quiet, sensing I had to give Rachel time to speak.

'Daniel was a biology tutor. He was staying with family in the area, on a gap year before he went to uni, and he was tutoring a few of the girls in our biology class, me included.'

I remembered now that the reports had talked of a nineteen-year-old man. If he was in the same class as the girls, Aaron would have been eighteen at most when Becky was killed. I wished I'd remembered that point when I was spiralling yesterday. 'And you're sure it was him?'

She rubbed a hand across her face. 'What does it matter?' she said. 'The aunt he was staying with swore he was home with her by the time Becky was killed. Becky called her mum at five past ten to say she was on her way home, and Daniel's aunt swore on her life that he was at her house, in the front room chatting with her as the opening credits of the *Ten o'Clock News* came on.'

'But you—'

'Becky had messaged me to say she wanted to tell me something important just before ten, so I'd sneaked out to meet her. I already told you Windmill Hill was our place. The Dell . . .' Her voice fractured. 'We spent so much time there over the years, and then he . . .' She covered her mouth. Tears seeped from the corners of her eyes.

I had to resist the urge to move to her and put my arm round her shoulders. I kept my voice quiet. 'What do you think she wanted to say?'

Rachel pulled her sleeve over the ball of her thumb and dabbed it on her wet face. 'At the time, I thought she wanted to tell me she'd got off with him. I knew she fancied Daniel. She couldn't talk about anything else.' She dropped her hand heavily into her lap. 'But after what happened, I don't know. It must've been something bad. Something he didn't want anyone else to know about. I don't know if he'd tried to . . .'

'Was there any sign that . . .' My mind conjured a moving image of Becky's assailant attempting to rape her before caving her head in. My stomach heaved.

'I don't know. If only I'd got there a bit earlier. I'll never forgive myself for going to the bathroom and putting on lip gloss before I left. If I hadn't been so vain, I might have got there in time to stop him. I can still see that reflection of myself now. It was probably the last time I looked at my face in the mirror and saw true happiness.'

My heart squeezed for her. 'You can't blame yourself for the abhorrent actions of someone else, Rachel. Please don't do that to yourself.'

'It's hard not to, especially when Becky never got justice.'

'So, you think his aunt was lying?'

She shrugged. 'The police didn't think so. But they didn't hear the sound of the rock on her skull. They didn't see him running away.'

The description of the noise made me wince again. 'How can you be sure it was him? Wasn't it dark?'

'He had very distinctive hair. I know it was him.'

'And there's no reason why Aaron would hold a grudge against you?' I had to put my suspicion to bed.

'I can't see why he would. Not unless he blamed me for Becky's killer getting away. I was the only witness, and I was made out to be a liar. Maybe he hates me for that. I don't know.'

That didn't seem like a strong enough reason to start tormenting her all these years later. The more I learned about this case, the more bewildered I was. 'They didn't find the murder weapon, did they?'

'No.' She wiped her sleeve across her nose. 'There's a lot of unanswered questions.' She rolled her shoulders. 'I was vilified for lying, even though I swear I wasn't. That's why I changed my name, and that's ultimately why I went into law. The injustice of what happened back then, of no one ever being caught for taking my best friend's life, and what I went through afterwards, made me want to make sure nobody else experienced anything like it.'

I understood completely. Moira's death had made me determined to be the best doctor I could be. We were driven by the same motivations – to help people who were suffering. That was another thing that connected us.

'I'm so sorry you went through all of that.'

'Thank you.'

We sat in silence until Rachel said, 'If it's okay with you, I think I'd like to be on my own for a while. This has brought up a lot of difficult stuff and I need time to sit with it.'

'Okay,' I said. I didn't want to leave. Nothing about our

conversation had convinced me she was safe. Even if Aaron wasn't a threat, I felt certain someone was. 'I could come back tonight if you like?'

She gave a sad smile. 'I think I need to be on my own for a while, if that's okay? Everything's getting on top of me. I had an email from Reece earlier in the week, asking how my sabbatical was going. I couldn't help feeling he knew more than he was letting on and was gloating. I feel like my chances of making partner are slipping through my fingers and I could scream with the frustration and unfairness of it all.' She smiled again, but it looked forced. 'I'm grateful to you, honestly, and knowing you believe me and want to help is everything, but I'm so depleted right now. I think I could sleep for a week.'

Her face was still pale, and I wanted to protest, but couldn't think of a way of insisting without letting her know I thought she could be in danger. 'Okay, I'll leave you to it,' I said. 'But remember you can call me any time. Any time at all.' I made my way to the door and shoved my feet into my trainers. 'I'll see myself out.' It was hard not to remind her to double-lock the door behind me.

In truth, the rejection burned, but I knew that was my issue, not hers. She didn't know that helping her had become the main focus of my life. I didn't understand why she was asking me to leave. She was making herself vulnerable, and the thought of her all alone, ruminating on that awful night, made my heart ache. I was unsettled by the mention of that awful man from her work too. If he really did know about what was happening to her, he might be the one taking advantage of the opportunity to prolong her condition. As the vicious wind slapped my hair around my face on my way back to the car, I had an idea. She might not want me inside her house, but there was more than one way to keep somebody safe.

Chapter Forty-Four

The Watcher

You've gone too far now, Beth. All your amateur digging around and insistence on vomiting out your half-baked theories to anyone who'll listen could ruin everything. You've fucked up my plans and forced my hand.

My fingers are itching to push you in the water as you flounce out of St Katharine Docks. You think you're some kind of Good Samaritan, doing your level best to help everyone, don't you?

But you're the one who's pushed me into taking action before I'm ready, and so the consequences will be yours too.

Chapter Forty-Five

I tried to watch a film that afternoon, but my mind wouldn't stop churning. I was a scientist at my core; observation, investigation and evidence were my staples. I was self-aware enough to know I should apply objectivity too, but also that objectivity was beyond me now when it came to working out what was going on. I was in too deep. The problem I had was that every bit of research I'd done on this situation threw up more questions, and the evidence I thought I'd found slipped through my fingers before it solidified. Max had me questioning whether I had actually seen Aaron in that school photo. Then Rachel confirmed it was him, but there was no way he would harm Becky. I was observing, I was investigating, but the only evidence I had was the connection between Aaron and Rachel. How could that simply be a coincidence? My gut told me it wasn't. I was increasingly frightened for my friend, so if she wouldn't accept my help I'd have to find another way to keep her safe.

When I got in the car ready to drive to Rachel's flat that

evening, the wind was still howling, and the temperature had dropped into the minuses. I keenly wished she'd agreed to let me stay. Since she hadn't, and I didn't want to let her know how concerned I was for her safety I was by insisting, I wrapped up warm in layers of clothes, pulled my big puffa jacket over the top, and prepared to keep an eye on her covertly.

My breath was visible almost all the way there, even with the car's heating on full blast, only melting away in the minutes before I arrived at Docklands. I was planning to park somewhere closer to her house that evening. Rachel had mentioned she rented a garage below the block of flats that was set back behind her short terrace. I'd scrutinised Google Maps and thought I could navigate my way through the warren of narrow side roads to the back of the house. If I could park there, I'd be able to spend most of the night in the car with the heater on but pop out regularly to scout around the house to make sure nothing nefarious was going on. Those enormous windows would be a boon at last, and it wasn't as if she was going to spot me since her eyes were clamped shut.

I drove at a snail's pace down Thomas More Street, peering into any gap between the flats to find the first entry point I needed. It all presented very differently to the images I'd examined on maps. Those street views were taken in daylight, but now it was dark, and cars and vans were parked in inconvenient places, blocking my view.

A car parked near the entrance to the East Dock caught my eye. It was a silver Mercedes Benz, sleek and low in comparison to most of the other vehicles lined up beside the pavement. A car like that belonged in a garage, not out on the street where anyone passing could scrape a key down its side. It looked like the one I took the piss out of Max for buying last year. I'd ribbed him for being such a stereotypical rich, single man with the fast car and private club membership. He didn't come from the same kind of background as Joel and me. He descended from generations of medics, the kind who went to public school, did ski seasons in their gap years. He embraced the kind of status symbols I was embarrassed by. If I even bought a nice suit for work, Mum's voice resounded in my head, telling me not to get above myself, thinking I was Miss La-di-da, when really I was a nobody from nowhere. Moira had tried to lift me up. She'd told me I deserved nice things, but Mum had been louder for longer and had become my inner voice, however hard I tried to expunge it.

I groaned inwardly as the T-junction came into view at the end of the street. I'd driven too far down. The entrance to the parking places behind East Dock couldn't be this far along the road. I pulled in and did what felt like a four-hundred-point turn, careful not to nudge any of the parked cars, and slowly set off in the direction I'd come from, anxiously scanning for the entrance I'd missed.

A flash of orange caught my eye. It was the indicators of the silver Mercedes Benz. A figure dressed in dark clothes, a black beanie pulled over their hair, emerged from the entrance to the East Dock. They looked back through the gap between the buildings that led to Rachel's house, then hurried across the road, opened the car door and climbed into the driver's side.

A pain filled my chest, compressing my lungs. I gasped for air, forcing my hands to remain steady on the steering wheel as I tucked my head down low into the collar of my coat and continued to drive. I glanced briefly at the driver's face as I passed, its pinched and angry expression chilling me to my core. The hat wasn't enough to disguise the person who had sat next to me in my flat last night. It was Max. For reasons I didn't understand, and could hardly bear to examine, Max was outside Rachel's house in the middle of the night, dressed head to toe in black, and the only word I could come up with to describe the look on his face was murderous.

Chapter Forty-Six

Hyper-aware of my hands gripping the steering wheel, my foot on the accelerator, trying not to push it down hard to speed away from what I'd seen, I drove on past Max, willing him not to turn his head in my direction. If he saw me, I wouldn't know how to react. My heart told me he was my closest friend, the man I cared about most in the world, but my head was screaming at me to get as far away from him as possible. At least my car was a nondescript old Audi A1, so unless he'd memorised my number plate, even if he acknowledged the car as it passed, he'd be unlikely to know it was me inside.

As soon as I was far enough away to be sure he wouldn't drive by and spot me, I clumsily pulled into the kerb and parked up. I rummaged in my coat pocket for my phone, swearing and unclipping the seatbelt when it trapped my hand. With fumbling fingers, I found Rachel's number and squeezed my eyes tight as the sound of the dial tone filled the car's interior. I exhaled, my whole body slumping in relief, when Rachel's voice said, 'Hello.'

'Hi, it's Beth,' I said, working hard to make my voice breezy. 'Just checking you're doing okay?'

'Ah, that's sweet of you, thank you. All good here. I've got a surprise visitor, actually. My friend Susie's over from Amsterdam, and she's staying tonight, so it's all good.' She spoke more quietly, and I imagined her turning away and shielding her mouth: 'She's not a lawyer, and she's heading back home tomorrow, so I'm hoping it's not too risky to let her see me like this.'

The relief that she was okay and had someone with her was tinged with a shot of envy. She didn't want me to stay, but she did want whoever this Susie was. 'Great. That's good. I'll let you get on. Glad you're okay.'

'Thanks, Beth. I really appreciate you thinking of me.'

'No worries, see you soon.' I ended the call. Sweat soaked the vest at the bottom layer of my clothes, and it stuck to my back as I sat up straight and clicked my seatbelt back into place. I'd been an idiot for bundling myself up like some kind of Arctic explorer and heading into the ice cold for a night of covert surveillance, an absolute fool. Rachel was in a nice warm house, probably sharing a bottle of wine and some girly chat with this friend I'd never heard of before.

Jealousy curdled in my gut as I drove back to Mile End, and questions about Max hurtled through my mind. It could be possible that this surprise guest had inadvertently saved Rachel. It was almost unthinkable, but the idea grew as I turned into Grove Road and drove under the railway bridge. It became a very real, horrifying possibility that Max, not Aaron, could be the threat. He'd been adamant

I'd made a mistake about that photograph. He'd insisted I should discharge Rachel and stop investigating her past. With a new foreboding, I remembered him standing over me when I was on my sofa, his face angrier than I'd ever seen it, until tonight. Maybe he had a motive I didn't know about. I needed to find out more about Max Larson, and what reason he could possibly have for being near Rachel Cartwright's home that night.

Back at my flat, I shed the layers and paced the sitting room, my thoughts tripping over themselves. Maybe I should have confronted Max. I could have stopped the car and asked what he was doing there. But he could have asked the same of me. He'd expressly told me to stop going to Rachel's house. But why had he done that? I'd thought he was acting as a concerned friend, as someone who cared about me, like I cared about him. But now, with a growing sense of dread, I asked myself if he might have another motive. I thought back to last night again, going over the conversation in detail. I recalled his tightly closed lids, the angry red patches on his cheeks. That wasn't a normal reaction from the calm, gentle man I'd fallen for. A shiver ran over my skin when it occurred to me that maybe I didn't know the real Max at all. I remembered how furious he'd been when I told him I'd stayed at Rachel's. It was out of all proportion. Why would he react like that? Could it be that he didn't want me there because he was the one watching Rachel, and didn't want me getting in the way?

I dropped on to the sofa, my hands clasped, kneading my

knuckles. How much did I actually know about Max? I'd met him when I started to work at Moorfields, but other than the fact he was from a medical family in New Zealand, had trained and worked there, until a post at Moorfields had tempted him to the UK, I knew very little about him. The time he admitted to being in love with me replayed in my mind. Was that the reason he was scoping out Rachel? Was he envious of the time I was spending there? The idea seemed preposterous. It couldn't be that. The only reason I started to stay at Rachel's was because she was sure she was being watched. She was certain an intruder had got into her home and was tormenting her. That began before Max knew I'd been anywhere near St Katharine Docks.

I lifted my laptop from the coffee table and opened it on my knees. When the screen came to life, I typed *Max Larson* into the search bar. Reams of entries filled the screen. There were bios on all the main private health websites, as well as the one from his own private practice. His face smiled at me from the screen, and I felt a surge of affection. It was the face of my friend, the man I would have chosen as a partner if I was capable of a healthy, loving relationship. But a voice was screaming in my head, telling me that Max wasn't the person I thought he was, and if that voice was right, I was an even worse judge of character than I thought. My experience with Simon suggested that may well be the case.

I scanned the reviews from his patients, all glowing, detailing his kindness, expertise and care. That was the Max I knew. I scrolled further down, eventually coming to his social media profiles. I should have started there. Had Aaron taught me nothing? The thought of Aaron made me pause. Where did he come into things? I stored that question for later and clicked on Max's Facebook account, but it was private. I logged into my own neglected Facebook page, allowing myself a minute to wallow in the pictures of my life three years ago. When Joel and I were together, I used to post regularly with pictures of us out and about, grinning or gurning into the camera. My throat clogged with tears when I came across a picture of us dangling a set of keys in front of the door of our flat in Tredegar Square.

Forcing my finger across the mousepad, I tapped Max's name into the search bar at the top. His profile came up straight away, and again I was greeted by his cheerful face. This time he appeared much more casual, in a white T-shirt, his smile more relaxed than in his professional shots. Remembering Aaron's concerns about Rachel's profile only going back around ten years, I clicked on to Max's information, stilling when I saw that he'd only started this profile six years ago, when he came to the UK. Surely people had Facebook profiles in New Zealand? It was the other side of the world, but it wasn't another planet. Had he created this page to stay in touch with people from overseas? I clearly hadn't given it a second thought when Max and I became friends. Now, it made my nerve endings twitch.

My eyes ached and I had to remind myself to blink as I navigated the arrow to his friends list. A lot of the people he knew were our mutual acquaintances, doctors and nurses from Moorfields. My heart tipped at the sight of Joel's name. It took all my strength not to tap on to his profile and see if he'd posted any pictures of himself with Chloe. I didn't. Instead, I scrolled further down Max's list, baulking at the number of attractive women on there. I had no right to have an emotional reaction, I knew that, but it still stung that it appeared that if a woman had a pretty face she was automatically accepted as his friend. That added to my suspicion that there might be more to him than he'd allowed me to see. My rising agitation merged with outrage as I imagined any of the women I knew gathering a list of attractive men. I could collect a thousand fake American airmen, or orthopaedic surgeons in a week if I wanted. The rules seemed different for men, as always.

I went back to Max's main page. He hadn't posted for a couple of months and, even then, it was just to share a birthday fundraiser for a male nurse whose name I vaguely recognised. Below that were about thirty posts wishing Max a happy birthday back at the start of December. From what I could see, he'd liked the first few but hadn't got to all of them. I scrolled through, torturing myself by checking out the ones from pretty women whose names I didn't recognise. One said, 'Happy birthday!' but where the other greetings were followed by balloon and cake emojis, this one had a broken heart emoji sitting after the exclamation mark. That seemed odd. There was a comment underneath. I opened it.

'Hello there, stranger. Remember me?' A devil's mask emoji sat next to one of a staring eye.

Chapter Forty-Seven

It was a matter of pride that I never called in to work sick, but following a completely sleepless night after seeing Max near Rachel's, I rang my NHS manager and asked them to get a locum doctor to cover for me. I would have been no use to patients. My eyes were gritty and my hands unsteady. That was no way to approach someone's precious eyes. I couldn't stop my mind from chewing over whether I really knew Max at all or why he was where he was last night. I needed to find out.

With a steaming coffee on my bedside table, I went back to thinking about the articles I'd read at Hitchin library. They were all by the same reporter. I'd made a note of his name in my phone. I opened the notes app. Vic Townsend. I typed his name into Google and a jolt of energy sparked through me when I found his website. He was a freelance journalist now. His email address was in the contact details, so I composed an email asking if he'd be willing to talk to me about Becky O'Gorman's unsolved murder, then dragged my weary bones out of bed and into the shower.

A reply was already in my inbox when I came out of the en suite. I dragged my towel tight around me and opened the email.

Hi Beth. That case still haunts me! I'm in London today, working on a piece at Spitalfields Market. Should be done at around 4pm. Any good?

Heart racing, I typed out a reply, hardly able to believe the man I wanted to talk to had been so easy to trace and was currently only twenty minutes from my flat.

I took the bus to Spitalfields rather than driving because the last time I'd visited the old market with Joel it had taken us half an hour to find a parking space. The pointed spire of Christ Church Spitalfields stood, chalky and imposing, against the brilliant blue winter sky. Its clock's Roman numerals told me it was three forty-five as I stepped from the bus and walked along Commercial Road, on the approach to the redbrick frontage of the market. I stood outside for a moment, taking in the unusual architecture above the gaping archway. The top third looked like the roof of a house with neat white dormers peeking out. I peered into the covered interior, which had been a market for centuries, this part rebuilt during the year of Queen Victoria's Jubilee, according to the plaque built into the ornate brickwork.

I momentarily felt very small, insignificant in the history of this ancient town, in the history of humanity. I was flooded with a sense of hopelessness. I was an inconsequential, transient mass of electrical impulses. I was no use. I couldn't help Rachel. I couldn't even help myself. What was I doing, trying to get to the bottom of a murder that may or may not have caused a delayed trauma response in my friend? The word *friend* repeated in my head. I was here because Rachel was my friend, and she might be in danger. I'd thought Max was my friend too, but now I had doubts about him, and that was shifting the foundations of my already unsteady self. That thought gave me the impetus to walk through the archway and into the belly of the market.

Once inside, the cacophony of smells from food stalls selling everything from artisan bread to noodles made my stomach roil. I hurried past, towards tables laid out with gold and silver jewellery and spools of vivid silks on tightly wound rolls. I stopped briefly at a stall with a beautiful watercolour painting propped up at the back. I recognised the scene immediately. It was the Palm Tree Pub in Mile End, sitting in its small park, Regent's Canal behind, a barge painted in watery reds on the canal to the left of the yellow-brick building. The stallholder shifted forward, clearly buoyed by my interest. I smiled briefly at her and moved away, feeling guilty for getting her hopes up when I wasn't there to buy paintings. I was there for answers.

I recognised Vic Townsend from his byline photo, although his hair was thinner and had crept further up his scalp in two sharp widow's peaks. He was sitting on a bench outside the café where we'd arranged to meet, wearing a black bomber jacket, which appeared too thin to combat February weather in the UK. No wonder his hands were wrapped round a paper cup. I made my way towards him.

'Mr Townsend?' I felt foolish as soon as I said it, like a child addressing one of their parents' friends.

'Call me Vic,' he said, his voice gruff. The films and TV shows I'd seen with stereotypical disaffected journalists lighting one Benson and Hedges off another as they scowled into the night occurred in my head. I could imagine him fitting right in. He offered a cold hand for me to shake. I wished he'd chosen somewhere warmer for us to meet than this bench outside a café. The glass ceiling above the indoor market did nothing to keep in the heat.

'I'm Beth, Beth Sanderson. Thank you for agreeing to meet with me.' I shifted from one hip to the other. This recent lack of certainty had turned me from an assured medical professional to someone who had forgotten how to stand normally. I held my hands in front of me, then shoved them in my pockets.

He smiled, showing uneven brown stained teeth. The lines on his cheeks deepened, and his heavy-lidded hazel eyes reflected the light, making them twinkle. 'No problem,' he said. 'This is one case I'm always up for discussing. Why don't you get us both a drink, and then you can tell me what you want to know.'

Chapter Forty-Eight

'Here you go.' I handed the black coffee to Vic, and he nodded his thanks then gestured for me to sit on the bench across the table from him. The rickety seat wobbled as I lowered myself on to the slats. I put my coffee in front of me on the table stained with various-sized brown rings and dried splashes.

'Right then, what do you want to know?' He rubbed his hands together, his palms making a papery sound.

I wished I'd written a list of questions. 'Everything, really. I want to understand what happened back then, from your perspective, I mean.' His eyebrows lifted minutely, and I felt like an amateur for being unprepared. This man asked questions for a living. *Tell me everything* wouldn't be an approach he respected.

'I've been thinking a lot about Becky O'Gorman since I got your email,' he said. 'I was so green, back when it all happened. I'd been on telesales at the *Come*t to start with, and the editor didn't think I had the chops to be a news reporter. When the story blew up, I wrote those pieces off my own bat and presented them to him, chest all puffed out, like' – he gestured to a pigeon pecking at the remains of a pastry scattered on the market's concrete floor – 'like a bloody pigeon. He printed my stuff rather than what the more experienced reporters wrote. Didn't make me popular, but I thought it was my big break, so I didn't care.' He scratched behind his ear. 'And it was, for a while. I'm a bit ashamed of that now, to be honest. I saw it as just a story.'

He took the lid off his coffee and we both watched the steam rise. 'I've got a sixteen-year-old daughter myself now, and when I heard from you this morning I couldn't help thinking about her, you know? I started to think about that poor girl's parents. I imagined how Becky would've felt in her final moments, if she was scared, or in pain.' He glanced up with watery eyes. 'It made me think about how her parents have had to live with those thoughts about their child for two decades. I don't know how you do that. I couldn't, if it was my girl.' He gave a wan smile. 'That editor was right. I don't have the chops for news, not since I had kids of my own, anyway. They give you thin skin, kids, don't they? That's why I mainly do lifestyle stuff now, like covering the opening of shops like that by social-media-famous pricks with more money than sense.' He pointed a square-nailed finger at a unit with colourful hand-blown bottles in the window and pink and white balloons around the door.

I nodded, understanding his words, even though I didn't have children of my own, and probably never would have now. I'd proved I couldn't cut it as a wife, and I sure as hell didn't have a good role model in my mother. Even though the thought hollowed me out, like it always did, it occurred to me now that maybe not having children was no bad thing for me. I was emotionally invested enough in Rachel; if a child of mine suffered, it would probably break me. No child deserved a mother who felt their pain as if it was their own. Good mothers needed to be emotionally strong for their offspring, to be able to carry the weight of their burdens without buckling. I thought again of my mother. There were so many ways to wreck a life, and it was a good thing I would never have the chance to ruin someone else's childhood. I'd always thought I'd learn from how she behaved towards me, and do my very utmost to be different, more like Moira, but the last weeks had taught me that I didn't learn from the lessons of my past. I went on repeating them, so it was better I didn't pass that damage on.

I started as the pigeon suddenly took flight, passing so close to my face I could feel the movement of the air disturbed by its wings. Vic laughed at my reaction, and I smiled and shook my head.

'I didn't ask why you're interested, did I?' Vic said, pushing his shoulders back in the way people who spend a lot of time at keyboards do. 'You're not a relative of Becky's or something, are you? God, sorry if I was insensitive, then.'

'No, nothing like that,' I said, thinking how he really wasn't cut out to be a reporter. 'I know the woman, the witness. I'm treating her, actually. I'm a doctor.'

'The girl who said she witnessed what happened?'

'Yes, Kate.' I didn't want to say the name she currently used. He was still a hack, albeit an unusually sensitive one.

He nodded slowly. 'I'm not surprised she needs a shrink.' I didn't correct him. 'Weird business, that was. She was adamant she'd seen that Daniel lad hit Becky. Swore blind it was him, but his aunt's alibi stood up, and there was some crude CCTV footage that backed up what they both said. He had been with Becky that night, he never denied that, and he was wearing dark, pretty nondescript clothes, but with what his aunt said and an albeit shitty CCTV image that could easily have been him on the right street, at exactly the time he said he walked home, there was enough evidence for him to walk free, or rather not enough evidence to charge him. There was no real motive, no murder weapon, no sign of a struggle, no DNA that showed anything beyond what the lad himself said.'

Daniel was the name Rachel had mentioned. My pulse increased. This was what I was there for. 'Can you tell me any more about Daniel?' The bench shook under me as a man with blond dreadlocks and an Aztec-print smock sat down further along and placed a cardboard container of falafel and salad on the table in front of him. The smell of the food made my stomach acid fizz. Maybe I should have bought one of the fat muffins I'd been tempted by when ordering our drinks.

Vic rolled his paper cup between his palms. 'He was on a gap year, staying with his aunt. He was some kind of science whiz, tutoring some of the students from the secondary school. There was a lot of talk about him having a relationship with Becky. He said they'd kissed for the first time in the Dell that night. People made a big deal of that at the time, but I didn't see why everyone was up in arms about it. He was nineteen and she was seventeen. Just because he was helping her with her exams, that didn't make him her teacher, not as far as I could see, anyway. Folk rattled on about a duty of care, and an inappropriate relationship, but he was just earning pocket money. He wasn't a middle-aged university don taking advantage of an innocent fresher or anything. I was only twenty-five myself back then, and it didn't seem like an issue to me, unless it was relevant to her death, which it didn't seem to be. A police source told me they were hoping to find out they'd had a big fight or something, so they had a motive, crime of passion kinda thing, you know, but they drew a blank on that and everything else.'

I was trying to keep up, sifting through for any information I didn't already know. 'He wasn't local, then?'

'No, he was on a gap year, like I said. He was a Kiwi, if I remember right.'

Sweat sprang up along my hairline. 'What was his full name?'

'Daniel Howard.' He sucked in a breath through his teeth. 'I mean, I shouldn't really be discussing him, since he wasn't even formally charged. It's just that the girl, Kate, your patient, seemed so sure it was him. I've always wondered if the CCTV timer could have been set five minutes off, or something like that. I mean, his aunt was bound to stand up for him, wasn't she? I remember doorstepping Mary Larson, and—'

'Mary Larson?' Cold fingers tightened around my throat.

'Yeah. He was staying with his mum's sister. The family on that side were called Larson. Like I said, I tried to talk to her, but she wasn't having any of it. The lad went back to New Zealand as soon as he was allowed out of the country. I don't blame him. Just wish I was more certain he wasn't involved. I've always wondered if he slipped through the net.' He rubbed his chin, dark stubble rasping on his palm. 'It's not as if he looked the same as every other lad, back then, you know, with all that long hair. I can't see how a girl who was tutored by the same fella could mistake him for someone else. There was something fishy about it; that's one of the reasons the case has stayed with me. There was something not right about the stories they were all telling. I wish I'd been able to work out what it was.' He slapped his hands on the table. 'But better men than me tried and failed. Doesn't stop me wondering, though. That poor girl. She was a lovely kid, by all accounts, a real sweetheart. She deserved better.'

Daniel Howard was from New Zealand, and he had long hair. He was related to a woman called Mary Larson. Max had told me on Saturday night that he had long hair when he was a teenager. A cold pool of terror collected in my chest and spread out through my veins. Could Daniel Howard really be Max Larson? And, if he was, is that why he was near Rachel's house last night? Was he the one she felt watching her? Now it looked like the case might reopen, did he want to silence the only eyewitness to his decades-old crime once and for all?

Chapter Forty-Nine

On the bus home from my meeting with Vic my nerves jangled with every jolt of the stop–start traffic. When I got off on Grove Road, I almost ran the short distance up to the lights, only stopping then because the flow of traffic was unremitting. I glanced left and right, then behind me, eyes peeled for a silver Mercedes, relieved when the lights changed and I could cross and turn left, finally arriving, breathless and harried, at the wrought-iron gates at the entrance to my block of flats.

I paused at the gates. After what had happened with Simon, one of the reasons I'd rented an apartment here when my home on Tredegar Square was sold was because it was gated. But, now I thought about it, I couldn't remember them ever being closed in all the time I'd lived there, despite being given a key fob for them when I moved in. Nothing happened when I pressed it, and after a few goes I'd given up. Now, anger rose like bile up my throat. What was the point of installing gates if they weren't maintained? What was to stop anyone walking in off the street and waiting for a conveniently open door? I couldn't believe I hadn't been moved to complain about this before. No woman could afford to be complacent. I should know. And now Rachel was learning the same lesson. Rage bubbled over as I slammed the front door of the flats and stormed upstairs to my apartment. Once inside, I checked every room, then double-locked my door and slid the chain across.

The fury didn't subside when I grabbed my laptop, fell on to the sofa and put the name Daniel Howard into the search engine. The screen filled instantly. There were too many entries to sift through. I needed to narrow the search. I added the words *New Zealand*, and pressed enter.

I stared at the first hit. It was an alumni page for the University of Auckland. There was a photograph of a man with shoulder-length dark hair. I would know those grey eyes anywhere. Underneath the photograph was the name Dr Daniel Maximillian Howard. My burning anger was extinguished by an avalanche of ice-cold fear. I clicked on the other links, each one making it absolutely clear to me that Daniel Howard and Max Larson were one and the same. My friend, the man I loved, the one who had originally referred Rachel to me, was the same man she'd accused of murder two decades before.

My clothes felt too tight. The neck of my jumper constricted my throat. I dragged it over my head and sat, sweating, in my T-shirt, staring at the screen as electrical currents of terror made my skin sting. He'd been here, on this sofa, with me on Saturday night. When I was frightened, he'd been the person I called, but, in truth, it was him who was the threat all along. His face when I talked about Rachel appeared in my mind's eye. I'd thought he was just frustrated with me for getting close to a patient again. I'd naïvely thought he had my best interests at heart. But now I knew who he was and understood, with a spear to my guts, that that frustration was actually rage at me interfering with his plan.

A new energy fuelled by fright drove me on to make the pieces of this awful jigsaw fit. I opened Facebook and went to Max's profile, pushing the mousepad until I found the birthday message that had struck me as odd. I read it again, "Hello there, stranger. Remember me?' The devil's mask emoji and the eye weren't a cheerful birthday greeting. That message had menace.

The name of the woman who posted the message was Didi George. That name meant nothing to me. I clicked on to her profile picture. On closer inspection, she could have been any one of thousands of generically attractive women in their late twenties and early thirties. Long dark hair draped slickly over her shoulders, her head was angled towards the camera, pouting lips slightly open, eyelashes like crow's wings framing unnaturally blue eyes. The more I enlarged it, the clearer it became that it wasn't a photograph at all. It was almost definitely an AI-generated image. I swallowed. Someone else was intentionally concealing their identity. I went to the profile and clicked on to Didi George's bio. 'From Hitchin' was the only thing there. If I hadn't been sure before, I was now. This was a pointed threat in a pretty disguise, and it seemed to be aimed at goading him.

I wiped sweat from my top lip, assessing what I'd learned.

Someone else knew Max was the murder suspect, and from the message they'd written, they seemed to think he was guilty. It briefly occurred to me that it could be Rachel, but I immediately discounted it. She'd made it patently clear that she was doing everything she could to put the awful event she witnessed behind her. My mind raced. I'd presumed that, because Max had liked other posts, but not this or any that followed, that he hadn't seen it. Maybe that wasn't the case. Perhaps he saw this as a malicious threat and this was what forced his hand. It was posted in December, around the same time Rachel said she started to feel like she was being watched. It was all beginning to make horrible, terrifying sense.

Aaron's name sprang into my mind. Where did he come into this? He loved Becky like a brother, according to Rachel, and I was now sure the woman he was caring for when he wasn't working for me was Becky's terminally ill mother. There was no doubt he'd have known who was questioned at the time of the murder. Could he have taken the job with me because he knew who Max really was and wanted to scope him out? Maybe he knew Rachel was in danger and wanted to watch out for her too. He hadn't been able to save Becky, so he wanted to look out for her best friend? Hesitantly, I lifted my phone and dialled his number, groaning when I heard the recorded message, 'The number you have dialled is unavailable. Please try again later.'

As I ended the call, my phone vibrated in my hand. Max's name flashed up on the screen. I dropped it on to the cushion. I watched, frozen, as the device jumped against the fabric, Max's name huge and insistent, the ringtone like a screaming alarm going off in my head.

The sound abruptly stopped, and the phone lay quiet and still on the cushion, like a child exhausted at the end of a tantrum. It gave one final alert as a voicemail notification brightened the screen. I touched it, then pressed the speaker icon, hugging my knees into my chest as Max's voice filled the room. 'Beth, I need to see you. Can I come round? Call me back when you get this. I really need to speak to you. It's urgent.'

Chapter Fifty
The Watcher

It's time. I'm ready. I'm going to finish this once and for all, and you're going to help me, sweet, innocent Saviour Beth, you fucking idiot.

Chapter Fifty-One

Max's message replayed in my mind as I dragged my jumper back over my head, shoved my toothbrush and some spare knickers into my bag and slid the chain back from the door with trembling fingers. I was frightened that he might not wait for me to reply to his message. He could just decide to turn up at any time in the camouflage of a caring friend. He didn't know that I'd found out who he really was underneath the carefully constructed disguise he wore. Every cell in my body screamed at me to get out of there immediately.

Once in my car, I glanced into the back seat to make sure it was empty, then pressed the central locking and started the engine. In my rush, I left the handbrake on. Metal squealed against the tyre rims and the car took stuttering jolts forwards. Tears blurred my vision. I was in no fit state to drive, but I had no choice.

Taylor Swift's 'Look What You Made Me Do' thumped through the car's speakers. I switched it off and tried to focus on the dark road ahead through the tears that kept coming, no matter how often I wiped them away with my hand. I kept in lane and stayed within the speed limit, the effort of concentrating making my head pound. The brake lights on the car ahead smudged into red blurs. I slashed more tears away, furious at myself for being weak. I was an adult, an educated professional, a doctor. I should be able to cope with a crisis situation. The waterfall of questions in my head had thrown me off kilter, though, and I couldn't think straight. I needed to get to Rachel's and tell her what I'd discovered. I was sure she would know what to do.

I didn't wait to find a suitable parking space outside St Katharine Docks. When I was sure there was no silver Mercedes anywhere nearby, I pulled up as close as I could to the entrance to East Dock, grabbed my bag and ran through the gap between the buildings, along the redbrick path and round to the back of the house. Convinced I heard running footsteps behind me, I picked up my pace, stumbling and almost falling before righting myself and staggering up the steps to Rachel's door. I hammered on the wood, eyes darting behind me, then to the left and right. I pressed the bell, the first joint of my finger bending back painfully with the pressure.

'Who is it?' Rachel shouted, the pitch of her voice high and sharp. She sounded terrified.

I took my finger off the bell, wiping it on my coat, as though that might ease the ache. My ears strained for the sound of steps, expecting a dark figure to round the corner any second and grab me. 'It's me, Beth. Can you let me in?'

The door opened a crack, and half of Rachel's face appeared, eyes closed. She wore forest-green pyjamas and a silky kimono, clearly ready for bed. 'What's going on?' she asked.

I pushed the door, feeling her resist for a moment before relenting and stepping back. I shoved it closed behind me, leaning my back against the solid wood. 'Sorry.' I paused to catch my breath. My heart pounded against my ribs. 'I need to talk to you.'

'You could have called. You scared the bloody life out of me, smashing on the door like that. My nerves are already shredded.'

'I'm sorry.' I closed my eyes and tried to pull more air into my lungs. 'I've been feeling like I'm being followed as well.' I opened my eyes and instantly regretted my words when I saw her mouth hanging open, her face a mask of fear with a film of skin where the eyes should be. 'We're inside now, though. We're safe.' I was no more convinced by my own words than she appeared to be.

'What do you mean?' Rachel crossed her arms, pushing herself back against the wall at the base of the stairs. She looked small and frightened. I imagined her next to Max and shuddered. He was inches taller, and broad. He regularly worked out, keeping himself lean and strong. I'd thought that was just because he liked to look after himself, but now I wondered if it was so he could intimidate women like her. How wrong I'd got it. What a gullible fool I'd been.

'Can we sit down?' Now I was inside, my head had started to spin. I held on to the banister, afraid my legs might give way. Rachel felt her way to the sofa facing away from the windows. I watched the Japanese-style tiger emblazoned on the back of her kimono stir like it was silently stalking prey as she moved. I took a seat on the other sofa, wishing I couldn't see out into the darkness of the evening, praying there was no one watching from outside in the black night.

'What's all this about, Beth? You're scaring me.' She folded her arms tightly across her chest.

'I'm sorry. I wouldn't be here if it wasn't urgent.' The word *urgent* brought Max's message back to me. I shuddered. 'I found something out that . . . that makes sense of what's been going on.'

'I don't know what you mean.' Rachel rocked gently, rolling from the ball of her feet to her heels. She was wearing soft-looking bed socks like the ones Moira used to love.

'Max, the doctor who referred you to me – what do you know about him?'

She shook her head. 'Nothing. My NHS GP had been worse than useless, so I went to a private GP and asked her to refer me to a private ophthalmologist. She said she usually referred patients to a doctor at Moorfields, so she emailed him to see if he could recommend a female colleague. He suggested you. Why are you asking?'

'So, you haven't had any contact with Max Larson?'

'Max Larson? No. Why?'

I placed my hands carefully on my lap and pushed down on my thighs, trying to ground myself. 'Max Larson changed his name. He used to be called Daniel Howard.'

She stopped moving. The muscles in her jaw twitched. 'Daniel Howard?'

'He's a New Zealander.'

Rachel's hand flew to her mouth. 'My GP got in touch with Daniel Howard? Why? Why would she go to him? She doesn't know who I am, who I was.'

'He has a good reputation. I'm sure he'd be the first on a lot of doctors' lists.' I wished I could pin the blame on someone else, but what was happening now was all down to me. 'I'm sorry, Rachel, but it looks like Max . . . Daniel, has been keeping tabs on you, and' – I burned with shame at what I was about to disclose – 'I think I must've unwittingly helped him. I shared a lot of stuff about your case with him. He's an experienced and well-respected doctor. I thought that by consulting with him, I was helping you. Now I'm scared I've inadvertently fed him information he could use.'

She dropped her hand and clasped the hem of her pyjama top. 'Use how?'

'I don't know. I've been trying to remember if I ever shared the exact times of your blepharospasms, the days and nights when your eyes would be closed. If I did, I'm so sorry. If he had that information, that could explain why you felt watched on those days.' I took a shallow breath and carried on, 'I saw him too, outside on the road, last time I came around. I realise I should have told you, but I didn't know what it meant before.'

'You saw Daniel Howard? Here?' Her voice was a terrified whisper.

'He was getting in his car; he'd parked on the road outside. I'd come over to check up on you . . . to make sure you were okay, I mean. I rang you after I saw him and you said you had a friend staying, so I didn't mention it. I didn't know who he really was then, just that it was weird. That's when I started to look into his background.'

Rachel gripped the edge of the cushion. 'Daniel Howard knows where I live, and knows exactly when I can't open my eyes?'

'I'm sorry.' I was terrified, so couldn't imagine how she must feel. 'I think we should go to the police.'

She lifted her hands. 'And say what? That the man who wasn't charged with a murder twenty years ago and is now an eminent and well-respected doctor happens to have been seen in a densely populated part of London?'

'He's been watching you.'

She gave a bitter laugh. 'I'm a lawyer, Beth. I know how the system works. I have zero evidence he even knows who I am, since I changed my name, never mind that he's been stalking or intimidating me.'

'I told him who you are,' I said, my voice wavering. 'I'm so sorry. I had no idea he was connected in any way, and he intentionally hid it from me when I told him what I knew. He never let on that he knew you, even when I told him about Aaron.'

'You told him about Aaron?' Her voice was sharp.

'I didn't know I was potentially putting him in danger too. I thought Aaron was the one spying on you.' How could I have fucked things up so completely?

'I suppose Aaron might have been watching me. It's not impossible, but if he was, it was most likely to be because he thought I needed protecting from Daniel.' She ran a hand over her face. 'Have you spoken to Aaron since?'

I heard the automated voice telling me Aaron's number was unavailable, and my throat closed. 'I couldn't get hold of him.'

'Shit, Beth.'

'I'll try again.' I took out my phone and pressed on Aaron's number. The same automated voice I'd heard before said, 'The number you have dialled is unavailable. Please try again later.' I terminated the call, and we sat in silence. Tears bubbled from my eyes. 'He'll be okay, won't he?' I said, eventually. 'Max wouldn't hurt him?'

'I have no idea.' She raked her fingers through her curls. 'I honestly don't know. We don't know what Max's agenda is, how far he'll go to cover up what he did.'

'We have to call the police. We can't deal with this on our own.'

'You don't get it, do you?' Rachel's voice was tight. 'If someone came to me with a story like this, I could dismantle it in seconds. He hasn't done a single thing that he could be questioned about, never mind charged.'

'But . . .' But what? When she phrased it like that, it was hard to put another side. 'There has to be something we can do.'

'We've got to plan our next move carefully,' she said. 'The law is only interested in evidence. There's absolutely nothing we can do without it, so we need to work out how to prove he's acting unlawfully.'

'So, what? We just wait for him to show his hand?'

'We think. We put our heads together and work out if there's anything at all we could build a convincing argument from.' After a moment, she said, 'Will you stay here with me tonight? There's no way I'm going to sleep now, but I'd feel a lot better if I knew I wasn't alone. We can try to work out a plan.'

My feet pulsed with the urge to run away. 'Of course,' I said. 'Of course I'll stay.'

Chapter Fifty-Two

The Watcher

You're so predictable, Beth. You've made this all so pathetically easy for me. I knew you'd go scurrying to St Katharine Docks tonight, your angel wings flapping in the breeze. I watched you running along the side of the dock, glancing behind you as if you were being chased by wolves.

You wouldn't recognise a wolf if it bit you, especially when it dresses as an innocent sheep so beautifully. Your neediness has blinded you to my fangs, my sweet friend. I almost feel sorry for you. Almost. But I won't let that get in the way of using you for my final, brilliant act. Bring it on.

Chapter Fifty-Three

We sat in silence, until Rachel eventually took a sharp breath in. 'I need sugar. I'll make a hot chocolate. Want one?' She stood and felt her way to the stairs. 'I actually need about half a bottle of neat whiskey, but I don't suppose that would be a wise idea.'

'Let me make it.' I followed her upstairs.

'No. You sit down,' she said, flicking on the kettle's switch and pointing vaguely towards the granite island at the front portion of the kitchen. 'My nerves are shot, and I can feel the anxiety coming off you in waves. We need a sugar spike and a plan. I won't burn myself this time, I promise.' She spooned heaps of brown powder into two mugs.

I cautiously approached the windows. The temperature dropped when I neared the glass. I stared out across the dock and tried to fill my lungs with air, to appear less frightened, less vulnerable than the wreck in my reflection. A few people were walking along the paths below. It was 10 p.m., so that wasn't unusual. Anyone looking in this direction would be able to see me, and I had the urge to cower back, but maybe it was a good thing I could be seen. If Max was watching, and saw we were both here, unafraid to show ourselves, he might think twice about trying anything. Strength in numbers. I felt anything but strong. I was shaking and my head buzzed with static. I stepped to the window on my left and stared past my reflection towards the Dickens Inn. Its windows glowed yellow against the black cladding. Beyond the pub, the turrets of Tower Bridge appeared like the top of a fairytale castle, and in the distance the Shard rose bright against the inky sky, its pinnacle illuminated like the triumphant tip of a shattered glass spear.

I could understand why Rachel loved it here, with all these vantage points out across centuries of London's past. As the sound of the kettle boiling filled the room, I gazed down at the boats moored below, imagining how different this view would have been when it was a commercial dock surrounded by slums. To put my fear in some sort of perspective, I made myself think of the bombing in this area during the Second World War. The first flying bomb hit London on Grove Road, five minutes from where I lived. I often walked past the blue commemoration plaque on the railway bridge. I imagined the inhabitants of Docklands cowering when they heard the buzz of a V1, their terror at the rasping sound, blood turning to ice as the engine cut out and they could do nothing but wait in eerie silence before the bomb struck.

That was a mistake. Thinking of someone else waiting for the axe to fall only exacerbated the same feeling in me.

The rumble of the boiling kettle stopped, and the room was silent. Now I was just waiting, every muscle in my body tensed, for the inevitable explosion.

'Come and get this.' Rachel's voice brought me out of my thoughts. I turned to see her holding out a mug. 'We'll take it downstairs and start to formulate a plan.' Her voice was calm. I took some strength from that.

I moved towards her and took the drink, wincing as the hot porcelain burned my fingers. I hooked my thumb and forefinger through the handle. 'Let me take yours too,' I said.

'You're all right. I've got this down to a fine art now,' she said, making her way towards the steps and taking them slowly, one by one. I followed, and we sat in the same position as before. 'What we need is something tangible to take to the police,' she said. 'If we can convince them to question him, even if it leads nowhere, then at least he'll have to think twice before coming anywhere near here again. They might even send a patrol round or keep an eye on him.' She let her head roll back. 'This probably sounds stupid, but even though I feel sick that he might try to do something tonight, I finally feel like this might come to an end at last. I've been on tenterhooks for months. I'm surprised I haven't had some kind of breakdown.'

I nodded, silently thinking that these blepharospasms could easily be a symptom of the breakdown she thought she was avoiding. The familiar way the inside of my head was stinging as my thoughts took uncontrollable turns made me wonder if I might be on my way to another one too.

This was how it started last time – the loss of control of my thoughts. Next came the sleeplessness, then the inability to eat. I couldn't go back to that place. I wouldn't. Rachel and I would get through this together. I didn't have a friend I could turn to last time. Now I did. I sipped the drink. It was sweet, almost sickly. I was grateful for the sugar hit. 'If we come up with something tangible we can take to the police, we should do it tonight. There's no point waiting here, wondering what his next move is like a pair of sitting ducks.'

'Absolutely.' She yawned. 'It's like there's fog in my head, though. My thoughts keep getting lost. Do you know what I mean?'

I knew exactly what she meant. 'Did you sleep well last night?'

She shook her head. 'Hardly at all.' She exhaled through her nose. 'I don't want you to see this as emotional blackmail, but I only sleep when you're here. You're the only person who makes me feel safe.'

Tears were already close to the surface. Now, one leaked out and slid down the side of my nose. Awful as our situation was, I was still grateful Rachel's condition had brought her to me. The connection I'd experienced over the last couple of months had nourished me. When this was all over, we could start our friendship properly, maybe take a break somewhere. I never took a break from work. I was due a holiday.

'I need my sharp lawyer's brain tonight, not this mess of cotton wool.' She tapped her temple with her finger before opening her mouth in another cavernous yawn.

She was right. She was the one who was used to putting together convincing cases. If we were going to come up with something that would make the police pay attention, she needed to be on better form. 'Why don't you go upstairs and get a couple of hours?' I said. 'It's not that late yet. People will still be coming out of the pubs and restaurants for at least an hour and a half, so even if Max is planning something, he'd be stupid to come before it was quieter out there.'

Her nose creased. 'I don't know. I don't want to leave you on your own.' She swayed slightly. She was too exhausted to even sit up straight.

'I'll get you up before midnight. I promise. Go on. Have a catnap.'

She put her hand to the cushion and started to lift herself, before sitting back down. 'No. I can't leave you down here.'

'I insist. Seriously. You're no use to me in this state. I need that sharp brain. Please, Rachel, try and get a bit of sleep. I'll keep watch. I'll keep my phone in my hand, okay?' I took my phone from my pocket and held it out, before remembering she couldn't see me. I wondered if she would be able to sleep. I knew I couldn't, and my eyes were fully functioning. How must it feel to be so scared and so vulnerable? I was relieved when she stood, stretching her arms as she yawned again.

'You are a total superstar, do you know that? My eyes will open tomorrow' – she crossed her fingers – 'and after we've been to the police I'm going to take you for the best lunch you've ever had.'

'I'll hold you to that,' I said. She turned, the tiger on her back appearing to prowl as she moved towards the door. I picked up my drink and took a gulp, trying to swallow down the lump in my throat that appeared when she began to walk away.

'I'm checking the door,' she said. I heard the rattle of the lock. 'All secure.' She stood on the first step and turned her head to the room. 'I don't know what I would have done without you these last couple of months, Beth. I hope you know how blessed I feel to have had you by my side.'

'That's what friends are for,' I said. I put my phone on the cushion beside me as she disappeared up the stairs and took another drink, the thick liquid warm and sweet in my mouth. As I finished the last of the hot chocolate, I was surprised to find I wasn't as terrified as I expected to be without Rachel here for support. I felt almost relaxed. I sat back, feeling the cortisol drain away. I'd got this. I was stronger than I thought.

Chapter Fifty-Four
The Watcher

Good girl. You're exactly where I need you to be. And now you're all alone.

Chapter Fifty-Five

A high-pitched scream pierced my dream. I jolted awake, blinking into bright light. I was in Rachel's sitting room. The overhead light was on, and Rachel was standing motionless, apart from the rapid rise and fall of her chest. Her eyes were closed, and she was holding something large in her hands.

My eyes tracked down to the floor. Bile flooded my mouth when I saw a prostrate, black-clad figure, a claret river seeping along the pale floorboards from its dark head. I knew, without seeing his face, that it was Max.

I leaped to my feet, swaying as the blood left my head. 'What happened?' Rachel didn't move. Instinctively, I rushed to her side. 'Rachel.' I put a hand on her shoulder. Her body was rigid. I forced my gaze down to the face I knew so well, the one I had thought I loved. His grey eyes were open, glassy and still, reflecting the light, despite the life having left them. I should kneel and try to stem the bleeding, but I was frozen, my feet too leaden to move. I held my breath and waited for him to blink, to sit up and put his hand to the huge gash I could see now above his temple. The smashed white bone of his skull was visible beyond the split skin. Blood flowed from the wound. He wasn't going to blink. He wouldn't sit up. It didn't take a doctor to know Max was dead. 'Rachel,' I said again, but she didn't move. The shock could have brought back the trauma of what happened to Becky and made her shut down, but I had to bring her round. I couldn't cope with this on my own. 'I need you to listen to me. What happened?' I raised my voice. 'Rachel.'

As if waking from a dream, Rachel came to life. Her shoulder trembled under my hand as her head slowly turned to me, her closed eyes making her face a death mask. 'I don't know.'

'Max,' I said, my gaze drawn to the railway-track bookend she was holding in her hand, and the dark, wet streak at its end. 'Daniel Howard, he's—'

'No!' She shook her head. 'No.' She took a step backwards and tottered as if she was going to collapse. I took the bookend from her hands. The iron was cold and heavy. I put it down on the floor beside my feet, retching when I noticed sticky redness on my palms.

'He can't be here,' said Rachel, her voice high and frantic. 'He wants to hurt us.'

'He's not going to hurt us.' Even as I said it, I willed Max to rear up and come at me. Anything would be less painful than the stillness.

'You don't understand—'

'He's dead, Rachel.'

She was silent for a beat, then let out a wail and crumpled

to her knees. 'He can't be. I couldn't . . . I'm not capable of . . .' She began to sob. 'Are you sure? You have to do CPR or something.'

Her words jolted me into action. 'Call an ambulance,' I said. 'Quick.' I knelt and held my fingers to Max's throat, eyes averted from his face and the skull wound I knew intuitively no one could survive. There was no pulse. I rolled him on to his back and felt his chest. Nothing. Ignoring the sickening wet sensation as blood soaked through the knees of my jeans, I put my mouth to his and blew. His lips were warm against mine. I'd stopped myself from kissing him so many times. We could have been partners, and now he was dead. The thought made my throat close and I had to pull back, lean away and retch. I forced myself to turn back to his body and put one hand on top of the other, pushing down with all my force on his chest, counting out loud. I knew the drill. I also knew it was pointless. Max wasn't coming back to life.

Eventually, I sat back. I became aware that Rachel was moving around the room, patting surfaces, and I realised she hadn't called for help because she couldn't find her phone with her eyes closed. 'There's nothing I could do,' I said, the urgency replaced by a billowing dread filling my head like smoke. 'I need to call an ambulance and the police.'

I stood. Rachel turned to me. 'Beth, I don't know.' Her voice was quiet and hesitant.

'What do you mean? I have to call 999. He's dead, Rachel. You killed him. What the fuck happened?'

She fell on to the sofa, covered her face and started to rock and sob. 'It was a mistake,' she spluttered. 'I didn't get to sleep when I went upstairs. I was too jittery. I was about to give up and come down when I heard the front door opening.'

'You heard the door?' I glanced at the door. It was closed and the wood and the lock appeared to be intact. 'How did he get in?'

'God knows, but I know it's not the first time. It was him all along, wasn't it? It's a rental property, so maybe there are ways – I don't know. I should have had the locks changed. Oh, God, Beth. I didn't mean to kill him. I didn't even know it was him for sure . . . but I thought . . . I just wanted to stop him hurting either of us.'

'What did you do?'

'I was terrified. I didn't know who'd come in or why you were silent. I wondered if you'd left for a second, but I knew you wouldn't just go. You wouldn't do that to me.' She took a heaving breath. 'I was expecting to hear raised voices or something, and when I didn't I knew he was here and that you weren't able to defend yourself. I knew it in my bones.' She put a hand to her chest. 'I was so scared he'd done something to you, Beth. Something awful.' A hiccupping sob made her pause briefly. She dragged in another deep breath and continued, 'I tiptoed downstairs, and I could tell the big light was on because it was brighter than usual through my eyelids. I turned so I was facing into the room.' Her voice faltered. 'Then it got darker, like I was in shadow. I could hear him breathing, then he said my name.' She was crying hard now, tears pouring from her closed eyes.

'He said Rachel?'

She shook her head fast. 'No. He said Kate. He said it so coldly. I could sense him getting closer, so I reached out and grabbed for something to protect myself. I picked up the bookend and swung it as hard as I could. I didn't aim it at his head, Beth, you have to believe me. I couldn't. I couldn't see anything except a dark shadow. I didn't mean to . . . to kill him.'

'I know that,' I said. I wanted to put my arms round her and comfort her, but there was no time. I had to act. 'I'll tell the police that.'

'You don't understand,' she said, her voice an anguished wail. 'The police will investigate. They have to by law. They'll discover who he was and who I am, and they'll think it was premeditated.'

'That won't happen,' I said, my eyes searching for my phone. It wasn't where I'd left it on the cushion next to me. I must've knocked it away when I was asleep. How the hell had I fallen asleep? 'And he was the one who was a murder suspect. He was intimidating you. I'll tell them how frightened you've been.'

'And will you tell them why you're here?'

The new edge to her voice made me turn back to her. 'What do you mean?'

'We both knew Max might come tonight, didn't we?'

Blood pooled close to my foot. I stepped back, shuddering as the sofa cushion touched my calf. My skin felt raw, like the top layer had been peeled off. 'Yes. But we can tell them that. That shows you acted in self-defence.'

Rachel shook her head. 'They'll say I was lying in wait. The law says that if there's forethought and planning before a crime, then it's premeditated.'

'But you can't even see.' Surely she couldn't be accused of aiming at his head when her eyes were clamped shut?

'No, but you can.'

A chill coated my body. 'But I didn't hit him.' Surely she wasn't going to say I did?

'God, no, that's not what I'm saying.'

I let out a breath, my knees weakening.

'But if I know one thing, it's the law, and if we go to the police with this, I will be tried for murder. They'll say I was lying in wait, that I intended to hurt him in revenge for what he did to Becky.'

'But . . .' I couldn't carry on the sentence, because it was dawning on me that she might well be right.

'And even you think my eye condition is caused by my mental state. They'll say I'm psychotic. They'll say I'm not a reliable witness because no one could find a medical reason for why I can't open my eyes. I'll end up in Rampton Secure Unit.'

'I won't let that happen,' I said. 'I'll tell them the truth.'

'What is the truth, Beth? Why can't I open my eyes now?'

I took in her wet cheeks, her closed lids, but I didn't have an answer. Desperate to call the emergency services, I tucked my hand between the sofa cushions and found my phone. I lifted it out and stared at the screen. 'There's a message from Max,' I said, taking a gulp of air. Seeing his name there, like I had hundreds of times before, made everything horrifyingly real. This could be the last message he ever sent. Max was dead and his lifeless body was on the floor in front of me. It wasn't a nightmare. Neither of us would ever wake up from this.

'What does it say?' Rachel rose unsteadily to her feet.

With a trembling finger, I opened the message and read. 'I'm coming to get you now.' Every hair on my scalp bristled. 'What did he mean, *coming to get me*?'

Rachel gasped. 'I don't know. They'll say that's proof that we knew he was coming.'

I gawped at Rachel's tear-stained face, panic pushing the air from my lungs. 'But I didn't see this before.' Before what? Before she caved in his skull with a wrought-iron railway track.

'I know that,' she said. 'But I don't know how we would ever convince anyone else.'

'Jesus, Rachel.' I dropped the phone back on the sofa cushion. 'What the hell are we going to do?'

Chapter Fifty-Six

Time stretched and warped. 'I could call Billy,' Rachel eventually said. Her voice had a new strength to it. She'd switched into lawyer mode. Thank God. I felt like a frightened child who needed an adult to tell them what to do.

'Billy?' Something moving across the floor caught my eye. The pool of red was growing, rivulets branching out and settling between the floorboards. There was so much blood.

She wiped her face dry in quick, deliberate movements. She'd shaken off the shock. She was stronger than me and I wanted her to take charge. 'Billy Galvin, the man we saw at the Palm Tree. He'll help us. He'll know what to do.' Her speech was staccato, words shooting out like bullets.

I didn't like the way she said *us*. I didn't want to be connected with this in any way. I lifted my hands, strangely hypnotised by the red that seemed to coat everything: my fingers, my clothes, the floorboards. I swooned and, for a moment, I thought I was going to faint. I fell back on to the sofa and closed my eyes.

The cushion sagged as Rachel sat beside me. 'I need you

to listen to me, Beth.' It was like we'd swapped places. She was in charge now and I relinquished all control, glad to be able to fall away from the horror. She put her hand on my thigh and squeezed it gently. 'Are you listening?'

I nodded, the motion worsening the nausea seething inside me. 'I'm listening.'

'I can't find my phone. Can you look for it for me?'

Unable to lift my heavy limbs off the sofa, I handed my phone to her. 'Use this.'

She took it and, through the ringing in my ears, I heard her ask Siri to call a number she seemed to know off by heart. She rose from the sofa and felt her way along the back to the furthest part of the room, where she spoke into the mouthpiece in hushed tones. I didn't strain to hear. I didn't want to know what she was arranging with Billy. I didn't want any of this.

'Beth,' she said, after she ended the call. 'Billy's given me some specific instructions and we both need to follow them to the letter. He says it's going to be okay, if we do exactly what he says. First, I need you to take off any clothes that have blood on them, okay?' She touched her way along the wall until she reached the light switch. She switched it off, leaving the room in the muted glow of the lamp.

'The light,' I said, head turning in horror to the window on to the dock. 'Anyone could have seen in.'

'I know it seems like hours, but it's only been a few minutes since I switched on the overhead light,' she said. 'It's one in the morning. No one was likely to be out there. If anyone had seen in, we'd be hearing sirens by now.' She sounded so sure of everything. 'Now take off your clothes, Beth.'

'My clothes?' I glanced down at myself. Everything was soiled with sticky red blood. I dry-heaved.

'That's right. I need you to follow my instructions exactly. It will be okay as long as we do everything Billy says. I promise you, Beth.' Her voice was soft and melodic, mesmerising. 'It will be all right, if you do what I ask.'

Nothing would ever be okay again. I pulled the jumper over my head. The wet fabric brushed against my lips and I could smell the metal tang of blood. I shivered, taking off my jeans, then my socks, laying them in a soggy pile at my feet.

'Good, that's good.' Her voice was soothing, dreamlike. 'Now I need you to go to my bedroom and take a shower. Wash carefully, get everything off you, scrub under your nails and wash your hair, okay?'

I stood, following her instructions like an automaton. I had left my body. I wasn't capable of independent thought.

'After you've showered, get into my bed and try to sleep. I don't want you to come down here again tonight. Do you understand me, Beth? You need to stay upstairs until I come for you. Okay?'

She was standing at the foot of the stairs. She held her arms out as I neared. I fell into them and her soft, warm hands on my back almost brought me back to life. But I resisted. I didn't want to be present in this horror. I released myself from her embrace and made my way upstairs.

Chapter Fifty-Seven

'Morning.' The door to the bedroom opened and Rachel stood, silhouetted against the bright light of the landing. 'Okay if I put the light on?'

'Yes.' My throat was thick with phlegm. I coughed. The blue lamp hanging in the centre of the ceiling sprang to life, illuminating the sparsely decorated room. I glanced around, wondering momentarily how Rachel managed to keep everything so minimal. It was almost like she didn't really live here.

'I'm glad you managed to sleep.' The smell of coffee came with her into the room. When my sight adjusted, I saw that her eyes were open and she was carrying one of the matching mugs. She put it down on a white bedside table. Dark rings circled her eyes, and her mouth was a set line. She looked changed, as if last night had erased the sheen from her. I understood that. I was sure the horror of what had happened in this house would be tattooed across my face for the rest of my life.

I wanted to correct her, to tell her I doubted I would ever

sleep again, but the words wouldn't come. The hours since I came upstairs and showered had stretched into years. Despite my best efforts, my ears had strained to make sense of the noises going on downstairs. For most of the night there'd been the rumble of baritone voices, and banging and scraping, every sound adding to the horror show going on in my imagination. *You should have called the police. You should have called an ambulance*, repeated in my head on a loop. I'd almost got up to ask Rachel if she remembered where I'd left my phone so I could unburden myself to a faceless voice at the end of the emergency services line. But something stopped me. Maybe it was the rumble of male voices downstairs. Maybe it was fear at what it would mean for Rachel and for me. Either way, the burden was still mine, and it was squatting heavy on my chest, crushing the air from my lungs.

I became aware of my nakedness under the sheets. I glanced down to where my white vest, bra and knickers were in an untidy pile by the side of the bed. Smears of reddish brown on the vest brought a scream tumbling into my mouth. I put a hand over my lips to stop it.

Rachel moved around the room, opening drawers and picking things out. She came over to the bed. 'Here's some clean underwear,' she said quietly, placing it on top of the duvet cover. I could feel it on top of my feet. She opened a built-in cupboard and plucked a navy sweatshirt and matching joggers from the almost empty shelves. 'These should do.' She dropped them on to the bed. She made for the door, then paused and looked back. 'I'll leave you to get dressed, then come down and we'll talk.'

My legs shook as I went down the first flight of stairs to the kitchen. I paused there and stared out across the dock. The leaden sky threatened rain. The ordinariness of the grey sky, of the man strolling along the path and the boats moored as if nothing cataclysmic had happened in the dark of the night was dizzying.

The smell of bleach stung my nostrils before I reached the ground floor. I paused halfway down the stairs, unable to make my feet travel the last few steps, terrified of what I would find.

'Beth.' Rachel's voice was soft. 'Come down. It's okay.'

I tried to poise myself and forced my feet to move. My reluctant gaze scanned the room. It was immaculate.

'They're good at what they do.' Rachel stood in the centre of the room and slowly turned. 'Not that I could see what it was like before, but I can imagine.' She shuddered and hugged herself.

In that moment, I envied her. I would give anything not to have the image of Max's lifeless body seared on to my retinas.

'Billy knows a company who do trauma cleaning. Can you believe that's a job? They get between the floorboards and everything.' She turned to me. 'I keep thinking about what you saw. I never in a million years thought I'd be grateful I couldn't open my eyes, but . . .' She let the sentence drift.

I stood at the bottom of the stairs, unable to move further into the room. Flashbacks of blood pooling at my feet made my breath falter. I trained my eyes on the spot where

Max's caved-in head had lain last night and found it hard to take in the clean polished wood. It was as if nothing had happened. 'Where is he?'

Rachel lowered her gaze. 'I didn't ask.'

Max's face when we had lunch on the Strand appeared in my mind. He was laughing. His eyes were bright, and he was happy. 'But . . . his family.'

'The family who harboured a murderer?' Rachel's tone was hard, and I didn't blame her. She'd been through so much because of that man. 'They knew what he was running away from when he went back to New Zealand. They let him get away with killing Becky. Don't let your sympathy settle in the wrong places, Beth. They saw what they wanted to see when they looked at him – I have no doubt about that. We're all good at self-denial. If we are convinced someone is good, our minds can trick our eyes into seeing goodness, even when the evidence is demonstrably different. You thought Max was your friend, but in reality you were a target, a victim of his deception, just like Becky and me.'

I shook my head to dislodge the dissonance. It was true: a part of me still viewed Max as a friend, loved him, even. He was a well-respected and well-liked doctor. But the truth was Rachel knew he was also a murderer. She'd seen him with her own eyes. He'd stalked and intimidated her and broken into her home, taking advantage of the fact she was vulnerable. His text said he was coming to get me.

'We had no choice, did we?' It came out as a whisper.

'We had no choice,' she repeated. She came to me and wrapped her warm arms round me. 'I've emailed your work and told them you'll be off for the rest of the week with a virus. I used your phone. I hope you don't mind.'

I rested my head on her shoulder, the smell of coconut from her hair momentarily masking the stench of bleach.

'You're going to stay here with me for a few days,' Rachel said into my ear. 'I'm going to take care of you. It will be all right. I'll look after you. Soon, this will all seem like a bad dream, and we'll be able to get on with our lives without fear.' She paused for a minute. 'I've got some diazepam, if you think that will help?'

I nodded. I wanted to blur reality. I needed to. Rachel brought me a tablet and a glass of water, then sat beside me and stroked my hair until the trembling in my body subsided. We had no choice, I told myself, over and over again. And the feeling of my friend's body next to mine made me almost believe it was true.

Chapter Fifty-Eight

I stayed at Rachel's house for a week. She made up the bed in the spare room since we no longer had to keep a night-time vigil, and gave me a small yellow tablet whenever I needed one. For the first day I stayed in bed, tossing and turning in a nightmarish half-sleep, unable even to eat or wash. I dragged myself into the kitchen on the next day, still not able to spend any time downstairs without the whole gory scene replaying in my head.

'I still haven't heard from Aaron,' I said. 'Do you think he's okay?'

Rachel nodded. 'I imagine he's gone back to Hitchin to look after Becky's mum. That's two more people who can rest more easily now.' She put a hand on my back. 'We've got to try to see it like that, otherwise it will send us mad.'

I wished I had her reframing skills. As I sat staring out across the dock, my phone began to vibrate on the granite counter. The screen lit up with a withheld number. My heart leaped up and lodged in my throat.

I looked at Rachel in panic. 'What should I do?'

She came over to where I was sitting and peered at the phone, tugging her bottom lip between her teeth. 'See if they leave a message.'

I wondered if she'd noted that no one else had called or messaged, if she understood my life before meeting her had shrunk to the extent that I could go missing for days and no one would notice. I was sure the same couldn't be said of Max. He would be missed by his work; his friends, and his family in New Zealand, would want to know why he hadn't been in touch.

The voicemail icon appeared. I glanced at Rachel again. I'd lost the ability to think for myself. She nodded. I opened the message. A woman's voice filled the room. 'Hi, Ms Sanderson. I'm PC Olivia Gifford. I've been told you're a friend of Max Larson's. His family have reported him missing, and I wanted to check whether you've seen him recently. Could you please give me a call on . . .' She reeled off a number, then repeated it.

My stomach balled. 'What do I do?'

Rachel wound a curl around her finger thoughtfully. 'Let's practise,' she said. She sat on the stool opposite me, clear blue eyes focused on mine. 'I'll be the police officer, and ask you questions, okay?'

I nodded. She asked when I'd last seen Max, then whether I could think of any reason why he hadn't been into work, or in touch with family or friends.

'No,' I said, struggling to keep my voice level. I wanted more valium, but it was too soon after my last one. 'He seemed fine.'

She pursed her lips. 'I wonder if you should say he wasn't himself. Open the door for a bit of speculation.'

'What do you mean?'

'If they think he could have been suicidal, then that might . . . help us.'

'But, if they find him.' I swallowed. 'His body, then they'll see straight away that he couldn't have inflicted that injury himself.'

She rubbed her hand over her face. 'They won't find him.'

My pulse sped up, the fear I'd been fighting every minute since I saw Max on the floor returning with force. 'How can you be so sure? Someone might have seen him coming here. There's CCTV everywhere.'

Rachel put a hand on my arm. 'Calm down, Beth. Billy sorted it all that night. There isn't a camera in East London he can't get access to, and if his people can't access the cameras he can get to the people who can. No one will know Max was here, and no one will find him. Not now, not ever.'

I tried not to think too hard about what she meant by *get to*. She seemed so sure, and oddly relaxed. I couldn't afford to dwell on that. After a moment, I said, 'I'll find it hard enough to talk to the police without adding extra lies.' In truth, I didn't want his parents to spend the rest of their lives thinking Max was so depressed he took his own life without ever reaching out to them.

'I'm a lawyer,' Rachel said. 'I know what I'm doing. Please trust me on this. I'm saying this for the good of both of us. Now, repeat what I say, using exactly the same intonation I do.' She stared at me expectantly, and I nodded. 'He'd been a bit low the last couple of times I saw him, but I didn't think much of it. It was out of character, now I come to think about it. I wish I'd asked more, now I look back. You don't think he might have—' She made her voice crack with pretend emotion. 'Now you try.'

'I can't.'

'You can.' Her voice was firm. If she could be so strong after what she'd been through, I could too. I put my shoulders back and repeated what she said.

'Again,' she said. 'Add a bit more emotion in that last bit.'

I tried again, and again, until there was little difference between my voice and hers. When I spoke to PC Gifford, I answered exactly as Rachel had taught me. She was a good lawyer. She was very convincing.

When Rachel's eyes closed on the third morning, she asked if I could make lunch, and slowly, by helping my friend with tasks she couldn't do, I came back to some kind of life.

Eventually, after a week of hiding from the world, I went back to my flat, but being alone was agony. Visions of Max plagued my waking hours as well as my dreams. Back at work, colleagues speculated where Mr Larson might be. I kept my head down, and soon everyone was sensitive enough to stop asking me. I overheard one nurse saying to another, 'I don't think we should mention Mr Larson in front of her again. She's finding it hard, poor lamb. They were close. I always thought they'd get together one day. She must be devastated by all this.' Guilt gnawed through my stomach and into my bones. I spent all my spare time with Rachel, because she was the only person on earth who understood the torment I was going through.

When I finally felt strong enough to see patients at Bath Street again, Darcy, one of the receptionists for another practice, knocked on my door in the late afternoon. I called for her to come in and registered the shock on her face when she saw me. I understood it. I couldn't eat. I couldn't sleep. I'd lost so much weight that when I dressed in the morning I looked like a child trying on her mother's suits.

She held a phone in her hand. 'I found this behind reception when you were off sick,' she said. 'I've checked with everyone else, and no one's lost one. No patients have asked for it. Do you know whose it is?'

I immediately recognised the black-and-white case. It was Aaron's. A new wave of fear slammed into me. I'd taken on board what Rachel had said, and visualised him back in his hometown, getting on with his life. But if his phone was there, where was Aaron? I'd tried ringing that phone the night . . . I had to stop my thoughts there in case Darcy read the horror on my face. I smiled and held out my hand, hoping she didn't notice the tremour. 'It's Aaron's, I think.' She passed it to me. I put it on my desk, face down. 'Thanks. I'll make sure he gets it.'

'It's a shame he didn't stick around. I liked him. Say hi, when you speak to him.' She turned to leave.

'I will. Thanks, Darcy.' New questions pulsed behind my throbbing brow. Aaron had been trying to help Rachel, hadn't he? He thought Max had murdered Becky too, and that's why he came here, to protect us. I'd exposed him to Max, and I hadn't heard from him since. In my near-fugue state, I hadn't really allowed my mind to ask why, just blindly accepting that he was safe and well.

When she closed the door behind her, I lifted the phone. It was a Samsung. I'd always had iPhones, so I pressed the unfamiliar buttons to try to bring it to life. When the screen didn't wake up when I'd tried everything, I sent a voice note to Rachel. It was a closed-eye day, so I was planning to go over after work. We both found it reassuring to be together when she couldn't open her eyes. I had secretly hoped the removal of the threat, as I called it in my head, would have cured her condition, but no such miracle had come about so far. 'Hi, hope you're doing okay,' I said into the phone's microphone. 'I've got Aaron's phone here. He must've left it behind, when he . . . I've been wondering where he might be, and . . . Anyway, it's got no charge. Do you have a Samsung charger? I want to charge it so we can call his family and see if he's with them. He will be, won't he? Let me know if you've got one handy, otherwise I'll try to buy one on the way to yours.'

Grey dots bounced in a speech bubble below my text, and I imagined her instructing Siri to open voice notes and dictating her reply.

I clicked the play icon and listened. 'I think I've got one. I definitely used to, so hope I didn't chuck it out. Don't buy one until we've checked. Will you take a look when you get here?'

'No problem. See you later,' I recorded, and pressed send. I dropped the phone in my bag and tried to force my thoughts away from why Aaron would have left his phone behind, and on to the notes for the patient waiting outside.

Chapter Fifty-Nine

When I couldn't find a Samsung charger anywhere Rachel directed me to look, I wished I'd taken a detour on the way to St Katharine Docks and bought one just in case. The fear that something might have happened to Aaron had swollen inside me, and now I was bloated with it.

'I need to know he's okay,' I said, opening the cutlery drawer and sighing at the neatly arranged knives and forks. 'What if I've inadvertently fed him to the lion?' The thought was threatening to overwhelm me. 'I'll go out and pick one up from somewhere,' I said, after inspecting the final drawer in the kitchen for the third time and finding nothing but cooking implements. The neatness of Rachel's kitchen baffled me. How had she avoided picking up at least one cupboard's worth of ephemera and squirrelling it away because it might come in useful one day, like everyone else I knew did?

'Please don't,' she said, sounding meeker than she had in a while. 'I didn't like to say, but when I'm on my own and my eyes are like this, I keep having these really distressing flashbacks. It's weird, because I didn't actually see anything, but I hear this echo of what happened, an awful smashing noise and screaming, and I feel this absolutely debilitating sense of dread. And it never happens when you're here. It's like my body knows it's safe with you around. Even the inside of my head, and my subconscious knows it. Honestly, I feel so much calmer when you're in the house with me.'

I strode over to where she was sitting at the island in front of the windows and put a hand on her back. 'I hear you,' I said. 'I'm finding it hard enough to fight the memories with my eyes open.'

'And it's dark outside, isn't it?'

I peered out into the night, suddenly less keen to leave the safety of the locked house.

'I don't like to think of you out there on your own in the dark. And we probably won't be able to unlock the phone, will we, even if we charge it, so I'm not sure how much good it will do. Can you get one tomorrow, or I could pick one up the day after when this bloody thing ends.' She put splayed fingers to her eyes, and I could feel her exasperation.

'Okay,' I said. She was right. She needed me, just as I had come to need her. 'I'll get one tomorrow.' A yawn tightened my jaw. 'I don't know about you, but I'm knackered. I'm ready for bed.'

'You're not eating enough,' she said gently. 'I'm not surprised you're tired. You'll get ill if you carry on like this.' She ran her fingers along my arm to my hand and held it. 'Promise me you'll try to keep your strength up. I need you, Beth. I don't know what would have happened to me without you.'

I hugged her, breathing in her coconut scent, feeling her soft curls flatten against my neck and absorbing the fact that she'd just expressed my thoughts out loud. Our synergy nourished me more than I could say.

'I'll try. Want me to help you with anything before you go up?'

'No, I'm good, thanks.' She gave my waist a squeeze. 'Sleep well, lovely.'

I kissed the top of her head. 'You too.' The one and only positive to come from the hell of the last few weeks was that the bond between us had grown even stronger. I couldn't imagine my life without Rachel now. I felt a tiny glimmer of hope that we might survive the horror of the last weeks as I made my way up the stairs to bed.

I tried to get to sleep in the narrow single bed in the spare room in the turret where I'd been spending most nights, but images of Max's lifeless eyes appeared behind mine every time I closed my lids. Thoughts of Aaron also swirled around my brain like poison gas. I was convinced now that Max had done something terrible to him. In any other circumstances, I would report Aaron missing, but I couldn't do that without explaining our involvement. That would be catastrophic for both me and Rachel. I turned my pillow over and pressed my cheek on to the cold cotton, trying to force my brain to create images of Aaron alive and well. He could have lost his phone and bought a new one. That was possible, wasn't it?

It was no good. My thoughts wouldn't be controlled, and I couldn't get comfortable on the thin mattress. My mouth tasted of mildew. Crusts had formed at the corners because I wasn't drinking enough water. Rachel was right: I needed to take better care of myself. What would be the point of surviving the horror of the last weeks if I gave up on myself anyway? I'd forgotten to bring a glass of water up with me, so I threw the duvet off and made for the stairs.

The floors below were in darkness. I flicked the switch to light the stairwell and tiptoed on bare feet down to the kitchen. Once there, I didn't turn the light on. There was enough of a glow from the stairs to allow me to see as far as the sink and I didn't want to light up the room when it was pitch black outside. I felt vulnerable at even the potential of being observed.

As I took a glass from the cupboard, the flicker of something behind me made me spin round. I flinched when I saw a figure, a dark silhouette against the window. The figure turned, its face illuminated by the eerie glow of a phone screen.

Chapter Sixty

I slapped my hand to my thundering chest. 'Rachel! You nearly gave me a heart attack.'

She didn't move. The phone's screen lit her face from beneath, accentuating the hollows below her cheek bones and her ocular cavities, giving her eyes an eerie blue glow.

Her eyes.

Her eyes were open.

'Your eyes.' I dropped my hand and took a step towards her, then stopped, confused by her expression of disdain. 'You can open your eyes.' There was hope in my words. My heart was still racing, joy adding to the adrenaline coursing through my system. Ordinarily, her blepharospasm wouldn't lift for another thirty hours. This was a breakthrough – maybe she was even cured. I expected to see my delight mirrored in her, but her face became impassive, and the smile that had blossomed on mine froze. 'Rachel?'

She let the arm holding the phone drop to her side and let out a huff of air. 'Well, I suppose the game's up now.'

I was acutely aware of my body, my bare feet on the cold

floorboards, my cheek muscles releasing as my smile faded, the sparking of my synapses, electrical impulses firing in my brain, trying to make sense of my friend's strange behaviour.

'I suppose it's for the best,' she said, dragging a stool from under the island and sitting. 'I was getting pretty bored of all your whining.' I didn't recognise the tone of her voice. It was derisive; cruel, even. 'Have you got any idea how much you complain?'

I blinked, my eyelids the only part of me capable of moving.

She held the phone screen out to me. 'Sweet, aren't they?' Her voice was sharp with sarcasm. The screensaver showed Aaron with his arm round an elderly woman, both of them smiling broadly. Rachel turned it back to herself. 'That's Becky's mum. Interfering old witch. This is all her fault, actually. If she'd just gone off and died like a good old lady, instead of digging up the past, I wouldn't have had to waste my time sorting everything out.'

'You didn't have a charger,' I stuttered. It sounded stupid as soon as it came out of my mouth, but my brain wouldn't allow me to process anything else she'd said.

The light from the screen was enough to show her sneer. 'I had a charger, Beth. I just didn't want you to find it.' She shook her head. 'Sweet Jesus, for a supposedly intelligent woman, you really will believe anything.' She stood and walked towards me, and I instinctively stepped away. I didn't know this woman. She scared me. 'Don't worry.' Her voice was mocking. 'I'm only going to put the light on.'

She flicked the switch and stood in front of me, a

self-satisfied smirk on her lips. 'You don't look great, Beth. You've gone very pale. Why don't we go downstairs and sit comfortably. Then, if you behave yourself, I'll tell you everything.' She walked past me towards the stairs. 'You may as well know the truth, I suppose. It's not as if you're going to share it with anyone. I had to keep you around long enough for things to die down, if you'll pardon the pun, but enough is enough. I'm so ready to get my life back. Babysitting you has been dull as fuck.'

Every nerve ending in my body told me I needed help. I visualised my phone, charging next to the bed upstairs. I made a move towards the first step.

She spoke over her shoulder, 'Before you think about ringing the police, you might want to consider what happened to the bookend with your fingerprints all over it, and those bloodied clothes you so dutifully stripped out of that night.' She held up a finger. 'And whose phone I used to call Billy Galvin too. Phone records are very useful in trials, you know.'

My mind catapulted back to that night. I saw Rachel standing, holding the wrought-iron bookend, sticky with parts of Max's skull. I felt the wet weight of it in my hands when I took it from her, followed by a vague memory of her speaking quietly into my phone. My mouth went dry. 'What have you done?'

She waved a hand for me to follow her. I had no choice. I took shaky steps, holding tight to the banister, frightened my unsteady legs might give way. As I reached the bottom, she ran a finger over the remaining bookend, and started to speak. 'Like I said, when Becky's mother started to bleat on about reopening the case, I had no choice but to cover my back.'

'But why?' My knees threatened to buckle. I sat on the sofa, every muscle taut. 'If Max killed Becky—' Rachel dropped her chin to her chest and viewed me through her eyelashes, and I knew then what she meant. 'Max didn't kill Becky, did he?' It came out as a whisper.

She gave a slow hand-clap. 'You're catching up. Well done.'

A juddering began in my core and spread out through my body. 'You killed Becky.' As soon as the words occurred to me, I knew it was true. Max wasn't a murderer. The woman in front of me was. A surge of electrified horror ran through me. 'Why?'

She blew out her cheeks. 'Max, or Daniel as we knew him back then, was supposed to be mine. Becky betrayed me and made a play for him, and he was too cuntstruck to realise he was making a mistake. I was watching them that night.' She fixed me with a cold stare. 'I've always been a watcher.' She left it a beat then continued. 'Becky promised me she wasn't interested in him, but she lied, and that night I caught her getting off with the boy she knew full well I was in love with.'

'Love?' The word escaped before I could stop it.

She flapped her hand. 'I was seventeen. I thought I was in love. Obviously, I've learned better since then. I mean, I wouldn't touch Max with a bargepole now. I saw how weak he was, how he always went for the nice girls, over the ones with a bit of . . . character.' She smiled. 'I saw the way he was with you, all doe-eyed and sappy. He hadn't changed.'

'You saw us?'

'I've been watching you, Beth, for, oh, so long.' Her voice was sing-song now. 'Every time you felt eyes on you, it was little old me. I could have dispensed with him the old-fashioned way, quick and easy, but I wanted to play with him a little first. I wanted him to be terrified that someone he cared about was in danger. I wanted to hurt him, like he and Becky hurt me. You were the perfect stooge, Beth. I'd dreamed of finding someone who was needy and gullible enough to go along with my plan, and, as if by magic, there you were. And when I found out Max cared about you more than anyone else, in this country at least, everything fell perfectly into place.'

I remembered the feeling of eyes on my back. It wasn't Max, or Aaron, it was her. 'It was you all along.'

'Yep. And guess what? You were the ideal mark.' A malicious grin spread across her face. 'I know all about Joel and Simon, you naughty girl.' She tutted and shook her head, a mocking smile playing on her lips. 'I know about your need to *save people*.' She made quote marks with her fingers. 'And the fact that Max was in love with you made it all so much easier. He was a sweetheart, really, if you like bland, dutiful men. He was one of the good guys. You really should have treated him better, Beth.'

He was good. Max was good. All the effort I'd put into trying not to love him so I didn't hurt him seemed so pathetic now. I'd done more than hurt him; I'd been complicit in his murder. I felt his still-warm mouth on mine again and wanted to rip my lips from my face.

'He knew I was out there somewhere because I'd left him a little clue on Facebook,' Rachel said smugly. 'That would have put him on his guard. As soon as you told him who I really was, he must've been scared to death I'd use you to get to him.'

Why hadn't Max told me that he'd known Rachel when she was called Kate, and that he was the one accused of Becky's murder? The realisation that he must've thought I would take Rachel's side made the blood drain from my face. I'd defended her relentlessly, refusing to heed any of his warnings. If only I'd let him in, been honest about how I felt, he might have trusted me to believe him. He might have still been alive.

'He started to keep an eye on you, just like I knew he would. So predictable. I'm surprised he didn't turn up on a white horse instead of that penis extension of a car. That's why he was outside the evening you saw him, you know? He suspected I killed Becky, right from the night she died. He just couldn't prove it. When he understood who I was, he followed you here in case I was a threat to you too. And when I sent him that message saying you were frightened and asking him to come—'

'What message?'

'The one he replied to saying he was coming to get you now. He wasn't coming to hurt you, Beth. He was coming to save you from me.'

'You sent him a message from my phone?'

'Yep. Remember when I pretended my phone was out of charge and I needed to check something or other online? You unlocked it and gave it straight to me. Such a trusting soul. I changed the setting so it would recognise you with your eyes closed, so I could message him when you were asleep. Fitting, right? Obviously, I deleted the message straight afterwards. And remember that hot chocolate, how sweet and strong it was? That was to disguise the sleeping tablet in it. That took an effort, actually, to get the dose right. I clearly overdid it because it took a few screams to wake you up. I thought you'd realise he'd been dead for over a minute when you saw how far across the floor the blood had travelled. But you didn't, did you?' She wrinkled her nose. 'Makes me wonder how good a doctor you are, actually.'

I put my hand to my mouth and swallowed down bile. The pieces of her fucked-up jigsaw were coming together in my mind. 'It was all staged. You planned everything.'

She threw her head back. 'Of course it was all staged. The whole thing was meticulously planned and executed.' She laughed. 'Executed, get it? I've been impressed with my own acting skills, to be honest, especially since I haven't trodden the boards since I was Lady Macbeth in the school production. It was an open-air performance in the Dell, where poor Becky met her tragic end. She was Duncan, by the way. So fitting. Life imitating art. I like that.' She looked at me, as if waiting for a round of applause.

'Your eyes were open when you hit Max. You murdered

him in cold blood.' I remembered the sound of her rattling the lock before she went upstairs. 'You didn't check the lock that night, did you? You opened the door so he could get in, and then you waited for him to arrive.'

'Like I said, all planned to a T.' She gave a self-congratulatory smile.

I hardly dared ask my next question. 'And Aaron?' Rachel's eyes were bright with excitement. She was enjoying this. She was sick.

'That was a surprise, to be fair. Finding out he was working for you almost threw me off my game. I was worried he might bump into Max and work out they'd both known Becky. I don't think they ever met back then, but I couldn't be certain, so that was a bit stressful, to be honest. Aaron was clever. He'd always suspected me too. He tried to warn Becky off me when we were kids, telling her I wasn't a good friend, never had her best interests at heart and all that bollocks. What seventeen-year-old does put other people first, for God's sake?' She smiled. 'Although even I have to admit I haven't changed much in that respect. I still like to be front and centre.' She gave a girlish sigh. 'Anyway, he must've been keeping an eye on me over the years. I have to give him credit for that. I always had him down as a bit of a helpless nerd, but he'd clearly cottoned on to me faking all the eye crap and got a job with you to keep tabs on me and gather evidence. He was probably trying to prove I was lying to make me look unreliable so he could accuse me again, and make it stick this time.'

The eye crap. I was only just allowing the truth to

permeate, and it soaked into me like acid. 'He was trying to warn me against you.' If only he'd told me directly, we could have stopped this. I doubt I would have listened, though. I was too sucked in by Rachel, too ready to defend her against Aaron, Max, everyone. I could see that now.

'Yeah, well, he should have stayed in his lane.' She raised her eyebrows. 'Honestly, Beth, I hinted at what was really going on often enough, but you seemed determined to see the best in people. Big mistake. The number of times I told you people aren't always who they seem, and not to believe everything you saw. I made it part of the game, challenged myself to shoehorn one into every conversation we had. You thought I was talking about Aaron and Max, when really it was this guy.' She swirled her finger, then pointed to herself, her relish terrifying.

I knew she was right, without searching back over our conversations. This was a twisted game to her, and had been all along. 'What did you do to him?'

'I didn't do anything,' she said sweetly. 'I left that to Billy and his friends. Aaron and Max are all cosied up together somewhere deep in Epping Forest, along with your soiled clothes and that bookend covered in your fingerprints and bits of Max's head. Not that anyone will find them. Billy's no amateur.' She tapped her finger on her chin and furrowed her brow, an exaggerated show of mulling something over. 'Unless someone were to try and implicate us in any wrongdoing. Then our friends on the murder squad might find some coordinates pinging on to their phones.'

'Aaron's dead too?' The horror of what she was telling

me filtered through my veins like poison. It was too much. I knew psychopaths existed, but I'd never truly seen one in action until now. 'Did Billy kill Aaron as a favour because of what you did for his daughter?' How could anyone take a life so lightly?

Rachel laughed. 'He killed him because I asked him to. Aaron was planning to expose me, and I couldn't let that happen. You completely swallowed that rubbish about Billy's sweet, innocent daughter, didn't you? The part about getting her off was true, but I'm afraid the rest was bullshit. She runs a gang that covers the whole of the East End. There isn't a man brave enough to cross her, especially not with Billy Galvin as a dad.' She put her shoulders back and lifted her chin. 'And, while we're on the subject of my work, I'm slightly insulted that you believed I wasn't a partner in my firm. I am the firm.' She tapped the bookend, clearly reminding me of what she was capable of.

I clenched my pelvic floor to stop my bladder emptying. 'There is no Reece, is there?'

She shook her head. 'A figment of my vivid imagination. Although it was hardly a stretch. There are plenty of Reece-like characters in the law game, just none who are stupid enough to stand against me. The ex who died in the hit and run was real, though. Such a shame they never caught the driver of that car.' She let her head tip and adopted a look of wide-eyed innocence that chilled my blood.

'But . . .' I tried to remember what I'd read about her on the internet. 'I read that . . .'

'You read what I wanted you to read. I was playing the

long game and so I had whatever suited my story put up there.' She let her head drop to the side and pursed her lips. She seemed to be waiting for me to say something, but my mind was filled with a high-pitched screaming. She sighed and carried on. 'So, let's recap the headlines.' She counted her points off on her fingers. 'I chose you to help me because you have a pathetic saviour complex, and Max was in love with you. Aaron was a fly in the ointment, but he's been dealt with. I am the firm, and Billy pays a very pretty retainer, and I'm keeping you around in case any fingers are ever pointed in my direction. I think that's it.' She peered around the room. 'Oh, and I don't live here.'

My eyes opened wider. All the clues I'd ignored tumbled into my head: the tidiness, the matching mugs and glasses. Of course this wasn't her home.

She sneered at the sofa I was sitting on. 'I wouldn't have chosen these sofas. So basic. No, my penthouse in Barbican is far more stylish than this.' She glanced past me to the window. 'It was nice to be on the water for a while, though. We actually considered weighing Max down and tipping him into the dock, but bodies do have a habit of bloating and floating.' She made rippling movements with her fingers as if what she'd said was a light-hearted joke.

'You're a sadist,' I said. 'There's something wrong with you.'

She arched her eyebrows. 'Is that your considered medical opinion?'

I stood on shaky legs and took a step towards the door. I

tried not to look at her face, but when I neared she bounced forward, then laughed as I jumped and let out a cry.

'Aw, you're so jittery. Don't be. You can go up and get your things,' she said, taking a step back. 'I won't stop you from leaving. I was all for putting you in the ground with your friends, but Billy said we should keep you around. One less missing person to be investigated, he said, and all the evidence points to you, so . . .' She lifted her hands. 'But do bear in mind what I said, Beth. I might be a shit-hot lawyer, but even I would struggle to get you off two murder charges when the bodies are buried with such compelling and damning evidence. Not that you'd last long enough to go to trial, obviously. Billy can be very protective, bless him. I'm a valuable asset. If he gets even a hint that you might blab, you'll be joining the gang in Epping Forest. He'll be keeping an eye on you. I might too. It's been such good fun. You might want to try to be a bit more interesting in future, though; give me something worth watching, eh?'

She was sitting, scrolling on her phone, when I came down minutes later with all my possessions shoved in my bag. She didn't look up when I turned the latch. 'Thanks for all your help, Doc,' she called as I stepped out into the icy February air. 'I couldn't have done it without you.'

Epilogue

Nine Months Later

The fresh mound of earth sparkled with a dusting of early-morning frost. There was no headstone yet. A bouquet of white roses wrapped in clear cellophane lay on top, petals limp and browning at the edges. Next to the freshly turned soil of her mother's grave, Becky's was flat and neat. The rectangle of gravel appeared to have been raked, the marble headstone wiped clean of grime. I was glad someone was tending to the graves. I'd been concerned that, since Aaron was gone, and now her mother too, Becky's resting place would become neglected and overgrown.

From the research I'd done, it seemed that the murder case had made no progress. Maybe now that no one was left to demand justice, it would be forgotten, by the police, at least. I would never forget. I couldn't.

I lay the pink and purple hydrangeas I'd bought when I arrived in Hitchin yesterday on the ground between the graves. I'd written 'I'm sorry' on the small rectangular card the florist had given to me, but now that I was here, it seemed too risky to leave it. I was a despicable coward.

That wasn't news. If I had any courage, I'd have exposed Rachel and Billy Galvin and taken the consequences, but whenever I came close fear overwhelmed me. I knew all too well what they were capable of. I dislodged the card from the brown wrapping paper and put it in my pocket. As I did, the crunch of footsteps on frosty grass made me freeze. A young man in a tracksuit, hands shoved deep in his pockets, walked slowly past. It was 7 a.m. The sun had only just risen. I'd expected to be alone to pay my tribute to the women whose lives had been taken and destroyed by Rachel.

But I was never truly alone any more. I felt eyes on me everywhere I went. I didn't even feel safe in my own home.

I straightened, adrenalin surging, and turned back to the path. In my pocket, I gripped my passport. I just needed to make it to the airport, and on to my flight to the Ivory Coast, then I could begin my life again. Joining Medecins Sans Frontières had seemed like the only way I could begin to cope with the part I'd played in the horror of nine months ago. Leaving my privileged life and putting myself in possible danger to help people suffering unimaginable trauma was my only hope of finding peace. The money from the sale of my flat should cover Mum's fees for long enough. I didn't tell her I was going away for good last time I visited. I couldn't bear the indifference I knew I'd see in her eyes.

The cab I'd ordered was waiting by the cemetery gate. I opened the door with trembling hands and told the driver which airport terminal I needed. I sat in the rear, glancing back at the graveyard as I reached for my seatbelt. The man in the tracksuit was standing at the entrance. He gave a small nod to the driver. My blood turned to ice as the central locking clicked and the car pulled away from the kerb.

Acknowledgements

My first thanks go to my brilliant editor, Lucy Dauman, who made my dream of writing crime fiction become a reality, and who has been a joy to work with at every stage.

Thank you to all the team at Headline for their insight, hard work and their generous comments about the book.

I owe a huge debt of gratitude to my fantastic agent, Laura Williams. She's the perfect combination of funny and fierce and there's no one I'd rather have at my back.

To my invaluable early readers – Suzy Oldfield, John Timoney and Claire McGlasson – thank you for your time and your honesty. I don't know what I'd do without you. Special thanks to Claire for inspiring some of the vocabulary.

My thanks also go to the fabulous online reading community, especially bloggers Nicola @nothing.beats.a.good.book, Emily @aquintillionwords, Rachel @rachel_loves_to_read and Angela @ang.all.about.books. Their support has blown me away. The following Facebook book groups are wonderful, and also instrumental in helping new readers find my books: the Bookload, Fiction Addicts Book Club, the Fiction Cafe Book Club and the Good Housekeeping Book Room. Huge thanks to their brilliant administration teams (especially Kate Rutherford, Teresa Nikolic and Trina Dixon) who give their time for free to spread the bookish-love. If you are looking for a place to share your love of books, I recommend these groups wholeheartedly.

The writing community is the most positive and supportive bunch of people you could hope to find. Both online and IRL, I've found my tribe, my strength and inspiration in the friends I have made since I began my writing life. There are too many to name individually, and I would hate to leave someone out, but if I've met you through writing, I'm talking about you.

Finally, my thanks go to my family. I am incredibly fortunate to live with people who make me laugh every day, ensure my feet are always firmly on the ground and fill my life with love.

If you enjoyed *The Eyewitness*, I would be very grateful if you could leave a brief review wherever you buy your books. Even a few words can make an author's day, and help new readers discover our books. Thank you!

Credits

Naomi Williams would like to thank everyone involved in the production of The Eyewitness

Editorial
Lucy Dauman
Ayana Playle

Copy-editor
Sarah Day

Proofreading
Sam Stewart

Audio
Ellie Wheeldon

Design
Alice Clark

Production
Victoria Lord

Marketing
Carmella Lowkis

Publicity
Khuriesh Farah

Sales
Becky Bader
Sinead White

Rights
Grace McCrum
Ruth Case-Green

Contracts
Rachel Monte

RAISING READERS
Books Build Bright Futures

Dear Reader,

We'd love your attention for one more page to tell you about the crisis in children's reading, and what we can all do.

Studies have shown that reading for fun is the **single biggest predictor of a child's future life chances** – more than family circumstance, parents' educational background or income. It improves academic results, mental health, wealth, communication skills, ambition and happiness.[1]

The number of children reading for fun is in rapid decline. Young people have a lot of competition for their time. In 2024, 1 in 10 children and young people in the UK aged 5 to 18 did not own a single book at home.[2]

Hachette works extensively with schools, libraries and literacy charities, but here are some ways we can all raise more readers:

- Reading to children for just 10 minutes a day makes a difference
- Don't give up if children aren't regular readers – there will be books for them!
- Visit bookshops and libraries to get recommendations
- Encourage them to listen to audiobooks
- Support school libraries
- Give books as gifts

There's a lot more information about how to encourage children to read on our website: **www.RaisingReaders.co.uk**

Thank you for reading.

hachette UK

---

[1] OECD, '21st-Century Readers: Developing Literacy Skills in a Digital World', 2021, https://www.oecd.org/en/publications/21st-century-readers_a83d84cb-en.html

[2] National Literacy Trust, 'Book Ownership in 2024', November 2024, https://literacytrust.org.uk/research-services/research-reports/book-ownership-in-2024